"Do you know how good you taste?"

"Probably as good as you taste. Although I'm infinitely sweeter." Abby laughed against the slightly rough skin of his throat.

"Lady, you have talents I never dreamed of," Zach said huskily, bringing her closer to him. "And I like them very much. We should do this more often."

Feeling more reckless than she had in a long time, Abby began a trail of kisses at the middle of his chin and ended with a nibble on his earlobe that she found equally sexy.

"Abby, you're driving me crazy."

Whatever Abby was about to say was halted when they heard the front door open and close. Her eyes opened wide, and she looked at Zach with shocked surprise.

"Beth?" he called out.

"Dad?" Zach's daughter appeared. The young girl didn't look happy....

ABOUT THE AUTHOR

Linda Randall Wisdom is a well-known name to readers of romance fiction. Long-term service in personnel, marketing and public relations gave her a wealth of experience on which to draw when creating characters. Linda knew she was destined to write romance novels when her first sale came on her wedding anniversary.

She lives in Southern California with her husband and a houseful of exotic birds.

Books by Linda Randall Wisdom

HARLEQUIN AMERICAN ROMANCE
250–WE GIVE THANKS

Lady's Choice
Linda Randall Wisdom

Harlequin Books

TORONTO • NEW YORK • LONDON
AMSTERDAM • PARIS • SYDNEY • HAMBURG
STOCKHOLM • ATHENS • TOKYO • MILAN

For my mother, Thelma Randall,
for putting up with a daughter
whose head was usually in the clouds
and making up stories as she went along.

Thanks, Mom.

Published February 1989

First printing December 1988

ISBN 0-373-16284-7

Chapter One

"Zach Randolph, I'll get you for this," Abby Townsend threatened with a laugh.

She always loved parties. After all, what better way was there to get together with friends. She *had* loved parties, until she was given one to celebrate her fortieth birthday when she really would have preferred to ignore it.

The room she stood in was decorated with black balloons, black crepe paper draped across the ceiling and artfully designed bouquets of dead flowers in black ceramic vases. The guests even wore mourning bands. She pointed an accusing finger at the man standing next to her.

He grinned unabashed. "You already did get me; on my fortieth birthday, remember?" He reached out and tweaked a curly lock of flame-red hair. "Three years later and the girls in the salon still haven't forgotten."

Abby nodded, recalling her macabre method of wishing Zach a happy birthday by sending an actor dressed as an undertaker driving a hearse. The ornate flower arrangement the man had delivered to Zach had been equally fitting for the occasion.

"At least I didn't send you a year's supply of Geritol," Zach countered, handing her a glass of champagne.

She sipped the bubbly liquid, grateful he hadn't decided to have it colored black. "No, you chose Ben Gay instead."

"If that's what she uses to look so great, I'm going to buy some first thing in the morning." A slender woman hugged Abby. "God, Abby, I hate you. How can you look this good when I literally fell apart on my fortieth." She speared Zach with a narrow-eyed gaze. "Unless it's because the two of you are indulging in a mad passionate affair as we've all prayed for these past years." She raised her eyebrows in a silent question.

"And ruin a wonderful friendship?" Abby bantered. "We know better than to mess that up, Donna."

Donna turned to Zach and eyed him appreciatively. "Zachary Randolph, if I wasn't a happily married woman I swear I'd go after you myself and let Abby suffer for not getting smart in time." She hugged Abby again and moved on.

Abby turned to Zach, lifting her champagne glass in a salute. "How many does that make it now?"

"Seven, if you want to count Craig Osbourne who suggested a torrid one-night stand with him if you didn't want to have one with me."

She gave Zach the same once-over Donna had. She saw a man a couple inches over six feet, silvery blond hair brushed back in a casual style and sea-green eyes a woman could lose herself in. Playing racquetball on a regular basis kept him lean and mean, as Abby enjoyed teasing him. She silently agreed he was a sexy man but she had known him too long to think of him as anyone other than a very good friend and the father of the girl her twenty-year-old son had dated for the past few years. The man who had been there with a handy shoulder to cry on when her husband died ten years before. As far as she was concerned he was her best friend.

"Yes, I guess you aren't too bad," she decided, her teal-blue eyes dancing with merriment. "So, if you're such a hot catch, why are you here without a date?"

"I'm here with a date," he argued amiably. "I've got you, don't I?"

"You told me you were taking me out to dinner for my birthday. I should have realized something was wrong when you said we had to come back to your house because you forgot your wallet. You've never forgotten anything because you're so well organized," Abby pointed out, leading him to the buffet table loaded with hot hors d'oeuvres. She gestured to the end of the table. "That cake is really sick."

Zach chuckled. "I don't know, I think it was a stroke of genius myself. I'll have you know I designed it."

She stared at the elaborate cake fashioned in the shape of a coffin with a headstone standing behind it with her name and birth date written on it in black frosting. "At least the cake I got you was more conventional."

"A conventional cake does not have drawings of old men in wheelchairs all over it."

She smiled, looking proud of herself. "Ah, yes, *that* was a stroke of genius." She turned when a man tapped her on the shoulder and kissed her lightly on the lips telling her she was still as sexy as she had been at thirty-nine.

An hour later, Abby stepped to the fringes of the party content to stand back and watch the festivities. She had been completely surprised by the party, much to Zach's delight. She slid her feet out of her taupe leather high heels and breathed a sigh of relief as her soles rubbed against the thick carpeting. Unconsciously her eyes followed Zach's progress through the crowd of people. She couldn't help but notice he was stopped by more women than men.

"How can you be such a saint?" Donna moaned, sidling up to Abby. "Go after the man, will you? Of course, I will want all the delicious details afterward."

"For a happily married woman you certainly think a lot about sex," Abby teased.

"It's just that the two of you make such a good-looking couple." She waved her champagne glass for emphasis. "And it's not as if you don't know each other. How long has it been?"

"More than twenty years," Abby murmured. "Since my sophomore year in high school."

"And she still doesn't trust me to cut her hair." Zach complained from behind.

Abby tipped her head back. "As I've told you so many times before, I can't afford your prices."

"If I can afford to pay your outrageous accounting fees, you can afford me. Hell, Abby, Sam lets me cut her hair."

"My daughter's haircuts are part of her salary for working as a shampoo girl for you," Abby pointed out. "You've never offered me the same deal."

"Fine, you can do my books in exchange for my doing your hair."

"I already do your books."

He shook his head. "You're incorrigible." He pulled her toward the family room that had been cleared for dancing. In honor of Abby's birthday, music from the sixties was played.

She moved her body to the rhythmic beat of Steppenwolf's "Magic Carpet Ride." "What, no Springsteen or Beastie Boys?" she shouted above the loud music.

"Those are saved for Beth's birthday."

FOR THE NEXT HOUR and a half Abby had more than her choice of dance partners, and her feet were starting to hurt.

"A great party, Abby," Dave Matthews, one of Zach's employees, told her as they undulated to Blood Sweat and Tears.

"Zach set up the party, I'm just the guest of honor," she replied, unable to stop staring at the earring dangling from his right ear, which resembled a small pair of handcuffs. She knew he worked in one of Zach's three hair salons and figured it had to be the one that catered to the New Wave or Punk teenagers, or whatever they called themselves now. She never could keep up with the new slang even with a teenager in the house consistently keeping her up to date.

"Still, it's hard to imagine you're forty." He looked her up and down. "Talk about looking well preserved."

Her smile froze on her face. "Thanks." She decided it was easy to hate anyone under the age of twenty-five.

By the time the last guests filtered out Abby was convinced her feet had run away to another state without her, and her face ached from so much smiling she doubted she would be able to move it come morning. She collapsed on the couch, propping her stockinged feet on the glass-topped coffee table.

"Tired?" Zach asked, handing her a cup of coffee.

"I'm past tired and well on my way to exhausted." She yawned. "I do hope you don't expect me to help clean up this mess. Guests of honor don't wash dishes."

He shook his head. "You're safe. I've got a cleaning crew coming in the morning." He picked up her legs and sat on the coffee table, cradling her feet in his lap as he rubbed the soreness from her aching insteps.

"Ahh," she moaned, throwing her head back. "With luck I'll be able to walk again in a few years."

"That's what happens when you're the belle of the ball," he teased, manipulating her toes in painful contortions. "Drink your coffee. I added a dollop of Irish Cream for flavor."

She sipped the hot brew gratefully. "Umm, just the way coffee should be made."

Zach concentrated on rubbing the sensitive arch. "Do you notice how our friends get more insistent about pairing us up," he commented, putting her feet back on the table and moving over a few inches.

"That's because most of them are married and can't stand seeing us run around single." Abby set her cup to one side.

He nodded. "Yet, in a way we are a couple. You attended that Heart Fund dinner with me last month."

"Only because you couldn't get a date."

"I could have gotten a date," he informed her huffily. "It was an important occasion and I didn't want to take just anyone."

Abby chuckled. "Remember right after your divorce when you dated that ditzy blonde who giggled all the time and called you sweet cheeks? And she wasn't talking about your face, either."

"Okay, so I made a mistake with her."

"A mistake? I noticed you didn't date for almost a year after she moved to Fiji to 'find herself.'"

"And what about Cameron?" Zach wasn't going to suffer alone during this trek down the memory lane.

She grimaced, thinking of the English professor she had dated a few times. "Okay, you've made your point, but you can blame Sally for him. She said he was a deep thinker. She forgot to mention he was also extremely stuffy."

"I think we were better off keeping track of the kids," he quipped. "How many times did I coach Matt's Little League team because no one else would?"

"More than either of us can count and only because he refused to have me do it." She laughed. "I can still remember one of the Girl Scout banquets I attended with your daughter where one of the other girls asked Beth what number wife I was! It appeared stepmothers were the norm there." She ran her fingers through her hair.

"Did you ever stop to think we would have ended up like this?" Zach asked lazily. "When Jason and I came back from 'Nam we figured we were lucky to be in one piece and just wanted to get on with our lives."

"Jason went to law school and you played the part of bum until you decided what you really wanted to do," Abby mused, continuing to sip her coffee. She chuckled. "I don't think any of us expected you to turn into one of the best-known hairdressers in San Diego." Her smile disappeared. "Or that I would end up a widow before I was ready."

"I figured if I was going to be a hairdresser I would be the best, and I had to become a success to afford Carolyn's alimony and Beth's clothing bills." Zach was determined to steer Abby away from less happy thoughts.

She smiled, well aware of his intent. "The three salons more than did that. Especially your latest one, by the university. Considering there're so many that deal with the young crowd yours has done very well for itself."

"I can't complain. I admit I don't go in that one too often. The bold color scheme and loud rock music are enough to make anyone from our generation crazy. But the kids like it and the stylists there are good, so I'm happy with it."

Abby stretched her arms over her head. "As much as I hate to move I think I should get going before I fall asleep here."

Zach stood up and held out his hand. She curled her fingers in his palm and allowed herself to be pulled up.

"Come on, old lady, let's get you home." He draped an arm around her shoulders.

"Very funny," she muttered, stooping to grab her shoes and purse.

He looked down at her, the hairdresser in him automatically restyling her red hair that hung down her back in loose waves. For more years than either cared to count they carried on a running joke as to why she didn't have him do her hair. He had to admit the tousled style suited her devil-may-care manner that contrasted sharply with her conservative occupation as a CPA.

They left Zach's ultramodern beachfront home in La Jolla for Abby's inland home.

"It appears someone's waiting up for me," she commented, seeing the lights glowing along the side of the house when Zach pulled into her driveway.

"The kids have got to make sure Mom gets home before curfew." They walked up to her front door. "Happy Birthday, Abby." Zach leaned down and brushed his lips across hers. For a moment he wanted to say something more, but he suddenly changed his mind. "Good night."

"Good night." She unlocked the door and slipped inside, locking the dead bolt immediately, knowing Zach would remain outside the door until he heard the telltale click of the lock. Sure enough, she didn't hear his footsteps until a moment later. She turned away walking toward the source of sound and light in the house. In the large den she found her son sprawled in a deep easy chair and her daughter curled up asleep on the couch.

"Hi," he greeted her, not bothering to look away from the television. "How was the party? Were you surprised? Beth said the cake was a real kick."

"I was shocked. And calling that cake a kick is an understatement," Abby admitted, looking at the array of empty potato-chip bags and cola cans littering the coffee table. "Just as I'm shocked by this mess. You know, Matt, I tried to teach you about picking up after yourself but I seem to have gone wrong somewhere."

"Blame half of this on Sam. She stuffed her face while complaining she was going to get zits from eating all that junk. Of course, the thought didn't stop her." He picked up the remote control and switched off the TV.

Abby chuckled. "I recall your doing the same when you were fifteen."

"I was never *that* bad," he spoke with the lofty authority of one who turned twenty a few months ago. He stood up and stretched his arms over his head. His lean build, blue eyes and dark auburn curly hair revealed his mother's heritage. "You going to wake up the kid or let her sleep here for the rest of the night?"

"What do you think? You should have told her to go to bed hours ago." Abby gently shook her daughter's shoulder. "Samantha."

The girl mumbled and turned over. "Mom?" Her voice was raspy with sleep as she pushed dark blond hair away from her sleep-flushed face. "What time is it?"

"Way past your bedtime."

Samantha stumbled to her feet. She aimed a kiss in Abby's direction. "G'night." She weaved her way out of the den.

Matt picked up the litter and tossed it in the wastebasket after a knowing look from his mother.

"What a shame you didn't do that in the beginning," Abby murmured.

Abby didn't get to bed for almost an hour by the time she shed her clothing and removed her makeup. She tucked her hair up in a towel to keep it dry before taking a quick shower. After she curled up in bed she thought over the events of the evening and smiled at the way Zach smoothly set her up.

She knew a lot of people thought of them as a couple in every sense of the word while they seemed to be more than careful to keep their friendship just that.

"He is sexy and good-looking," she admitted to the room. "Successful, a good father and a good friend." And when he kissed her she could have sworn there was just the faintest hint of a tingle between them. Nothing solid, just a bare suggestion, so that she wasn't sure if it was fact or just wishful thinking on her part.

Perhaps if things had been different Abby might have thought of considering Zach on a more intimate level years ago, but she knew only too well how his marriage and divorce had left him scarred and with no desire to remarry while her own marriage had been the stuff dreams were made of and she wouldn't mind having a second marriage just like it. Perhaps that was why her brain always fit Zach in the slot labeled "good buddy." After all, they were all more like one big happy family, especially with Matt and Beth dating for the past three years. During that time Abby

hadn't bothered wondering why she and Zach never deepened their friendship because she already knew. Giving in to
the lassitude taking over her body she soon closed her eyes
and fell asleep.

"YOU'RE UP EARLY," Matt greeted a sleepy looking Abby
around a mouthful of warm cinnamon roll. "Coffee's already made."

"Just because I turned forty doesn't mean I'll spend the
rest of my life in bed." She poured herself a cup of coffee,
turning when the back door opened revealing a gray-haired
woman. "Hi, Estelle."

The woman stared down at Matt. "You cleaned up that
mess you and your sister began last night, didn't you?"

"I cleaned up all of it," he replied. "Sam fell asleep on
the couch and Mom didn't force her to help out."

The housekeeper turned to Abby, then looked at the coffee maker then back to Abby. "Abby, you didn't try to make
coffee again, did you?" she asked softly.

Matt guffawed, earning a murderous glare from his
mother.

"Nah, we're safe, Estelle. I made it," he assured her.

"There is nothing all that difficult about making coffee," Abby enunciated every word.

Matt and the housekeeper exchanged knowing looks.

"Mom, every time you've tried to make coffee we've
either almost had a fire or ended up with a ruined coffee
maker," he reminded her. "We're on our sixth one now."

"Seventh," Estelle corrected, much to Abby's mortifi-
cation. "You forgot two months ago when she wanted to try
that new gourmet coffee and no one was home."

"All right, I get the message," Abby said hastily. "I
promised I wouldn't do it again, didn't I?"

"You did the other six times, too," Estelle spoke with the
familiarity of one who had been with the family for years.

"Don't sweat it, Mom," Matt consoled, unaware he was only making matters worse. "Not everyone can cook."

Abby sighed. No matter how much it hurt, her son was right; she had no culinary aptitude whatsoever. She had suffered the humiliation of flunking Home Economics in school and was known to have trouble even boiling water. As a result Estelle arrived early enough in the morning to cook breakfast and stayed until after dinnertime before retiring to her apartment over the large detached garage in the back.

"If you're all through insulting me I think I'll return to my room to dress," Abby said haughtily.

"She's getting touchy in her old age, Estelle," Matt confided. "We're going to have to humor her now that she's reached the big four-oh."

"Watch who you're calling old, buster," she retorted, pulling a frying pan out of the cabinet. "You gonna be here for lunch?"

He shook his head. "Beth and I are driving up to the mountains. We probably won't be back until late."

"Hi!" a raspy voice shouted, before a large macaw with a brilliant red-feathered head, blue and green wing feathers and long blue tail waddled into the kitchen and sidled up to Abby. "Hi." This time his greeting sounded more like a lover's call.

"Max, you're supposed to be in your cage," she scolded the bird while lifting her head to glare at her son. "Didn't you make sure he was locked up last night?"

"No, it was Sam's turn. And you know how she feels about Max."

Abby did indeed. The friendly macaw had discovered early on that Samantha was easily intimidated by him and he took every available chance to rattle her. The only human he more than tolerated was Abby, whom he had fallen in love with at first sight. One of her clients bred macaws and cockatoos, and during one of Abby's visits to the aviary she had met Max who immediately swooped down to perch on her shoulder and coo and regurgitate on her blouse. She couldn't help but be wary even after being told how she was honored by the normally shy bird. In the end she got out her checkbook. After almost a year in the Townsend household, Max acted more like another son than a bird. And he took every chance he got to be with his favorite human. He flapped his brilliant-colored wings and seemed to hug her leg.

"Come on, lover boy." Abby bent down to allow him to step onto her arm as she settled him on a large perch set in a corner of the kitchen.

"Breakfast," the bird demanded, his red head fuzzed up with excitement at being with the rest of the family.

"You want breakfast you can cook it yourself," Estelle informed him, then muttered, "I still can't believe I'm talking to him as if he understands."

"That's the problem, he does." Abby grabbed a walnut out of a nearby basket and handed it to Max. "I won't be here, either. I promised to take Sam shopping for new school clothes today. That is, if she plans to get up within the next half hour. Knowing her we'll be hitting every mall within a one-hundred-mile radius so we should make an early start."

"How was the party?" Estelle asked, as she began frying sausage.

"Wonderful. Zach got more than even with me for what I did on his fortieth, but I'll get back at him when he turns fifty."

"Knowing you, you'll come up with something appropriate."

"After last night everyone will suspect the worst. For some crazy reason they feel we should become a couple. I swear we were their prime subject the entire evening."

Matt choked. "No way. Zach prefers to remain single. Plus you and him getting it on just doesn't cut it."

Abby's eyes narrowed. "Would you please explain that last statement?" she asked sweetly.

"No offense, Mom, but the two of you are practically brother and sister. Besides, you're not his type."

"Zach doesn't have a specific type."

"Sure he does. While he may not date a lot, the women he does go out with are usually stacked and know the score."

Abby's gaze fell to her own faint curves, or lack thereof. "Matt, you really know how to make a woman feel good. If this is the way you refer to Beth I'm surprised she has anything to do with you." Carrying her coffee cup she left the kitchen.

Within ten seconds Max had hopped off his perch and was practically running through the house after Abby. Matt and Estelle laughed as they heard Abby order Max out, then the audible click of a lock snapping on what was Max's cage door and his sorrowful mutterings. Then they heard Abby's knock on Samantha's bedroom door and her reminder that the girl should be up soon if she wanted to go shopping that day.

"Something tells me this isn't going to be a good day," Estelle murmured.

"Mom will agree with you after she sees the shopping list Sam made out." Matt tackled the eggs and sausage the housekeeper set in front of him.

"HI, MR. RANDOLPH, can Beth come out to play?" Matt called, climbing out of his black sports car. He walked up the driveway to watch Zach maneuver a motorized lawn mower.

"Hi, Matt," he greeted the younger man. "Beth, Matt's here," he called through an open window.

"Okay," a young feminine voice filtered out. "Be right out."

"What happened to your gardening service?" Matt gestured toward the lawn mower.

"They messed up the lawn the last two times so I cancelled them and I haven't had the time to find anyone new." He wiped the perspiration from his brow. "My first appointment isn't until ten so I figured the exercise would do me good. Your mom sleeping in after her big night?"

Matt shook his head. "She's taking Sam shopping for school clothes."

Zach winced. "That's going to be an expensive day."

"Yeah, I didn't tell Mom that Sam made a list last night of what stores she wants to hit today." He grinned.

"I'm sorry, sir, but buttering up my father won't get you anywhere," a girl called out gaily, sauntering out of the house. Tall, slim with shoulder-length golden blond hair pulled back in an intricate braid, she was a feminine version of Zach. "'Bye, Dad, see you tonight."

Zach looked at Matt. "Any idea when you'll be back?" he asked, ignoring Beth's groan of dismay.

He shrugged. "Probably not until seven or eight." Keeping his arm around Beth's shoulders they walked down to his car. He stopped. "Hey, I hear everyone's on your case for you and Mom to get it on." He chuckled. "Funny, huh?"

"Funny?" Zach didn't think it was that humorous an idea. "Why do you think it's funny?"

Matt laughed. "Hey, Zach, you have to admit Mom's not your type and you're not hers. Gotta go. See ya."

"'Bye, Dad." Beth waved as they drove off.

Zach watched the car until he could see it no more before returning to his work. Just before switching the lawn mower on again he halted, bracing his hands on his hips.

"We're not each other's type," Zach echoed. "Amazing that we get along so well then." The changed feelings about Abby weren't sudden. In fact, they had been building up for quite a while now, but Zach was a cautious man and preferred considering his options first. Abby had always been a very good friend. If something happened to turn that friendship into something more intimate would they lose something or gain even more? Only time would tell.

"Now this is the way a lawn should look." He stood back, looking at his work with supreme pride. Needing to cool off, he turned on the hose and stuck his head under the flowing water, sputtering when it turned too cold.

"Harrumph!"

Zach looked up, finding a tiny silver-haired lady staring at him with pinched-mouth disapproval.

"Good morning, Miss Howard," he greeted her with a broad smile.

"Mr. Randolph," she spoke in a frosty, broad Boston accent. "Aren't you afraid of catching a chill?" She silently referred to his bare chest and legs.

As the August morning temperature was already topping the eighties Zach knew he didn't have anything to worry about. "No, ma'am, my family have always been extremely healthy," he spoke respectfully. He privately considered the snoopy old lady a royal pain in the butt but she always acted like the proper lady, so he refused to act impolitely toward her no matter how much she irritated him.

She stamped the tip of her walking stick against the ground. "I just hope you don't plan on having more of those wild parties."

Zach turned away, ostensibly to turn off the water, so she couldn't see the grin hovering on his lips. "No, Miss Howard, I merely held a surprise birthday party for Abby Townsend."

A delicate sniff was his answer. Zach was given the impression that Miss Howard's imagination had them acting in a highly "improper manner."

"Hell," he muttered to himself. "Everyone's got us in bed." Seeing that Miss Howard was already marching toward her front door he made his escape, putting the lawn mower away before showering and changing his clothes. The more he thought about it the more he began to wonder if the others didn't have the right idea about him and Abby. Now, if he could only convince Abby to give it fair consideration!

"MY FEET ARE DEAD, Samantha Townsend," Abby complained, after they left another boutique without success. "I can't walk another step."

When their shopping trip began that morning Abby laid down the law, saying she would only spend a specified amount of money and not a cent more. As a result, Sam turned into a very discriminating shopper.

"Here." Samantha urged her into another store but Abby hung back shaking her head.

"You look around. I'll wait out here." Abby searched for a nearby bench and collapsed, piling packages around her. "I should have enrolled her in a private school where uniforms are required. It would save so much time... and money," she muttered, pushing a lock of hair out of her eyes.

"I found two blouses, a pair of cords, jeans and a sweater," Samantha reported forty minutes later.

Abby nodded wearily as she slowly got to her feet. "Dare I hope this will finish our shopping?"

Samantha shook her head. "I still need shoes," she explained.

Abby groaned. "A nice pair of white tennis shoes would go with everything."

Samantha shot her an exasperated look. "Get real, Mom. Say, can we have lunch first? I'm starved."

"Only if we can find a restaurant that won't care if I take off my shoes and soak them in a tub of ice." Abby, and her well-used charge cards, marched on looking like a soldier going off to war.

When they finally limped home Abby could only think longingly of a hot bath and spending the evening with her feet elevated.

"Matt called," Estelle announced when they entered the house. "Something happened to the car and he isn't sure when he'll be back." She looked at their piles of packages. "Did you leave anything in the stores?"

"Empty hangers," Abby said wearily, setting her armful of bags on the kitchen table. "Do I have time for a bath before dinner?"

"More than enough."

"Wait until you see what I got, Estelle," Samantha announced, carrying in her second pile of bags.

"This wardrobe has to last her until her twenty-first birthday." Abby poured herself a cup of coffee. "Sam, I want those clothes hung up before dinner."

The girl nodded as she left the kitchen, her arms filled with shopping bags.

"Want some help? I'll make the salad," Abby offered, then quickly rescinded it when she saw the knowing look on her housekeeper's face. "Sorry, I forgot myself."

Estelle reached over and held up Abby's hand pointing out a thin white line along the third finger. "The last time you tried to fix a salad you almost amputated that finger. Please, Abby, don't do me any favors."

"The knife was too sharp," Abby said defensively.

"It's supposed to be."

Sensing her dismissal, Abby left the room. She stopped by Samantha's bedroom to make sure her daughter was doing as requested. True to form, Samantha was curled up on the bed, her phone plastered to her ear.

"That shop in the mall has the cutest sweaters," she rambled on. "I got a pastel striped one and a pair of pale pink cords to go with it."

Abby knocked lightly on the door, mouthing her previous order before moving down the hall to her bedroom.

"I'm getting too old for shopping marathons. From now on we order out of catalogs," she muttered, turning the tub taps on full blast and stripping off her clothes. She eased her tired body into the steaming water with a sigh of relief. When she began to feel drowsy she climbed out and quickly dried off before pulling on a yellow cotton robe.

"I WONDER IF I shouldn't have gotten that pink sweater at Nordstrom," Samantha thought out loud as she helped herself to the lasagna.

Abby rolled her eyes. "Forget it. As it is, you'll have to clean out your closet to put away what you bought today."

"Already done." Samantha looked unbearably smug.

"And now all the clothes she suddenly hates are all over her bed." Estelle set a basket of warm garlic bread on the table before sitting down. "Am I right?"

"I had to put them somewhere. Don't worry, I've got it all under control."

"So why am I worried?" Abby muttered.

After dinner, Abby sent Samantha upstairs with the request to fold her discarded clothing neatly and put the items in a box. She couldn't stop glancing at the clock every few minutes wondering when Matt would get home.

"You're worried about Matt and Beth, aren't you?" Estelle easily read her thoughts.

"Yes, and I don't know why," she admitted. "I feel so uneasy."

"It's just the mother complex you were born with. Relax, everything's fine. He's never given you any problems before, has he?"

"No. All right, I promise not to worry until midnight, is that fair?"

"More than fair."

Abby kept repeating her vow even as the clock hands pointed to one. By then she was ready to call the police.

When the telephone rang she jumped. Picturing visions of multiple car pileups and worse, she picked up the receiver.

"Hello?"

"Abby, it's me." Zach's voice was quiet. "I wanted you to know Matt just dropped Beth off."

"Is everything all right?" She still feared the worse.

"Yes. Good night, Abby."

She slowly replaced the receiver, puzzling over Zach's unusual tone. It seemed no time at all before she heard Matt's car in the driveway. She appeared in the kitchen doorway when the back door opened and closed. The young man looked up, flashing her a sheepish grin.

"Hi."

"Hi, yourself." She entered the kitchen. "Everything all right with the car?"

"Yeah, it was the clutch acting up."

"You were going to work on it this weekend."

He grimaced. "I know, it got fixed a little early. I'm afraid I had to put the repairs on the Master Card you gave me 'cause they wouldn't take a check. I'll give you the money tomorrow." He turned to the refrigerator and pulled out a cola can. "I'm really bushed, Mom, so I'm going to bed." He left the kitchen.

Abby sighed. "It's times like this that turn a mother's hair gray."

"IT WAS MY THIRD STROKE!" Abby stood nose to nose with Zach.

"Fourth."

"Third."

"Fourth."

Her gaze refused to leave his. "What if I pick up the ball and take it over?" Abby suggested slyly.

"Mom, we're getting old waiting here," Samantha called out.

Muttering to herself, Abby picked up the ball and snatched the scorecard out of Zach's hand.

"When I asked you to come along with us I didn't realize you'd take this game so seriously."

He grinned at her aggrieved tone. "If you're going to do something, do it right."

"I heartily dislike high-minded people." Abby caught the attention of her giggling daughter and friend who were occupied ogling a couple of boys who were playing nearby and obviously showing off for their enthralled audience. "Okay girls, put the hormones on hold," she ordered crisply. "We're playing as a foursome here."

For the remainder of the game Abby and Zach good-naturedly squabbled.

"Abby, that's the third ball you've hit into the pond!" Zach exploded.

"I never claimed to be good at this game," she argued. "I just come here to have fun."

"Good thing because your golfing skills are about as good as your cooking."

She looked at him fit to kill. "That was cold, Zach. Very cold."

"And very true."

Connie, Samantha's friend, watched the heated exchange with awe. "They sound like my parents," she told Samantha.

"Yeah, and they don't even date," she sighed. "Come on, let's get a soda."

Zach turned to watch the two girls walk away, their golf clubs resting nonchalantly on their shoulders. "They're probably letting us know, in their own subtle way, that they're embarrassed to be seen with us."

Abby shrugged. "I wouldn't worry. When I was seeing Brian, Sam once informed me she refused to be seen with us unless she could wear a bag over her head and walk on the opposite side of the street." Her lips twitched.

Zach nodded, recalling the no-nonsense computer programmer Abby had dated on and off for about two years. "She had the right idea." He grabbed her hand and led her off the colorful course.

"At least he didn't call me 'sweet cheeks,'" Abby said sweetly as they approached the snack bar where Samantha and Connie were already enjoying their drinks.

Zach rolled his eyes. "We'll just forget that, shall we?"

Abby thought differently but she wasn't about to say so. "Two attractive, fairly sane people with above-average skills and we can't find Mr. and Ms. Right if our lives depended on it."

"Trust me, we're better off." Zach glared at two young boys who were tentatively approaching the girls and hoped they would get the message to back off.

Samantha wrinkled her nose at him. "That is the last time you two play miniature golf with us. It's too embarrassing."

"Fine, next time we'll play on the other course," Zach said easily.

Abby chuckled. "Let's go. Since Zach lost he's paying for the hamburgers."

"Who lost?"

"I told you, I only took three strokes on that hole."

"Four, but I'm feeling magnanimous so I'll forget you tried to cheat and let you pay," he told her as they walked out to the car.

Connie nodded at Samantha. "Yeah, just like my parents."

Chapter Two

"Now look here, Mrs. Townsend, I kept all my receipts and now you're telling me my trip last month can't be written off? It was a business trip!" he blustered. "What kind of service do you run here?"

Abby faced the irate man seated across the broad expanse of her desk. Gone was the laughing, mischievous sometimes scatterbrained woman her family knew so well. Dressed in navy-tailored slacks, a pale gold silk blouse and her hair pulled up in a loose knot, she looked like a no-nonsense CPA.

She silently counted to ten. "Mr. Moore, we've been through all of this before." She forced herself to sound reasonable when all she wanted to do was tell the rude man exactly what she thought of him. "You own five men's clothing stores. That kind of business doesn't necessitate a trip to Club Med."

His plump face grew a dull red.

"Not to mention a majority of those receipts were bar bills signed by Mrs. Moore," she went on. "Mr. Moore, you've been divorced for six years and your ex-wife practically let the entire world know what she thought of you at that time."

"I have to entertain clients," he muttered, staring down at his hands clasped in his lap.

"Give me some credit, Mr. Moore," Abby told him. "A man whose clothing stores specialize in attire for the conservative businessman does not make business trips to Club Med. The IRS certainly wouldn't see it your way."

Defeated, he pushed back his chair. "It would have worked." He paused to have the last word. "Every chance I've taken has come out in my favor. You've got to go for the gusto, Mrs. Townsend. Grab the brass ring. That's how you get ahead in this world, not by hiding out." With that, he took his leave.

Grateful to be alone after an hour of what was probably fruitless arguing, Abby rummaged through her desk drawer. "Estelle!"

The housekeeper appeared in the doorway separating Abby's office from the rest of the house. "You ran out of aspirin last Thursday when Mrs. Powell kept trying to convince you her little Fluffy is a dependent."

Abby closed her eyes and groaned. "A twenty-pound Persian cat, no less. Why am I so lucky to get clients like these?"

Estelle handed her an aspirin bottle and a large glass of water; clearly, she had anticipated Abby's request. "It seems to me your normal clients are a distinct minority. You've got to work harder at getting a better class of clientele. Perhaps I should say normal."

Abby rolled her eyes. "I have enough problems now, thank you." She popped two aspirin into her mouth and lifted the glass to her lips. "Thank you, you've saved my life."

"You stopping long enough to eat a proper lunch?"

Abby looked down at her appointment calendar and shook her head. "I've got to get some end-of-month reports out in this afternoon's mail, so I guess I'll just have a sandwich in here." Abby switched on her computer and searched through her index of floppy disks for the appropriate one.

"That's a sure way to get indigestion," Estelle muttered, leaving the office.

"If you don't want to fix me anything to eat in here, I'll do it," she sang out.

"Fat chance. I'll bring something in, then I'm going grocery shopping and you stay out of my kitchen!"

Lost in a maze of profit-and-loss statements, Abby merely nodded. She worked on her reports and stopped only when Estelle returned with a bacon, lettuce and tomato sandwich.

"It's amazing all that numbers stuff doesn't faze you, while you can't handle a simple microwave," Estelle commented, setting the plate on the desk.

"Computers are safer."

"Computers lose information."

"A red piece of clothing in the wrong laundry load turns everything pink."

"Computers send you the wrong statements." Estelle referred to a multicharge account statement Abby had received a few months earlier that included more than one customer's statement.

"Dishwashers break glasses," Abby countered with a grin, enjoying the verbal battle.

"Not if you put them in the right way. Besides, that's one thing you've never done. The dishwasher is about the only appliance I can trust you with."

"Blame my mother. She always said it was easier to do it herself than to teach me." Abby made a face. "She also said it had been amazing Jason hadn't died from food poisoning early on in our marriage." Her expression sobered. "Instead it had to be from some kid high on drugs. If Adam hadn't called him that night to bail him out of the drunk tank he wouldn't have been there when the police brought in that kid. How that teenager got that policeman's gun no one will ever know."

Estelle shook her head at the memory of the senseless death. "Jason was always there for his friends. The kid should have been taken to the hospital, but he hadn't been. So do yourself a favor and stop thinking about it. It's a beautiful day out. Think of that, instead."

Abby smiled at the housekeeper. "Okay, boss."

"Harrumph! I should be so lucky. See you in a few hours." She left the office.

With a sigh Abby returned to her work. Even though she ran her business out of her home she kept herself on a strict schedule except during tax season when she burned the midnight oil on a regular basis. A little after five o'clock she switched on her answering machine and left her office.

After changing into jeans and a pale green cotton top, Abby went outside where she found Matt clipping the hedge separating their yard from their neighbor's.

"Hi," she greeted her son, kissing him on the cheek. "My, aren't we busy."

"It looked pretty bad, so I decided it was time to do it before you told me to." He grinned.

"Hmm, you must want something pretty badly if you're willing to butter me up by doing something without me screaming at you first," she teased.

"There's our next Perry Mason!" A woman in her late twenties waved as she walked out of the neighboring house. "Hi, Abby, Matt."

"You said it, Sandi," Abby called out laughing. "And when he's a rich and famous lawyer he's going to support his aging mother in the style she'd like to become accustomed to."

"You'd be better off finding a rich husband," Matt retorted, putting down the hedge clippers.

"No such animal," Sandi declared with the knowledge of one who knew. "I should know. I've been looking for the past three years." When her teacher husband ran off with one of his high-school students, Sandi had promptly di-

vorced him and decided to find a husband who wasn't
looking at younger women all the time. Like Abby she was
discriminating in her choice of men but still enjoyed the
search for Mr. Right.

"If you two want dinner you better get in here now." Estelle stood in the back door. Her gaze sliced in Matt's direction. "But *you* clean up first."

"Yes, ma'am, anything you say, ma'am." Matt saluted
smartly.

"Smart aleck," she muttered before turning away.

After dinner Matt closeted himself in his room to talk to
Beth on the phone and Samantha and Abby watched television in the den with Max perched on the couch arm. As
they sat there Abby watched her daughter with uncon-
cealed pride. While Matt shared Abby's auburn coloring,
Samantha took after her father with thick, dark blond hair
that swung loose around her cheeks, gold-flecked brown
eyes and a bit stockier build than Abby's and Matt's slim
ones. While Samantha looked like her father, she inherited
her mother's temperament and could fly off the handle easily. But she was a good kid who didn't hold grudges and had
friends whom she enjoyed being with. Abby was more than
glad for that after seeing how many of Samantha's school-
mates were nothing more than snobs.

When Matt walked in a few hours later Samantha micro-
waved a package of popcorn for them to snack on. Abby
enjoyed their quiet time together even as she wondered when
it would end. They were growing up all too fast.

ZACH ENJOYED SATURDAYS because they were so profit-
able and hated them because he always seemed to be over-
booked, since a majority of his clients were standing
appointments. At the moment he stood back waiting for the
silver-haired woman's judgement on her new hairstyle. She
turned her head from one side to the other gazing into the
hand mirror so she could see the way the back was styled.

"I don't know, Zach, don't you feel it's a bit, well, extreme?" She looked up at him with a worried look on her lightly wrinkled face.

"You wanted something new, Marjorie," he pointed out gently. "You also said you were tired of pinning your hair up in a twist when your arthritis has been acting up. With it short and curly all you have to do is wash it and fluff it up with your fingers. That's why we've talked this over for so long before doing it."

She still didn't look convinced although Zach knew he was right. Marjorie Brennan had been complaining for a long time that she had trouble with her long hair when her fingers were aching on cold mornings, so he suggested a shorter cut.

"Mrs. Brennan, that looks great," Susan, one of Zach's hairdressers who doubled as salon manager, complimented the older woman. "If your husband doesn't take one look and demand to take you out to dinner to show you off he's crazy." Zach shot her a look of gratitude.

She still didn't look entirely convinced. "Well, we'll see," she murmured, then turned to Zach. "It's not that I don't like it, Zach. It's just that it's so new."

He nodded. This was something he was used to.

"You're losing your touch, Zach," Susan teased, after the woman left.

"It never fails. They come in demanding a new look, something entirely different, but if you give it to them they practically have a heart attack," he groused.

"Next time she comes in she'll be beaming as if this was all her idea. That never fails, either." Susan took his hands and they executed a couple of jitterbug steps to the forties swing tune playing, much to the amusement of the patrons. Zach catered to his clients' tastes and this salon reflected quiet colors, a few World War II era posters and music from the same time period. Situated in an older, more established part of San Diego, the salon was popular.

"I don't know how you keep up your pace," Susan told him, filling her coffee cup as they took a much-needed five-minute break. "There are some days I'm lucky if I can make it home and walk in the door under my own power."

He hugged her briefly. She had been one of the first stylists to come to work for him and the two had always been more like close friends than employer and employee. "Eight hours sleep, a proper diet, a rigorous exercise program and just plain old-fashioned clean living."

Susan's reply was brief and to the point. Zach laughed and returned to his station to double-check his appointment book. He had almost called Abby that morning to see if she'd like to meet him for lunch, but Saturdays were too busy for him to have more than just a quick sandwich.

"Idiot, you could have seen if she was free for dinner," he muttered with a disgusted shake of the head.

ZACH STRODE OVER to the pay phone in the back of the shop and probed his pockets for change. He swore under his breath when he came up with a few pennies and a nickel.

"Anybody got change for the phone?" he called out and received hoots and laughter in return.

"Is there something wrong with the phone up front?" someone teased. "Oh, that's right, the boss doesn't want the help to use the front-desk phone."

"I think it's admirable that you're observing your own rules, Zach. It looks good for us peons," another joked.

"We're in trouble if the boss can't even cough up twenty-five cents. Has anyone tried to cash their pay checks yet?" one of the stylists joked.

He simply stood there waiting for their good-natured teasing to wind down. Susan finally took pity on him and tossed him a quarter.

"I expect the change," she told him with a deadpan expression.

"A man wants some privacy and he gets Don Rickles instead," Zach muttered under his breath turning back to the phone, dialing quickly.

"Townsend residence."

Zach grinned. Estelle always answered the phone sounding as if the caller had pulled her away from some very important task when usually, it was her favorite soap opera or movie.

"Hi, darlin'," Zach crooned into the receiver. "How's the sexiest woman in the world?"

"Don't you try to sweet-talk me, Zach Randolph," she retorted. "Shouldn't you be cutting or coloring someone's hair or whatever you're doing?"

"I've got a few minutes. Is Abby around?" He shifted from one foot to the other.

"She's here somewhere. Just a second." Estelle put him on hold while she searched for her boss.

"Zach, hi." Abby sounded breathless. "I'm honored."

He frowned, confused by her statement. "Honored, why?"

She laughed softly. "Are you kidding? Zach, it's Saturday, your busiest day. Shouldn't you be standing over a hot curling iron?"

"Cute, Abby. I thought I'd see how a night out on the town sounded to you."

"It sounds good, but aren't Matt and Beth going to that party tonight? And Sam's having Melanie over for dinner and they're going to the movies afterward."

He exhaled. "Actually, I thought just you and I could go out. And no, this isn't for a fund-raiser or any other social event where I need a last-minute date."

"I see." She sounded more than a little surprised. "Zach, are you asking me for a date?"

"Yeah, I think I am."

Abby was silent for a moment. She hadn't expected this at all. Their evenings out were usually family affairs. "Is this to be a dress-up dinner where we have to act like adults with impeccable table manners, or a casual dinner where anything goes?''

''How about we start out casual and work our way up to formal?'' Zach suggested. ''Maybe it will be easier for us that way.''

Easier for what? she thought to herself. ''Sounds good to me.''

''Zach, your two-o'clock is here,'' a disembodied voice announced over the speaker. ''Zach.''

''Abby, I've got to run. I'll pick you up at seven, okay?''

''See you then.''

When Zach hung up he was unaware of a grin hovering on the edge of his lips. ''All right,'' he murmured, leaving the room.

''Did I hear right, Zach asked you out on a real date?'' Estelle asked Abby the minute she hung up.

''You're eavesdropping again.'' It was clear this was an old battle between them.

''Housekeepers are supposed to eavesdrop, it's in their by-laws,'' she said unperturbed. ''How else can we know what's going on?''

Abby pinched off a corner of the spice cake Estelle had just finished frosting and got her hand slapped in the process.

''That's for dinner,'' Estelle informed her.

''But I won't be here for dinner so I may as well have my share now.''

''No. Samantha asked me to bake this cake for Melanie and she deserves an unspoiled cake.''

Abby grinned. ''Spoilsport.''

''So where's Zach taking you? Some place real fancy?''

''I have no idea. I'm just supposed to dress casual. We're probably going out for hamburgers. Maybe he has a problem with Beth he wants to talk over.'' For some reason Abby felt a little uneasy thinking about this being a *real* date, yet if he had asked her to help him out for a social occasion she wouldn't have thought twice about it.

Estelle's eyes glittered. "And maybe he doesn't. Don't mind me, I'll think positive. Now, get out of here so I can get this kitchen cleaned."

Abby walked into the den where a five-foot-tall, wrought-iron dome-shaped cage domineered one corner. At the moment the perch inside stood empty while Max stood in the middle of the coffee table happily tearing magazines into confetti.

"Max!" Abby shouted.

"Hi!" His exuberant greeting echoed throughout the room. He lifted one foot in a silent plea to be picked up. "What a good boy!"

Abby held out her arm and he climbed on, his wings spread out in a brilliant display. He tipped his head to one side in hopes she would scratch the tiny lines of red feathers along his face.

"That's a very bad boy, Max," she scolded angrily, looking down at the scraps littering the table. "Look at this mess you made." He made the crooning sounds of a happy macaw, unrepentant of the destruction he had just caused.

"My magazines!" Samantha yelled, running into the room. She turned to glare at Max who now sat on his perch inside his cage. "Look what you did, you dumb bird!"

"Samantha, his cage door wasn't locked and you know he's been able to get out from almost the beginning," Abby intervened, before Samantha completely lost her temper. "He's at fault, yes, but I can't blame him entirely since you cleaned his cage today but forgot to secure the lock. He probably escaped the first chance he got and took advantage of his freedom."

The girl glared at the bird who seemed to smirk back at her. She turned back to the pile picking up several of the magazines that hadn't been touched. "I see he didn't get any of yours."

"Probably because I caught him before he got to them."

Samantha held one magazine up high. "This one was on the top. I remembered stacking them earlier today. He only tore up mine and it was deliberate." She shot the bird a dirty look. He fluffed his feathers in a threatening display and screamed at her. She stepped back one pace and his head snapped up in pride of intimidating her so easily.

Abby sighed. She wanted to tell her daughter it couldn't be true, that Max couldn't have known which was whose, but she knew better. Over the past year she had come to learn just how intelligent he was. And it did appear he always knew what he was doing. His last crime wave consisted of getting into Samantha's bedroom and chewing several holes in her quilt. She kept her door closed after that. But he never touched any of Abby's belongings and Matt's only on a rare occasion.

"Max, tell Sam you're sorry for tearing up her magazines," Abby ordered.

His head feathers fluffed up, showing his displeasure at such a request.

"He's worse than a three-year-old child. And if he touches one more thing of mine I'm going to roast him!" Samantha stormed out of the room.

"Hello Max," he rasped. "Max is a good boy."

Abby scowled at him. "Not today you aren't. I just wish I could make you clean this." She began picking up the shredded paper and tossed it in a nearby wastebasket and rearranged the remaining magazines before going to her room to decide what to wear that evening. Just because it was a casual date didn't mean she had to wear a sweatshirt and jeans.

Zach appeared at Abby's house promptly at seven although he knew from past experience she wouldn't be ready. Samantha came to the door and suggested he come back to the kitchen where she and her friend were having dinner before going to the movies.

"Hello, Melanie," he greeted the dark-haired girl seated at the table.

She smiled up at him. "Hello, Zach." Only the slow cadence and slightly slurred speech revealed she was mentally handicapped. "Do you want to have cake with us? 'Stelle made my favorite."

He placed his hand on top of her head, ruffling the black curls. "No thanks, hon, it might spoil my dinner. What are you two up to tonight?"

Melanie smiled. "Sam and I are going to the movies and I get to spend the night here."

"That sounds like fun." He looked up when Abby, wearing khaki, tan twill slacks and a red-and-khaki-striped cotton top, entered the room, then glanced down at his watch. "Not bad, you're only ten minutes late."

She wrinkled her nose at him. "Cute."

Zach opened his mouth to say something else but a pained grimace marred his face. He looked down to see Max's beak holding his ankle in what had to be a painful pressure bite. "Hello, Max," he sighed.

"Max, let him go," Abby ordered.

The macaw looked up at her and deliberated before slowly releasing his prey. Giving Zach an aggrieved look he walked out of the kitchen.

"That bird is a menace," Zach declared.

"You can say that again," Samantha spoke up.

"He just has a different way of saying hello," Abby replied, walking over to the table and hugging each girl. "Have a good time at the movies."

"I'm surprised Melanie's mother is allowing her to go out at night," Zach commented as they climbed into his car. "She's always been so protective about her."

"Lara knows Estelle is taking them and picking them up. She also knows Sam wouldn't allow anyone to make fun of Melanie or try to hurt her."

Zach chuckled as he set the car in gear. "Yeah, the last time she almost got suspended from school for giving one of the boys a bloody nose after he teased Melanie until she cried."

Abby sighed, remembering the episode only too well. She had been proud of her daughter for defending her friend so valiantly, but talked to her about finding another, less violent way the next time. "Melanie is a beautiful fifteen-year-old girl who will never grow beyond the age of seven. It's so sad and yet I'm thankful it isn't my Samantha. And then I feel guilty for feeling that way."

"Don't," he ordered gently. "It's a perfectly natural feeling. All parents want their children to be perfect in every way. Just consider the good you've done in allowing Sam to associate with Melanie and for Sam to have the good sense in realizing being different doesn't mean being inferior. Not to mention Melanie's gained a good friend. How many mothers allow their children to be with her even now in these supposedly enlightened times? It says a lot that you saw more than a little girl who will always remain a little girl."

She tipped her head to one side. "My, you really know how to flatter a lady. Now you can tell me how gorgeous I am," she prompted hopefully.

"Are you kidding? There'd be no living with you then."

"Then you should be thankful that you don't have to live with me."

He grinned at her pert reply and switched on the engine.

"So, where are we going for dinner?" Abby asked as his Corvette roared down the street.

"How hungry are you?" Zach asked, turning left.

"Not starving, why? Are we eating in a different state?" She couldn't understand the need for secrecy.

"No, but I thought we could do something first to work up more of an appetite."

She was beginning to grow suspicious. What was he up to? "Such as?"

"You'll see soon enough." Zach slowed at the next intersection and turned again.

"I didn't realize our evening was going to be a mystery," she commented, hoping to take her mind off the flexing muscles so near her hand resting on the corner of her seat.

"It's not, I just wanted to give you something special. Let's just say our first date will be something to remember."

Ten minutes later, Zach pulled into a fairly crowded parking lot and parked the car. Abby looked up at the neon sign with disbelief.

Chapter Three

"You're right. This is a first date I'll never forget." Abby looked around the noisy smoke-filled interior. She patted Zach's cheek. "I'll give you credit, Zach. You're certainly not pulling out all the stops to impress me."

"Ah, but as you said, you won't forget it." He spoke to a balding heavy-set man behind a large desk and received a large sheet of paper and two pair of shoes, one of which he handed to Abby. "Shall we see if your bowling skills are any better than your golf?"

She stopped, placing her hands on her hips. "Watch out, Randolph, because I'm going to cream you."

Abby enjoyed herself until the neighboring lane's occupants appeared. She was jumping up and down in glee after rolling her first strike when two young women sat down on the other side of the curved bench.

"It was a fluke," Zach announced solemnly. "I demand a recount."

"That was a perfectly good strike and you know it." She playfully bopped him on the head. "So mark the X in the proper box. No, not next to your name, mine!" She draped her arm across his back.

"Excuse me." A woman's husky voice broke in.

Abby and Zach turned their heads to view a tall slim blond woman wearing tight white shorts and a bright blue bandeau top barely covering her generous curves while the other woman wore equally tight jeans and a skimpy tank top over voluptuous breasts. Abby clenched her teeth before her jaw dropped.

"How do you know which balls are the lightest?" the young woman asked with an inviting smile.

Abby rolled her eyes and bit her lip to keep from saying anything.

"The balls with the colored swirls," he replied with a brief smile and turned back to Abby.

Within minutes the two women returned with their balls and placed them on the return with appreciative sidelong glances at Zach.

"If the one in blue can bowl without splitting anything I'll be very surprised," Abby murmured in Zach's ear.

His eyes lit up. "Hmm, the prospect sounds interesting."

"Pull the eyeballs back in, Zachary," she ordered sweetly, unconsciously exhaling to push her meager chest out as far as possible, which wasn't all that far.

It wasn't the first time a strange woman had flirted with Zach in front of Abby but it was the first time it irritated her. For the next twenty minutes she watched them watch Zach, which also prompted her to watch him. She silently admitted to herself he looked very well in his jeans and aqua polo shirt and certainly didn't look his age.

"A forty-three-year-old man shouldn't look so good," she muttered, marking down his score with jabbing strokes. "Why can't he be balding with a pot belly, jowls and flat feet?"

"Who should have flat feet?" Zach came up and placed his hands on the tiny table next to her.

"You probably do from all the standing you do."

"Nope, my feet are in excellent health as is the rest of me."

Abby's eyes swept over him. She decided she would be better off not to say anything further on that subject.

"Zach, perhaps I should call and check on the children?" she suggested, coating each word with sugar.

He lifted an eyebrow. "The children?"

"Yes, dear, *our* children. All *three* of them."

He nodded. "Ah, yes, little Matt, Bethy and Samantha. Perhaps you're right. They do have a nasty habit of terrorizing the baby-sitter." He smiled at the two young women who listened to every word and started laughing as if they realized the reason behind it.

"Honestly, Zach, you should be ashamed of yourself." Abby clucked as they crossed the parking lot.

"Me? *You* were the one talking about our *three* children."

"That's not at all what I'm talking about. That girl wasn't that much older than Beth."

"So she liked older men. Nothing wrong in that." He unlocked the passenger door for her. "After all, we seasoned men have experience, we have savoir faire, we have . . ."

"A load of bull."

He shot her a pained look. "That really hurts, Abigail."

"Zach, their tongues were hanging out, not to mention a few other parts of their anatomy."

"Do I hear envy speaking?"

Abby laughed. She didn't want to admit that the emotion clutching a corner of her stomach just might have been jealousy. "You're talking to a woman whose daughter's bra size is larger than her own. I don't think you could call it envy or I would have bound Sam's breasts years ago."

Zach was silent for a few minutes. "Does it bother you, Abby?" he asked quietly.

She didn't hesitate with her answer. "Not really. At least, I don't think so." She didn't notice his gaze briefly sliding across her chest. "Oh, I did mind when I was in school because that was all the boys cared about. You could have the greatest legs in the world but if you couldn't fill out your sweater without the use of wads of tissue you couldn't become popular. You just weren't worth their time."

Zach winced. He remembered being guilty of just that during his teen years. It had taken him a long time before he learned quantity didn't necessarily mean quality. "Yeah, well, what do kids with overactive hormones know? We were too busy concentrating on finding somebody to make it with to wonder if the girl could talk halfway intelligently."

"And most of us girls were learning fifty ways to say no," Abby mused, then burst out laughing.

"What's so funny?"

"I was remembering this guy I once dated when I was seventeen. It was right before I met Jason. Naturally after an evening out we parked near my parents' house. The trouble was, he got more familiar than I cared for, but I had trouble making him understand I didn't want the extra attention."

Zach hated to hear a description of what could have been him once upon a time. "What happened?" He silently reassured himself it couldn't have been bad if she laughed about it now.

She shook her head, still chuckling at the memory. "A cat jumped in through the open car window."

His lips twitched. "A cat?"

Abby nodded. "Right smack in between us. It appeared he was allergic to cats so I hugged that sweet feline as if she was my very best friend and asked to be taken home. Needless to say he never asked me out again."

"No wonder why. You're a cruel woman, Abby."

"Just one who turned into a cat lover real fast."

Zach pulled into the crowded parking lot of what was probably one of the last old-fashioned drive-in fast-food restaurants.

Abby's eyes danced with amusement as she turned to Zach. "Are we eating inside or in the car?" She smiled since she already knew his reply.

"And spill chili on this upholstery? Give me a break."

"Hey, you're the messy one, not me."

Fred's Drive-In was well-known for its chili burgers and chili dogs that would eat out your insides and have you coming back for more, so finding an empty table inside the area recently built for those who didn't want to eat in their cars was difficult. Luckily Abby spied a table and pointed it out to Zach as he stood in line to order their food. Tapping her fingers on the tabletop in time to the music, she watched him stand in line and couldn't help but notice him as an attractive man. Abby knew the idea of Zach as a desirable man had always been in the back of her mind but she always seemed to prefer to push him into the niche as a good friend. Was it because she feared she would lose him as a friend if the relationship took another turn? After all, it had done that with another man she had always seen as a friend until they deepened that relationship. In the end they couldn't even remain friends. And she valued Zach's friendship too much to lose it. But the feelings she had been hiding for so long were working hard to surface and she was finding it difficult to keep them hidden. She feared soon she would have to make a choice.

When Zach brought the food he was struck by the strange look in Abby's eyes. "Are you all right?" He set the tray down and slid across the bench until he sat next to her.

She managed a smile. "I was just trying to count how many chili burgers I've eaten here over the years. The thought brought on a horrendous case of heartburn," she lied without a qualm. She certainly wasn't going to confess that she suddenly decided this man had much more to offer than she thought he did!

Zach sensed it was more than that but he wasn't going to pursue the subject.

"Is Beth getting excited about starting college this year?" Abby asked brightly.

Zach shook his head. "No talk about the kids," he ordered. "As far as we're concerned they don't even exist tonight."

"Does that mean I'll go home to find my refrigerator filled with food for once?"

Zach chuckled as he picked up a French fry and popped it in her mouth. "Instead, why don't we talk business so I can write this meal off."

Abby picked up the receipt and carefully tore it into tiny pieces. "Go ahead, talk about your shops all you want," she invited, biting into her messy hamburger. In no time she finished her burger and looked at Zach with pleading eyes.

"Seconds?" he looked astounded.

"I wouldn't turn it down."

He laughed as he got up to order two more burgers. "I should have remembered your stomach turns into a bottomless pit when you come here."

"How's business going for you?" Zach asked as they finished their food.

"Not bad, although too many clients want to take the most ridiculous deductions," Abby sighed. "Estelle figures I'm going through a bottle of aspirin a week. Of course, she's happy as long as I stay away from the kitchen."

"Blow up any microwaves lately?"

She wrinkled her nose at him. "Very funny. Estelle claims I'm on Litton's Christmas-card list."

"I wouldn't be surprised. The local salesman bought a new house thanks to you."

"Are you this funny at the salon or does it have something to do with the food here?"

"A comedian could make a fortune coming up with cooking jokes where you're concerned," he teased, reaching for the last fry, but Abby beat him to it, smirking as she bit into the seasoned potato.

Zach glanced at his watch. "Since we don't have a curfew to worry about and it's still fairly early want to see where else we can go to get into trouble?"

"Sounds fine to me as long as it isn't miniature golf."

"That's because you cheat," he pointed out.

"You're the one who can't count."

They continued their amiable argument as they walked outside to Zach's car.

"We could shoot some pool," he suggested.

"No way. You change the rules every time I knock a ball in one of the pockets," she retorted.

"How about a late movie? There's a good comedy playing down the street. There's no score to keep, no ball to hit there."

"As long as you buy me popcorn."

"After two chili burgers and a large order of fries you're still hungry?"

"I need my fiber," she intoned.

When they later entered the darkened theater, Abby stopped a moment to allow her eyes to adjust to the lack of light as the previews played on the screen. "Do you see any seats?" she whispered.

"Yeah, on the left side near the middle." He took her hand and led the way.

When Abby settled back in her seat she immediately straightened up when she discovered the back was loose.

"Abby." Zach's low voice sounded strained. "Would you take my soda please?"

Abby turned her head but at first couldn't see Zach until she looked down. She bit down on her lower lip to keep from laughing but couldn't stop. Zach's seat back was also broken but he hadn't found out in time. He lay almost prone, his head practically in the lap of the person behind him. In the end Abby lost the battle for composure. She quickly rose from her seat and ran out of the theater into the lobby with Zach eventually following her.

"Thanks for the help," he muttered, scowling at her as she leaned against the wall while she gave in to her laughter.

"If—if you could have seen your face," she choked, holding her sides. "Not to mention the guy sitting behind you!" She wiped her tears away with her fingertips. "This is priceless, Zach. Out of all the seats in that theater you would choose broken ones."

"I'm going to tell someone about the seats, then I'd like to see the movie," he informed her, before trying to find the manager. "By the time I get back I hope you will have been able to calm yourself sufficiently."

By the time Abby and Zach reentered the theater she felt composed; until she looked at Zach. Then she burst out laughing again and continued choking back giggles during the film.

"It's a good thing we didn't see a murder mystery," Zach muttered, as they walked out of the theater. "As it was, we were almost thrown out because of you."

"Come on, Zach, you have to admit it was funny," she retorted, grabbing hold of his arm. "Besides, I was laughing at the movie, not you. You're much too sensitive."

"You're really enjoying this, aren't you?" he demanded, almost stripping the gears as he raced down the street.

"Yes."

"You have a very perverted sense of humor."

"It came from being around you so much."

Zach slowed the car a few houses away from Abby's and stopped in front of a large tree. She turned halfway in the seat and looked at him questioningly.

"First off I want to remind you that I'm not allergic to cats," he grinned, loosening his seat belt and shifting to face her.

Abby remained still for a moment. "Zach, are you flirting with me?"

He considered her words. "Yeah, in a way I guess I am."

"Why?"

"Why not?"

"I asked you first."

Zach faced the windshield, his hands draped over the steering wheel. "Beats me. I guess it's because we've known each other for so long and yet we've never been more than good friends."

She smiled. "You sound as if it's some kind of crime."

"Far from it, I enjoy what we have, Abby," he assured her. "And I feel we probably have a closer relationship than most married couples."

"That certainly doesn't say much for marriage, does it?"

Zach grimaced. "I don't seem to be doing this very well."

Abby took pity on him. "It's because of all the cracks made at my birthday party, isn't it? They all seemed to think we're better off as a couple and not just friends. Right?"

"Partially," he admitted. "But that's not the entire reason. I mean, we share a lot. Why not see where it leads?"

Abby looked down at her nails, idly chipping the polish from her forefinger. "You make it sound so easy," she murmured.

"In a way it is," he replied. "Abby, I'm not talking about a full-blown affair. At least, I'm not saying let's have one here and now. What I would like, if you agree, is for us to start dating. And I don't mean taking the kids as we usually do, but for us to go out maybe once or twice a week and get to know each other as a man and woman. We've known each other for more than half our lives. Don't you think there's more to our relationship than our kids and a friendship that began in high school? Why can't we give it a chance?"

She thought about what he said but still had trouble taking it all in. *Hey, Abby, isn't this exactly what you want?* a little voice demanded. *You've been thinking about him as an attractive man for a long time now but you've kept it to yourself because deep down you're afraid he would reject you as anything more than a good buddy. Take it, Abby. Grab the gold ring.* She swallowed, wondering if she could speak past the lump in her throat. "Well, you are attractive and you do use the proper utensils when you eat and don't pick your nose, but Zach, this is so sudden! Can you understand why I feel a little confused?" she pleaded with him.

He had the grace to look sheepish. "I didn't phrase any of this very well, did I? I'm the guy who used to be called a silver-tongued devil and I messed up royally."

"No, you didn't. This is just a surprise." Abby leaned over to place her hand on his arm, unaware her fingers were trembling. "Zach, I've always enjoyed your company more than anyone else's, and maybe that's why this is hard to take in." *Liar. Go for it!* "Perhaps as a self-defense mechanism we've always viewed each other in a certain light and now it's changing. Maybe it's been slowly changing without our being aware of it." Her face lit up with her smile. "As my daughter has informed me I've entered my golden years. She seems to think I'm going to fall apart within the next few days. I guess I shouldn't pass up the opportunity to be seen with such a handsome gentleman, although I'll be honest with you, I can't see how different it will be from the times we've gone out in the past."

He relaxed the moment he heard her answer. "Trust me, Abby, it will be different."

She stared at him, finding herself drowning in his sea-green eyes as he gazed at her. "Yes, I guess it will be," she whispered, still under his spell.

"We'll work on keeping it casual in the beginning and see what develops, okay?" Zach started up the engine and drove down the street parking in her driveway. He helped her out of the car and walked with her to the door.

"Would you like to come in?" Abby asked, turning to face him after unlocking the door.

He shook his head. "No, thanks. Are you free tomorrow?"

"You're not wasting any time, are you?"

"Nope."

"So you don't get too hung up on our togetherness, I think I should warn you we'll be together on Monday for our annual Labor Day barbecue."

"Right, I forgot about that. Is it your house or mine this year?"

"Mine."

"Then I bring the eats." He recalled their annual trade of food and services. "Okay, why don't we wait until next weekend then."

"The fair," she reminded him.

Zach laughed, feeling as if his best-laid plans were falling apart before he could institute them. "Okay, but this year Matt and Beth can take Samantha and her friend and we'll ride alone. I'll take the 'Vette so no one can horn in. Deal?"

"Sounds wonderful," she agreed.

Zach placed his hands on her shoulders and looked down at her.

This is it, Abby thought. *He's going to kiss me, really kiss me instead of those brotherly pecks I usually get. Rumor has it he's a great kisser. Now I'll be able to find out if the rumors are true.*

"Abby," he murmured in a husky voice he had never used with her before.

"Yes," she replied in a like manner.

"I just want you to know I enjoyed our evening together. Oh yes, I have a rule—I don't kiss on the first date. Good night, Abby." He squeezed her shoulder and walked swiftly away.

Chapter Four

"Amazing that we call it Labor Day when we don't do anything except have picnics and play," Abby muttered, rummaging for underwear.

In deference to the heat Abby wore pale gray shorts and a cotton T-shirt in mint-green and gray stripes. She kept telling herself she wasn't wearing a new outfit just because Zach was coming over. Not to mention that his comment about not kissing on the first date had teased her mind all this time. Determined to ban all thoughts of him, she busied herself weaving her hair into a single braid as she walked into the kitchen where Estelle was placing plates filled with blueberry pancakes and bacon in front of Samantha and Matt.

"Yours will be ready soon," the housekeeper told her, watching Abby pour herself a cup of coffee. "What time will Beth and Zach get here?"

"Around eleven," Matt spoke up. "Beth told me last night on the phone."

"No wonder I don't get any calls," Samantha muttered. "No one can reach me."

"Are you kidding? Because of the call-waiting we get interrupted more than we can talk," he groused, buttering his pancakes.

Samantha eyed her mother slyly. "Maybe it would be more beneficial if I got my own phone."

"You'll have my blessing when you can afford the installation fee and the bill." Abby bestowed a bright smile on her daughter, which promptly silenced her. She looked up when the housekeeper set a plate in front of her before taking the empty chair next to Samantha.

"Ma-ma!" A raspy voice sounded just before a feathered body engulfed Abby's leg.

Abby turned an accusing gaze at Samantha as Matt hurriedly spoke up.

"My fault," he admitted, holding his hands up in surrender. "I gave him fresh food after I uncovered him and I must not have made sure the lock was secure. Sorry."

Abby cut off a good-sized piece of pancake without syrup on it and handed it to the macaw who accepted it with delicate finesse.

"It's not right," Estelle announced. "Birds should eat bird food."

"The more healthy human food they eat, the healthier they'll be," Abby replied. "That was one thing Chris explained in great detail when she came out to help me work with him."

"Yeah, but he doesn't fight *you* when we have pizza," Samantha insisted, glaring at the colorful macaw. "Karen's cat just had kittens and she said there would be no problem if I wanted one." She smiled when the large bird made a growling sound at her as if guessing the direction of her thoughts.

"I swear there're three children in this house instead of two." Abby stood up to refill her coffee cup.

"Maybe we'd be better off if we kept Sam in the cage," Matt quipped, earning a screech of outrage from his sister.

"Our best bet would be to sneak out in the middle of the night and not leave a forwarding address," Estelle suggested.

Abby chuckled. "Good idea. I'll pack right after breakfast."

"On that note I'm going to clean the pool." Matt stood up and carried his dishes over to the sink and rinsed them off.

"Estelle, I feel old," Abby confided ten minutes later after Samantha had left the table to do her chores.

"You just *think* you feel old. You hear everyone saying forty is over the hill and you believe them. I don't think Joan Collins, Linda Evans or Sally Field believe that." Estelle began stacking the dishes in the dishwasher. "Shall I go on?"

Abby sighed, resting her chin in her cupped palm. "No thanks, I'll only end up feeling more depressed."

"You have one of the best-looking men in town wanting to take you out and you're worrying about falling apart?" It was obvious Estelle wasn't going to be sympathetic. "You have a successful career, two fairly normal children, a not-so-normal bird and a typical nosy housekeeper. You certainly haven't lost your looks and you still get wolf whistles when you wear shorts. What's to complain about?"

Abby thought long and hard. "The way you make it sound I should be grateful I have all my teeth."

Estelle thought of the upper plate she felt cursed with. "You should be."

"Okay, I get the message. No more self-pity." She stood up. "Is there anything you want me to help you with?"

"Not in the kitchen. Why don't you take that feathered brat back to his cage before he takes another chunk out of the kitchen chair. I've got baking to do." Estelle turned on the oven.

Abby thought it ironic that she kept glancing out the window to see if Zach and Beth had arrived yet and then hated herself for acting like a giddy teenager. In fact, she decided Samantha would probably act a great deal more sophisticated if she were in the same situation.

"Abigail, you are forty years old and should know better," she scolded herself as she set out clean towels in the guest bathroom for want of better things to do.

"They say one of the first signs is talking to yourself," an amused male voice said from behind. "Just make sure not to answer yourself."

Abby gasped and spun around, clutching a powder-blue hand towel. "You could have given me a heart attack sneaking up like that!" she accused.

Zach, lounging indolently in the doorway, didn't look repentant.

"Ah, Abby, you're so easy to agitate," he teased, grabbing hold of her braid and yanking on it gently. "Why don't you put the towel down and we'll go outside to enjoy the sun. In fact, put on a bikini so I can lay around and ogle you."

"Fat chance."

They walked through the house with Zach's arm draped around Abby's shoulders. They stopped in the kitchen long enough to pick up a large bowl of potato chips and several smaller bowls of dip.

"Estelle, my love, leave this dreary place and come away with me." Zach hugged the older woman. "I'll give you everything your heart desires."

"If you think sweet talk will get you a piece of cake, you're wrong."

He hung his head. "You wound me, truly wound me. As if I would have an ulterior motive where you're concerned."

"I know you well enough to know you'll say anything to get a piece of my Mississippi mud cake." Her eyes twinkled. "You better get those snacks outside before the kids starve to death. Matt already took out the drinks."

"Are you coming out?" Abby asked.

"Just as soon as I finish seasoning the steaks."

Abby and Zach walked outside to find Matt, Beth and Samantha playing basketball with the hoop set in the deep end of the pool next to the slide.

"Come on!" Beth shouted, waving her arms over her head.

Abby smiled and shook her head. "Maybe later. Right now all I want to do is play lazy and enjoy the sun."

"Did you remember to put on sunscreen?" Zach called out to his daughter.

She made a face. "Of course I did. Give me a break, Dad."

"She thinks a diploma means instant common sense," he muttered, setting the bowl of chips down on the rectangular patio table beside the bowls of dip Abby had already set down next to a large cooler filled with cans of beer and soft drinks. He pulled out a can of beer and popped the tab.

"It's the magic age that does it," Abby replied, choosing diet cola and taking the chair next to him. "They reach eighteen and immediately become convinced they know everything about life. What I'm afraid of is Sam *will* know everything when she hits eighteen."

Zach watched the three play enthusiastically. His eyes widened a fraction when Samantha climbed out of the pool and ascended the slide's ladder.

"My God," he breathed, watching her slim body. "When did that happen?" He drank deeply of his beer.

Abby gazed at her bikini-clad daughter. "If you're trying to say that she's bloomed, it seemed to suddenly happen overnight."

"I sure won't feel right calling her Sam anymore," he muttered in his beer.

"Why is it such a shock to you? You went though this with Beth a few years ago. Of course, you didn't take it very well, as I recall, but you survived," Abby reminded him.

"Yeah, but I always saw Sam as a scrawny kid playing girls' softball and soccer. Now she's . . ." he waved his hand in the air for better lack of words.

"Now she's deciding boys aren't so bad after all and she spends hours in the bathroom experimenting with makeup, usually mine," Abby said dryly, dunking a potato chip in the cheese dip and munching on it. "And she gives me an average of five new gray hairs a day. I'm sure once the school year begins it will more than double."

"Better make an appointment with me for a color job," he advised kindly. "Let's tackle it before it's too late."

Abby raised her eyes heavenward. "When time comes I'll find what I need at the drugstore, thank you."

"You're a stubborn lady, Abigail."

She shrugged. "I work hard at it."

Zach looked Abby over with more than clinical interest. Her bare long legs were stretched out in front of her, rose-polished toes peeking out of her sandals. He remembered her infectious enthusiasm when they were out Saturday night and was surprised to feel a twinge of jealousy that she might act that way with any of her dates.

"Hey, Zach, come in and even up the odds," Matt yelled, who was under attack by a laughing Beth and Samantha. "They're murdering me!"

"Go ahead," Abby urged. "He looks like he needs help."

"Only if you come, too," he told her.

"I'll hit the spa later. I just want to soak up the sun for now."

Zach stood up, pushing off each deck shoe with the opposite foot and pulling off his shorts and T-shirt before running across the grass and diving into the water. Samantha squealed when he surfaced next to her and grabbed her by the waist and tossed her a short distance away into the water.

"The two of you would have great-looking kids." Estelle sat down next to Abby.

Her head whipped around at the remark. "Why is everyone trying to give me heart failure today?" Abby demanded. "First Zach walks in on me without any warning and now you drop a bomb like that."

"You're not too old to still have kids," Estelle decided mildly. "It happens to a lot of women your age."

"No thanks, I've already done my share of diaper duty."

Abby spent the next half hour watching the foursome horse around in the pool, but her gaze lingered mostly on Zach. Finally she escaped to the kitchen where Estelle graciously allowed her to dish up various salads into serving bowls.

"I thought you weren't allowed to do anything the least bit domestic."

Abby turned her head to watch Zach walk in. "If you get the floor wet Estelle will have your head," she informed him, returning to her duties.

"Don't worry, I dried off before coming in." He walked up behind her, bracing a hand on the counter on each side of her.

Abby's hands faltered for just a second before she resumed spooning potato salad into a bowl. She swore under her breath as the spoon hit the side of the bowl spilling some of the salad on the counter.

Zach grinned. The lady wasn't as calm as she pretended to be. He decided to keep her off balance a bit longer.

"So." He nudged her braid to one side and brushed his fingertips across her nape. "What did you contribute to the party?"

"Just my charming presence," she said lightly.

"Charming is a good description," he murmured, his breath warm on her ear. "You smell good."

"It's the same cologne I've worn for years," Abby said dryly.

"Shalimar," he breathed. "Warm and womanly."

Recognizing it as an old line, Abby spun around prepared to tell Zach to back off. The trouble was she didn't expect to find him standing so close to her, the smell of chlorine mixed with his own skin's scent.

"The least you can do is come up with a new line."

He considered her request and nodded. "Fair enough. How about your perfume drives me wild with uncontrollable lust?"

"How about you're full of bull?" she suggested sweetly.

Zach threw back his head and laughed. "Ah, Abby, you're good for me. You always keep my feet on the ground."

"Where they belong." Whatever else she might have said was halted by the warm pressure of his mouth on hers.

Abby's eyes widened as she stared into the warm green eyes staring back at her.

"Just relax and enjoy it, Abby," he advised against her mouth, bringing his hands to rest on her wrists pulling them slowly around his bare waist. He angled his mouth against hers and rubbed gently, his tongue tracing the outline of her lips but not slipping inside. Instead he kept teasing her mouth with delicate nibbles on each corner until Abby thought she'd scream.

They were right, she thought wildly. The man deserves a gold medal in the Olympic art of kissing! Her fingers dug into his waist afraid if she didn't hold on her gelatin-encased knees would collapse.

Zach still didn't try to take their kiss any further, as he alternately licked and nibbled every inch of Abby's mouth. With excruciating slowness he lifted his head.

"I—" Abby blinked rapidly in hopes of restoring her equilibrium. "I thought you didn't kiss on the first date."

His teeth shone white in his tanned face. "You forget, this isn't our first date." He tapped his forefinger against the tip of her nose before straightening up and walking out of the house.

Abby collapsed against the counter. "Whew!" She fanned her face with her hand.

"You can't be that hot," Estelle told her, entering the kitchen.

"You'd be surprised," she muttered, wiping off the side of the bowl before finishing her task.

"I DON'T SEE WHY you have to go all the way up there for school," Beth complained, resting her chin on her laced fingers. She and Matt had stretched out on their towels along the side of the house where they felt they could have some privacy.

"Beth, you and I've talked about this before. I'm going to law school, I'm not just getting a regular degree," he said wearily, resting his hand against the back of her neck that was warm from the sun.

"You'll probably meet all those gorgeous girls and forget all about me," she mourned, staring down at her clenched hands.

"Beth, I'm not even going for a couple of years. Why are you worrying so much now. I'm sure not looking at other girls now, am I?"

She straightened up, bracing her upper body on her forearms. "You'll meet older girls there, prettier ones."

He shot up into a sitting position. "Now you listen to me, Elizabeth Marie Randolph. I've been stuck on you since my junior year in high school and I haven't dated anyone but you since then and if that doesn't tell you something maybe this will." His hands fastened on her shoulders and he dragged her toward him for a kiss that fairly sizzled.

"Matt, I wish we were here alone," she moaned, twining her arms around his neck and practically lying on top of him. They were soon lost in their own world, murmuring words of love and affection.

"Matt, Mom—wow!" Samantha skidded to a stop as she ran around the corner and almost stumbled over the couple and quickly backed up a few steps. "Sorry."

Matt raised his head. His face flamed a bright red. He was shifting his position so Samantha couldn't see where his hand was before he carefully withdrew it.

"What the hell do you want?" His fierce look sent her back a couple steps.

"Uh, Mom said something's wrong with the barbecue." she blushed.

Matt swore under his breath feeling frustration at the world well up inside. Why couldn't Beth believe him when he told her he loved her? "Zach knows what to do. Why not have him take a look at it?" He finally stood up pointing a finger at Samantha. "Not one word of what you saw. Understand? *Not one word.* Or so help me you're dead meat." He waited for her nod before heading for the patio.

Samantha stood there uncertainly watching Beth rise to her feet and pick up the two towels. "I'm sorry." She couldn't look the older girl in the eye. "If I had known I wouldn't have . . . well . . . you know."

"That's all right, Sam. Better you than one of our parents." Beth reassured her, as she folded the towels. "I guess we should see what we can do to help." They looked across the yard where Abby and Matt were standing by the gas barbecue.

"Why do I have to do everything? Zach's here, right? He can handle it just as well as I can," Matt shouted at his mother, feeling the need to take his anger out on someone even if that someone was an innocent party.

"I suggest you calm down this minute, Matthew. I don't appreciate being treated like some kind of idiot." She glared back.

"Then don't act like one!"

Abby's features tightened. "Inside, now." Her tone brooked no disobedience. Luckily, Matt didn't argue further but stalked toward the house. Estelle took one look at their faces and instantly vacated the kitchen. Matt faced one of the counters, his hands braced on the edges.

"First of all I want an apology for your unforgivable behavior. Second, I want to know what the problem is because I will not have your ruining this day," Abby said, cold fury lacing her voice.

He heaved a deep sigh. "Beth seems to think if I go to law school I'll forget all about her and find someone new. She won't believe me that it won't happen."

Abby nodded. "Then that's Beth's problem, not yours."

He turned around. "But I love her. Shouldn't that be enough?"

"Yes, but she's also young and her love for you is still in the insecure stages. If your love is strong enough neither of you have anything to worry about. Show her how much you love her. But if it's going to tear you apart this way then break it off now, because I won't stand for this kind of behavior. All it will do is destroy the two of you. Do you understand me?"

Matt nodded. He walked over and put his arms around his mother, holding her tightly. "I'm sorry, Mom," he muttered. "I was mad at Beth and at myself, but I took it out on you. That wasn't right."

"No, it wasn't. I'm just glad you realized it. And apology accepted. Let's try to enjoy the rest of the day, okay?" She kissed his cheek. "Oh, Matt, it's times like this I wish you weren't too big to spank."

He laughed shakily. "If it came to that I don't think my size would stop you."

With the air cleared they were able to return outdoors in hopes of recapturing the earlier holiday spirit.

"Abby, are we eating soon?" Beth stood nearby still carrying the two oversize towels. She looked a bit uncomfortable as if she realized she had something to do with the argument.

"It looks like it." Abby didn't say anything about the faint purple mark she noticed on the side of Beth's throat and carefully schooled her expression so the young woman couldn't read her thoughts.

"I guess I'll go in and see if Estelle needs any help," Beth said as she walked toward the house.

Abby watched her with slightly narrowed eyes. Zach may feel that Samantha had grown up suddenly but she sensed that Beth had matured even more over the summer. Her delicate features appeared just a bit more womanly than the girlish aura she exuded at her high school graduation. And that worried her. "Damn it, he has law school to get through," Abby muttered.

In record time the patio table was filled with baked potatoes, three different salads, corn on the cob, a fudgy Mississippi mud cake and apple pie.

"We always have too much food," Abby complained, as she helped herself to small portions of everything.

"Maybe so, but there's never enough left to count as leftovers," Zach pointed out.

"That's because the guys always eat so much," Samantha piped up.

Abby eyed her daughter's overloaded plate. "You should talk."

"Holidays are a great reason to go off a diet." Estelle handed out drinks.

"Mom does it every time Estelle makes her milk-chocolate cake," Matt joked, earning a good-natured cuff from his mother. "That's probably why Estelle doesn't make it anymore. To keep Mom honest."

After the meal the kids performed KP duty, then Matt and Beth went off on their own and Samantha asked to go down the street to a friend's house; Estelle retired to the den and Zach collapsed in the hammock under a tree with Abby ensconced in a nearby chair with her legs stretched out on another one to catch the afternoon sun.

"We should do something energetic," she mumbled, her eyes closed as slumber threatened to overtake.

"We are."

"We are?"

"Sure, we're breathing, aren't we? That can get pretty energetic." He yawned. "Did you happen to notice your son gave my daughter a hickey."

"Couldn't help but notice. Why?" Abby silently decided a nap was highly preferable to this conversation.

"What are you going to do about it?" Zach's words sounded slurred as if he was going under fast.

"Suggest to Beth she wear turtlenecks for a while. She could try makeup to cover it but I always found I emphasized the mark more." She thought about dumping Zach out of the hammock and taking it over for herself but promptly decided she didn't want to make the effort.

"Hickeys happen because of kissing, you know."

"Give me a break, Zach. They've been dating for what, three years? I'm sure they've kissed before and I doubt this is her first hickey, so I don't know why you brought it up."

"No wonder Samantha's the way she is. You're as irreverent as hell. I just forgot how purple hickeys look. Do you think they're still a sort of badge of honor the way they were with us?"

"I don't know." Abby thought longingly of the hammock. "You wouldn't care to trade, would you?"

"Trade what?"

"Your hammock for my chairs?"

"Fat chance."

"That's what I was afraid of." Abby drifted off to sleep unaware Estelle had overheard their conversation through the open den window.

"They couldn't have shared?" she murmured, turning on ESPN and settling back to watch Australian football.

ZACH RUMMAGED THROUGH the main bathroom's medicine cabinet with no luck.

"Beth, do you know where that swimmer's ear stuff is?" he called out.

"My bathroom," she replied. "I had to use it last week when we got back from the Thompsons."

He cursed softly as he rummaged through the feminine paraphernalia every young adult woman seemed to require.

"She's got enough makeup in here to last her the next fifty years," he muttered, pushing aside cases of eye shadow and lipsticks. He froze when a pale blue, narrow plastic box caught his eye. He picked it up and opened it. Only seven tiny white pills remained.

Zach knew what they were. He even remembered when a pink-faced Beth approached him several months ago explaining the doctor suggesting putting her on birth-control pills to regulate her erratic periods. Back then he had been pleased she felt comfortable enough to talk to him about it. So why did it make him feel uncomfortable to look at them? He carefully replaced the case and pulled out the small plastic bottle he was looking for.

He was tempted to call Abby right away and talk to her but decided to wait a bit. He had been wanting to push for more from her for quite a while now but he sensed a reserve on her part.

"Of all the women in the world why did I have to pick one who continues to treat me like a brother?" he muttered. "I guess I'll just have to work harder on my charm."

Later on when Zach talked to Abby on the telephone he brought up his earlier feelings about his daughter.

"This is scary, Abby. Beth's all grown-up now. I don't know if I'm going to survive this."

"That's because she isn't your little girl anymore. Zach, you felt this way the day she had her first period, remember? And she was too embarrassed to come to you." He groaned. "And I felt that way when Matt's voice started changing and he began shaving. I'm sure our parents suffered the same fears. And in a few years I'll be agonizing over Sam. It's a vicious circle. Our parents went crazy when we became teenagers so we're obliged to do the same when our children grow up. Besides, you have nothing to worry about with her. Right now, all she wants to do is work for her degree so she can become a physical therapist. So relax."

He chuckled. "When did you turn so wise?"

"It's part of being a mother. I think it's in the genes." Abby curled up on the bed, cradling the phone in the crook of her shoulder. "My turn for hysteria is coming now that Sam's decided boys are more fun than softball. It's bad enough some of her friends have been dating for a while."

"She'll be sixteen next year. You started dating then. Of course, if you're worried I'll check out the boys when she starts going out," Zach offered.

Abby laughed. "I'm sure she'd love that. What time are we leaving for the fair on Sunday?"

"How about we leave at eight? That way we can stop for breakfast first," he suggested.

"Sounds good to me." She glanced at the clock. "I better check on Sam and make sure she's finished her homework. She's been complaining about her math all week."

"Abby." His low voice stopped her beginning farewell. She paused. "Yes?"

"Just think, this will be our third date."

"Meaning?"

"Don't worry, you'll find out soon enough."

Abby didn't know how long she held the receiver before the loud buzz roused her.

"The man is dangerous," she murmured, hanging up the phone. "Dangerous, but a great kisser."

THE FOURSOME FACING Abby and Zach in Abby's kitchen were not happy.

"How come we get stuck with them?" Matt demanded. "What's wrong with them going with you like always?"

"*You?* Do you think we want to go around with you guys?" Samantha glared at her older brother. "All you do is treat us like we're five years old." She turned to her mother. "Mom, we really don't have to go with them, do we?"

Abby closed her eyes and counted to ten. She held her hands up asking for silence. "Okay, here's the plan."

"No plan is going to stop her from making snide remarks behind our backs," Matt argued.

"Give me a break, I haven't done anything that juvenile in years," Samantha shot back.

"That's enough!" Abby's voice snapped out like a whip cracking over their heads.

"They won't fit in the back of my car." Matt tried one last time.

The look on Abby's face was more than enough to silence her son. "You can take my car. I won't even ask you to refill the gas tank. Besides, once you reach the fair you can part company as long as the girls check in with us at appointed times." Abby turned to Samantha and Melanie for confirmation, waiting until they nodded. "Fine, then let's head for the restaurant because I'm not going to hear another word about this."

"Are you sure you weren't a marine drill instructor in another life?" Zach teased as he helped her into his silver Corvette. "Talk about organizing them in a hurry."

"You could have backed me up instead of standing there like a bump on the log," she groused, buckling the seat belt and dropping her purse on the floor.

"Maybe so, but it was more fun listening to you." He watched Matt back Abby's car down the driveway, a dark look on the young man's face. He may have given in but he didn't look as if he liked it. "I had every confidence in you."

"Thanks a lot." Each word dripped with sarcasm.

"Hey, I had to listen to my esteemed neighbor, Miss Howard, lecture me on Beth's inappropriate attire. You'd think she'd be used to women wearing shorts by now. Since you're on a roll I can't wait to watch you oversee breakfast." He grinned at her glare.

Abby was relieved there were no further repercussions during breakfast. She decided it was more Beth's doing than Matt seeing the error of his ways, since the young woman kept touching his arm every time he tensed. Abby could only breathe a sigh of relief as the meal passed pleasantly.

"I want you to meet us at the clock tower at two," She instructed Samantha and Melanie.

"Don't talk to strangers, no staring at guys," Samantha said glibly, then clapped her mouth shut under her mother's fit-to-kill look. "No problem." She shifted her eyes toward Melanie, silently assuring her mother she'd watch after her.

"Why do I worry when she says that?" Abby mourned, watching them drive away.

Zach caught her neck in the crook of his arm and steered her toward his car. "Because you're a mother. It's in the genes," he teased.

She wrinkled her nose at his throwing back her words. "That doesn't make me feel better."

He started up the engine. "Know what we're doing first?"

"What?"

He turned his head, a strange gleam in his eye. "We're going to the midway first and I'm getting you in the dungeon of horrors where it's dark and scary and I'm going to..."

Abby licked dry lips. "Going to what?" she ventured.

He didn't reply but just kept flashing a wicked smile as he drove out of the restaurant's parking lot.

"Don't you want to know?" Zach asked much later as they parked in the fairground's parking lot.

She turned and blessed him with an enigmatic smile of her own. "No thanks, I'll just wait to be surprised."

"Oh, you'll be surprised, all right."

Chapter Five

Zach liked to walk slightly behind Abby just to watch the easy way her body moved. Since the day was hot she had chosen pale mint-green shorts and a pastel-striped polo shirt. She had pulled her hair back, anchoring it high off her neck with a pale green plastic banana clip and wore an off-white straw hat to shield her face from the sun. He also couldn't help but notice other men didn't mind looking at Abby's long legs, either.

"When we have a fair so close to us why do we come all the way up to Pomona for theirs?" she asked him.

"Old habits die hard, I guess," he said absently, quickly raising his eyes from her slim ankles and changing the direction of his gaze to another interesting sight.

Abby looked up to see what had caught his attention and smiled. Zach's eyes had settled with delight on the various speedboats and camping gear displayed under a canvas cover.

"They have the same thing every year," she pointed out, allowing him to steer her toward one sleek boat.

"They just look the same to you." He fairly drooled over the boat.

"That's because all they do is change the colors. They're all the same, Zach," Abby commented when they left the display twenty minutes later.

He bent his head whispering in her ear, "I bet you don't even look at the boats. I bet you're just looking at my legs, aren't you?"

She rolled her eyes. "That does not even merit a reply."

"A-ha, evasion means I was right. You're turning into a dirty old lady."

"It must be the company I keep." She dragged him toward one of the many lemonade stands dotting the grounds. "You want one? My treat."

"Sure."

They wandered through the various exhibit halls listening to people extol the virtues of their massage pad, jewelry cleaner, knitting machines and cookware, along with many others. As was Abby's annual habit, she bought a pound of fudge from one booth and generously offered to share it with Zach.

"You're worse than the kids when it comes to junk food," he teased, nipping off a small corner of the fudge. "Every year you seem to go crazy the minute we hit here."

"And I'll be downing Alka Seltzer all night to pay for it, but I don't care. It's worth it," she declared airily. "You know, this is the first time it's been just you and me wandering around."

"Yeah, nice, isn't it?" He spied a stand selling foreign beer and guided her over to it. Abby turned down the beer and settled for a diet soda instead.

After checking the time, they wandered over to the outdoor display of swimming pools and spas.

"Why do we look at these when we both have them?" Abby asked, studying the ornate tile work in one spa.

"I've been debating about building a gazebo over the spa," he explained, looking at one redwood gazebo and picking up a brochure, tucking it in the outside pocket of Abby's canvas tote bag.

She looked down, saying wryly. "I'm glad I brought this along. After all, you wouldn't have anywhere to put all the brochures you collect, would you?"

He grinned. "That's why I bring you."

Zach either kept his arm around Abby's shoulders or held her hand as they wandered through the crowded fair-grounds. He usually inclined his head when he said something to her or listened to her words so he could also inhale the light sensual fragrance of her cologne.

"Shalimar," he murmured. "I still remember Matt picking it out for your birthday. He was ten years old and he had saved the money he earned from his paper route."

Abby smiled. "And I'm sure you made up the difference. Matt was so proud of himself. And he gives me a new bottle every year. He likes to tease me saying it's an easy gift to buy."

During their wanderings they stopped for cold drinks and Abby also purchased a warm cinnamon roll, which she greedily consumed as they sat on a shady rock wall.

"How long have we been coming here?" Abby asked.

Zach's expression briefly sombered. "Ten years."

Her smile faltered. "That's right, Jason had been dead for about two months and we had done everything possible to keep the kids busy. I swear, we hit every tourist spot in Southern California that summer, which only left us with sore feet and empty wallets. I don't know who was more tired, them or us."

He chuckled. "Yeah, and afterward you and I wondered why we went to so much trouble when Matt and Sam bounced back so easily. We forgot about the resiliency of youth." He stood up and held out his hand. "Come on, we've got lots more to see before meeting the kids."

Samantha and Melanie were waiting at the clock tower when Abby and Zach arrived.

"Matt and Beth said they were going off on their own for lunch." Samantha told them. "And we're to meet them here at seven."

Abby chuckled. "Heaven forbid they associate with we adults."

"They're probably afraid something will wear off on them," Zach reminded her. "How about some lunch? Of course, I know of one person who won't be interested since she's been eating junk food all morning."

"I wasn't the one who bought the salt-water taffy," Abby said smugly.

"No, but that didn't stop you from eating half of it."

It took ten minutes before they all decided to try the barbecued sandwiches after smelling the rich aroma coming their way.

"The one near the animal barns?" Abby didn't look pleased as they walked along.

"They have the best," Zach assured her.

"Don't worry, Mom," Samantha told her. "We'll sit upwind."

"How comforting."

In spite of the atmosphere Abby enjoyed her messy barbecue beef sandwich and coleslaw. "What have you two been up to?" she asked the girls.

"Looking at the boys," Melanie said, earning a jab in the ribs from Samantha. "Sam, that hurt! Oh, I wasn't supposed to tell, was I?"

Abby's smile froze. "Just be sure you only look and don't touch or talk," she said softly, her meaning very clear.

After they ate, they wandered through the animal barns, not one of Abby's favorite activities since she saw nothing exciting about sheep, pigs and cows. They also halted by a large riding ring, watching riders school their horses.

"Maybe I could have a horse for my sixteenth birthday instead of a car," Samantha brought up with a sly glance in her mother's direction.

"Consider yourself lucky if you receive a card," Abby advised kindly.

"You said I can have my ears pierced then." She looked at a girl's dangling earrings with undisguised envy.

"That's right. And I have the needle all picked out for you, too." Abby wiggled her eyebrows.

"Abby, you're terrible." Zach chuckled when they parted from the two girls who were eager to visit a wild-life exhibit featuring live animals.

"It's self-defense," she countered, content to follow him as they walked through the midway with the hawkers shouting the prizes that could be so "easily" won.

"It always looks sort of tawdry during the day and gaudy at night," Abby commented, watching a teenage boy try to toss rings over the lip of Coke bottles.

"That's the attraction. Especially when an elegant lady like you comes along to give the place some class." He leaned over kissing her on the cheek.

She laughed. "Me, elegant? My nose is sunburned. I feel gritty and I'm sure there's a pound of dust in my hair."

Zach disagreed. "No, it's your manner. Even now you look like some very cool-mannered lady who's got it all together."

"If I had it all together I wouldn't be getting gray hairs every day from my kids." Abby stopped when she realized where Zach was leading her. "Oh, no, I'm not going in there."

"Come on, Abby, I'll protect you," Zach crooned, climbing the first step toward the gray-painted exterior boasting the Dungeon of Terror.

She burst out laughing. "Give me a break. I may have more to worry about with you than whatever they have in there." She hung back. "I'm too young to die, Zach."

In the end, Abby allowed Zach to lead her into the pitch-black tunnel as long as he walked ahead of her. She hung on to his hand, her eyes darting every which way to make sure she saw whatever might jump out to scare her before it happened. But she wasn't quick enough.

"Augh!" she screeched when something cold and slimy slithered across her face. *"Eech!"* This time a skeleton's hand rested on her shoulder. *"Zach!"* she screamed when cobwebs appeared caught on her face. "Damn you, stop laughing!" She punched him on the arm as hard as she could then almost fell into that same arm as a squeaky being skittered across her toes.

By the time they left the dungeon Zach was laughing and Abby was furious with him.

"You do this to me every year," she stormed. "This is it, never again."

"You said that last year and the year before that and the—"

"I don't care what I always say, this will be the last year," she insisted. "And now I want you to win me that large lion over there and I don't care how much it costs you."

He looked dismayed at the variation on a baseball game. "Not fair, Abby."

"You chose the dungeon, I choose the games." She stood back, her arms crossed in front of her, tapping her foot.

Zach sighed and dug into his pocket. "I hope he'll take a credit card when I run out of cash."

He didn't run out of cash, but he grumbled she was going to have to pay for dinner. Abby carried the large stuffed lion since Zach refused to have anything to do with it.

"You wanted that thing badly enough, you can carry it," he informed her.

"Zach." She looked at him over the tawny animal's head. "I know I gave you a bad time about it, but thank you. This is the first time anyone has won something for me."

He smiled and reached out to touch her cheek. "Then I'm glad I was the first."

She returned his smile. "So am I."

Abby was ready for a rest when it was time for them to meet the others. She had wanted to make sure Matt and Beth would show up for Samantha and Melanie. When she and Zach got near the clock tower she noticed two young men wearing red T-shirts with the gold marine emblem on the front talking to the girls. She pushed the lion at Zach to rush toward them but he grabbed her hand to halt her flight.

"We're close enough if they need us, but let's just stand back and see what happens, okay?" he suggested.

Within a few minutes the two young men walked away with a wave of the hand. Abby and Zach then walked toward the girls.

"We saw you two standing over there," Samantha informed them. "Don't worry, they were just asking us where the photography exhibit hall was."

"Oh, I wasn't worried," Abby said airily, but the three sets of eyes directed at her said something else. She glanced down at her watch and discovered it was ten minutes past the meeting time. "Where are those two?"

"Probably on their way," he replied.

When Matt and Beth showed up thirty minutes later they looked strained as if they had been arguing.

"Sorry, we got sidetracked at the horse barns," Matt said gruffly.

"Matt." Abby took him to one side. "Are you all right?"

"Yeah, fine."

Abby handed him some money. "I'm sure you'll want to stop for something to eat on the way back."

His smile was strained. "You think the girls are going to break the bank?"

"With the way they eat, yes. This way, if you want to go to somewhere halfway nice you can. Okay?"

He nodded. "Okay."

Abby noticed Zach had taken Beth aside while she talked to Matt. He didn't seem to be any more successful at finding out the problem as she had.

"Did you learn anything?" he asked as they later walked out to the parking lot.

She shook her head. "I gather you didn't, either."

"Nope." Zach sighed. "But I feel as if she has a lot bottled up inside and doesn't know how to release it. I sure don't have the right words anymore to approach her."

"I think a good part of it is the fact Matt's going away to law school," Abby thought out loud as she settled herself in the low-slung car. "And Beth's afraid she'll lose him."

Zach's head whipped around at that revelation. "You think they're that involved?"

She smiled wryly. "How many years have they been dating? Three? And they've gone out exclusively with each other for the past two. Oh, yes, they're definitely involved. Don't act like the typical father who hides his head in the sand, Zach. You want to keep Beth your little girl and you can't. She and Matt share something special and Beth doesn't want to lose him. That's not so wrong."

He cursed under his breath. "I knew I should have insisted she see other guys."

"And have her defy you the way so many kids defy their parents? No, let them work this out themselves."

Zach started up the car and put it in gear. "Why couldn't fathers have inherited some of those genes that keep mothers so sane?" he muttered.

Abby put a tape in the tape deck and curled up in the seat. "Wake me when we get to the house."

Zach turned up the volume to an ear-splitting blast. Abby yelped and quickly turned it down.

"Okay, I get the hint," she grumbled, sitting up. "The driver does not appreciate the passenger taking naps."

"Do you want to stop off somewhere for dinner?" He accelerated when he pulled onto the freeway.

Abby looked down at her grubby clothes and grimaced. "As long as we don't have to go inside."

"If you can wait long enough, we can pick something up and eat at my place," he suggested.

Abby thought about what it could mean, discarded pros and cons and decided she was better off not looking at it that way. "All right," she agreed.

They later carried in the red-and-white containers of chicken and accompaniments into Zach's kitchen and set them in the middle of the table. Zach brought out the drinks while Abby found paper plates and eating utensils.

"Only the colonel makes chicken this good." She carefully tore the skin off a chicken breast.

"You're throwing away the best part," Zach protested, grabbing the crispy skin and popping it in his mouth.

"Are you kidding? It's so loaded with calories it's not even funny." Abby smeared honey on a biscuit.

He looked at her with disbelief. "Says the woman who ate six million calories today."

"Junk food consumed during a day's outing doesn't count," Abby said primly.

"Then if you're smart you won't step on the scales tomorrow."

"Were you always this crass?"

Zach grinned. "You mean you never noticed before? I'm crushed. And here I worked so hard to have it down to a fine art."

Their cleanup was taken care of in minutes and they carried their coffee into the den.

"I have an idea this may have been our last year of family togetherness," she said sadly. "Everyone is growing up and growing away from us."

"You felt it, too?" Zach sat in the chair next to her and stretched his legs out in front of him. "Yeah, old lady, no more trips to Disneyland or Sea World. We may not even have our regular family barbecues next summer."

Abby closed her eyes, listening to Zach's deep rumble. She wondered if he realized he made them sound as if they were one big happy family. But they weren't, she told herself. And she should continue to remember that. "Our nests are shrinking by the minute," she said out loud. "And before I grow too maudlin I think I'd better have you drive me home." She finished her coffee and stood up, carrying the cup into the kitchen.

Zach looked after her quizzically. This wasn't the Abby he knew so well. Where was her usual zest? "Sure," he said slowly. "I had hoped you could stay longer."

"It's almost midnight and I have a busy day tomorrow, even if you get to sleep late." She grabbed her tote bag.

"Sleep late? Mondays are the only day I can catch up on my paperwork," he retorted. "And even if a lot of salons are closed on Mondays, mine aren't." They walked outside to the Corvette parked in the driveway.

"I have a new client coming in at eight and I'm scared to death he'll bring all his paperwork to me in shoe boxes." She looked over where a tiny figure stood on the neighboring porch watching them. "Good evening, Miss Howard. Nice night, isn't it?"

Caught at her eavesdropping, the elderly woman sniffed loudly and spun around, entering her house so quickly the air seemed to tremble around her.

"Mean, Abby, real mean," Zach pronounced, chuckling under his breath. "You know how much she enjoys sitting on that porch learning all the dirt she can."

"She wants to believe you're the typical swinging bachelor and I'm just helping to perpetuate the myth." She slid into the passenger seat. "Just think of the thrill I gave her."

"Yeah, making me out like some kind of mindless stud." He backed out of the driveway.

The drive to Abby's house was made in comparative silence. She noted the entry light was on as they walked up the brick-lined pathway, thanks to Estelle.

Zach stopped Abby before she unlocked the door. He slid his hands up and down her arms, finally stopping at her wrists, holding them lightly at her sides.

"I thought we were going to give this dating bit a serious try?" he said quietly.

"We are."

He shook his head. "Are we? Abby, you suddenly acted as if you were afraid I was going to pounce on you and carry you off to my bedroom to have my way with you as Miss Howard believes I do with any woman who enters my house." Her blush confirmed his suspicion.

"You forget I've seen you in an entirely different light for so many years, it's difficult to see you as the man I'm dating." She shook her head feeling at a loss for the proper words.

His grip tightened. "It's too late to back out. We're committed now, Abby." He pressed a brief hard kiss against her lips and walked away.

Abby let herself into the house, waiting by the door until she heard the purr of Zach's car driving away. She ran her tongue over her lips to recreate the taste of his kiss as she headed for her bedroom and hopefully a good night's sleep.

"I'M LATE," Samantha called out, running through the kitchen. "'Bye."

"Wait a minute," Abby ordered. She looked at the pale pink cotton short skirt and print cotton sweater. "I believe this is mine, not to mention that is brand new. I haven't even had a chance to wear it yet!" She only wished she'd finished another cup of coffee so she could think a bit more coherently.

"Oh, I know, but don't you agree it looks better on me?" She blew her mother a kiss and sailed out the door. "'Bye."

"She's going to put bumps in that sweater that will never come out," Abby grumbled, feeding Max a piece of toast covered with egg.

Estelle chuckled. "Maybe you should put a lock on your closet door."

Abby sighed. "The trouble is, she's right. It does look better on her. Just don't tell her I said so or I'll never see that sweater again."

"You never really said how yesterday went." Estelle glared at Max, who was trying to climb up one of the chairs. "Tell that bird he doesn't belong at the table."

"Why not? He has better table manners than a lot of people I know." Abby fed the macaw another piece of toast. "I brought you two large bags of butter-toffee peanuts and some fudge."

"I hate to think how much junk food you ate. You're usually worse than the kids."

"Hey, the fair's only once a year." Abby glanced at the clock, then down at the robe she still wore. "I'd better get dressed. New clients deserve a good first impression."

"Then don't wear that yellowish dress," Estelle advised, turning back to the dishes she was loading in the dishwasher.

Abby frowned as she tried to recall the outfit. "Wait a minute, are you talking about the dress I bought at Bullock's that cost me a small fortune even on sale?"

"If I had been with you, I would have talked you out of it."

"Yellow is an excellent color for redheads," she argued.

"Not that yellow. There's a hint of something in it that makes your skin look pasty," Estelle said bluntly.

"Go ahead and tell me the truth, Estelle, don't hold anything back," Abby said wryly. "I'll make sure not to wear that dress."

Abby's fears weren't unfounded. Her new client, the owner of three clothing boutiques, brought her paperwork in two large dress boxes with the apology that her former accountant had messed everything up and she sincerely hoped Abby could straighten it out. Abby was flattered the woman had such confidence in her, but still felt a bit overwhelmed by all the work ahead.

Mondays were always the busiest for her as she began her workweek meeting with clients and continually working on month-end reports and profit-and-loss statements.

"I'm going to the grocery store, cleaners and video store to return those tapes," Estelle announced, bringing in a carafe of coffee. "You need anything while I'm out?"

"Max needs more monkey chow," Abby reminded her.

"It's on my list."

"I'm on my last tube of toothpaste."

"Got it."

Abby thought it over. "Peanut butter?"

Estelle looked wry at the mention of the family's favorite food product. "Surely you jest."

"If you're so well organized why are you asking me if there's anything we need?" Abby demanded.

Estelle's lips curved. "Call it an attempt to make the boss feel important."

"Call it bull. No, there's nothing else I can think of." Abby returned to her work.

"When I come back why don't you take a break and tell me all about yesterday," Estelle suggested.

Abby grimaced. "Yesterday was a disaster. Matt didn't want to drive Sam and Melanie, and I'm sure they fought all the way up to Pomona and probably all the way back last night. It was one of those days when I wished I wasn't a mother."

"That's nothing new," Estelle chuckled. "I'm off. See you later."

As Abby worked that afternoon, she decided Estelle was having more fun than she was as she took calls and pulled out blank work sheets for her new client.

"Judging from the prices of her clothing she must only sell designer originals," she muttered, inserting her pencil in the electric pencil sharpener.

During dinner Abby noticed Matt's appetite wasn't as hearty as usual and commented on it.

"We had a pop quiz in one of my classes today," he mumbled, staring down at his plate. "I guess I'm just not very hungry."

Abby's brow wrinkled in a frown. If Samantha and her insatiable curiosity hadn't been present she would have asked him what was wrong. "When you finish rinsing off the dishes, I want you to do your homework," she instructed her daughter, who was carrying the empty plates to the sink.

"As most of my homework is from biology class, I doubt I'll be seen for the rest of the night," she moaned, but couldn't find any sympathy from the other three.

"Just be grateful you have Mr. Lorne instead of old man Grant," Matt told her. "Grant loves to give pop quizzes and used to hold them almost every other day."

"Yeah, but Mr. Lorne likes everyone to write long papers."

"It's better than the quizzes," he advised.

Abby waited until Matt was settled down in the den before approaching him.

"Are you going to see Beth tonight?" she asked, curling up in a corner of the couch.

He shook his head. "She's got homework, too, so we're not going out until Friday."

She nodded as she sipped her coffee. "What about you?"

"I finished mine when I got home."

"Matt, are you and Beth having problems? Is it something you'd like to talk about?"

He shrugged. "Just the usual. She's convinced if I go up to L.A. for school I'll find someone else and forget all about her." He leaned forward, his clasped hands hanging between his knees. "Mom, I love Beth. I'm not going up there just to find someone else. Why can't she believe me?" He seemed to plead for all the right answers.

Abby wished she had them, just as she used to be able to tell Matt what caused the thunder and lightning and why birds ate worms. "She just feels insecure right now, it's perfectly natural. Within the space of three months she's graduated from high school and entered college. You've been there. You know how different it is for a teenager. She's in a new world and because of her classes I doubt she even sees you on campus, does she? She probably feels you've always been there for her and before long you'll soon be leaving to take an even bigger step." She made a helpless gesture. "I honestly don't know, Matt. There can be a lot of things bothering her, but she's going to have to settle them herself, because you have more than enough ahead of you." She paused. "And as much as I hate to say it, absence doesn't always make the heart grow fonder. There are no guarantees, Matt. You just might go up there and meet someone else."

He jumped to his feet, his face dark with anger. "No way! I love Beth and I want to marry her."

Abby's eyes widened at that bombshell, although deep down she expected it. "Marriage? Matt, you're only twenty years old. You have your whole life ahead of you." She inwardly winced at the same phrase her parents had once spouted at her.

"I'm talking about when I graduate, not tomorrow."

"Have you and Beth discussed this?" It took every ounce of self-control to keep her voice low and even.

He exhaled. "Some, but I didn't want to say too much until I had something to offer her."

"Thank God for that," she murmured. "Oh, Matt, I wish I knew all the right words to say and had all the right answers, but I don't. All I can say is to think things over very carefully. Law school isn't easy at the best and even rougher for someone married. Your father and I did a lot of struggling back then, and when you announced you wanted to go into law, I vowed to ensure you would have it easier."

He smiled wryly. "Sorry, Mom, but this isn't a skinned knee or a problem in school. Whatever happens I'll have to work it out for myself."

Abby's eyes filled with tears. "You're right, you're no longer my little boy and I can't protect you from the world's evils. I just have to remember that."

Matt got up and leaned over, hugging her tightly.

"Don't worry, Mom, I won't do anything without talking to you first. I promise." He left her with that vow hanging in the air.

Abby sighed. "Why couldn't Dr. Spock have written about this?"

Chapter Six

The manicurist stared silently at Abby's hands, which boasted six broken nails.

"Had a rough week, did we?" She soaked cotton in polish remover and cleaned each nail.

"Sorry about this, Carla. Let's just say it wasn't one of my best," Abby admitted ruefully, looking around the second of Zach's salons as she liked to call it. This one catered to what he whimsically called the baby boomers. Decorations were in bright colors, soft rock played on the sound system and Perrier and wine was available to those who chose to indulge. Along with hair and nail services, he also employed a facialist.

"I hear you're dating Zach now."

Abby chuckled. "I see the grapevine is as efficient as ever, although I wouldn't exactly call it dating."

Carla shook her head as she clipped away the old acrylic closer to Abby's cuticles and filled in each nail with new material. "You're going out together, aren't you? The man calls you from the salon. He never used to do that with anyone he saw in the past. I've been doing your nails for what, six years? And I've worked for Zach for seven, so I should be able to read between the lines pretty well by now." She grinned. "You'll come to his salon to have your nails done and an occasional facial, but you won't let him do your hair. Sounds a bit strange to me. Or are you afraid?''

Abby's eyes widened with amusement. "Afraid? That's a new one. You're right, I'm afraid he'll decide to give me a Mohawk if not shave my head completely. What person would trust a CPA with a Mohawk?''

Carla flashed her a long-suffering look. "You know very well what I mean. You see it as something intimate. You're afraid to have him touch you.''

"You still seeing Gary?" Abby asked brightly, trying to change the subject.

Carla shook her head, her sun-streaked brown hair brushing her shoulders. She bent over slightly, smoothing each new acrylic nail. "He started out telling me how much he wanted an independent woman and then he found out how independent I am. He's now seeing someone who has the brains of a Barbie doll. Come to think of it, I'm probably insulting the doll.''

Abby laughed as she stood up to walk back to the rear of the salon to wash her hands free of the dust before having them polished. "I know just the kind you mean.''

Carla uncapped the bottle of nail polish and began brushing a peach color on Abby's nails.

"Why don't you give Zach a break?" she went on. "You, of all people, should know what a great guy he is. He deserves someone nice and the two of you already know each other so well that the rest should be easy.''

"Too bad it doesn't work that way." Abby sat in another chair where she could place her nails under a small dryer.

"For once why don't you sit there for the full five minutes so they'll be perfectly dry," Carla suggested. "And no fooling around with them until they snap.''

"Yes, Mother.''

"No wonder Zach is hot to trot. You're the perfect type for him." Carla switched on the dryer and began to walk away.

Abby looked around and realizing no one was in the immediate area called Carla back. "What do you mean his type? The kids explain I'm basically too old for him, and I've seen some of the women he's dated in the past and I'm not anywhere near like them."

She smiled. "And who said they were his type?"

Abby opened her mouth to answer, but unable to think exactly what to say, she closed it again.

"You keep him on his toes, Abby," Carla told her. "He likes that. Take care, and I'll see you in two weeks."

Abby kept her eyes on the clock and as soon as three minutes passed, she left the salon and walked right into Zach.

"Hey, where's the fire?" he laughed, grabbing on to her arms.

"Oh, sorry," she apologized, making sure her slightly damp nails were kept out of the way, her key ring dangling from one hand. "That's what happens when I'm in a hurry."

He looked down at her sage-green cotton sundress. "Meeting a client?"

She shook her head. "The one coming in today canceled, so I thought I'd get a bit of shopping in."

Zach glanced at his watch. "I have a customer coming in about ten minutes. How about you meet me back here in about an hour and I'll buy you lunch? I want to assure you, you won't get a better offer."

She pretended to consider his offer. "Actually, I was planning on meeting Mel Gibson at some little, out-of-the-way place, but I could be persuaded to cancel."

"Clam chowder, scallops and shrimp, fresh-baked sourdough bread," he tempted. "A nice bottle of Chablis. Cheesecake for dessert."

Abby exhaled. "Mel can wait."

Zach's smile lit up his entire face. "Great. I'll see you back here in an hour then."

She nodded. "With a lunch like that waiting for me, I'll be back in fifty minutes."

Abby drove to a nearby shopping mall and dispensed with her errands in record time; new underwear—something she never seemed to buy until she absolutely needed it—face cleanser and a birthday gift for a friend. She was walking past one boutique when the dress in the window caught her eye. She backed up and studied it carefully. The bronze silk was certainly perfect for her coloring, the style a little more daring than she might usually wear, but she seemed to grow more daring every day. She entered the shop, was pleased to discover it came in her size and immediately tried it on.

"It's certainly made for you," the sales clerk told her as she stood in front of a discreetly lit mirror.

The simple slip-styled dress had a jacquard jacket that just skimmed her waist and covered all the bare skin the dress revealed.

"The price isn't," Abby said dryly, thinking of the shoes and bag she'd have to buy to go with the dress and, ironically, what shop she had seen them in. "And I'm sure you take all major credit cards."

"You bet," she said brightly.

"That's what I was afraid of."

Abby made a quick stop to buy the shoes and bag and feeling much poorer drove back to Zach's shop. When she entered, Carla greeted her with a knowing smile.

"He's almost finished with the dragon lady," she murmured. "If you're as smart as I know you are, I'd make my presence known."

"Why?"

"Just go on back and let Zach know you're here," she advised.

Abby walked to the rear of the salon where she could see Zach finishing blow-drying a woman's shoulder-length ash blond hair into a tousled style.

One look at the woman and she understood why Carla called her the dragon lady. Very long, red nails topped slender hands gesturing languidly as she talked to Zach in low tones.

Sensing she was there Zach looked up and smiled.

"Hi," he greeted her. "I'll be through in a minute."

The woman looked up at the intrusion, glanced Abby up and down and immediately ignored her.

Zach switched off the blow dryer and stood back. "There you go, Helene. Gorgeous as always."

The woman smiled at him as if she already knew that. She wrote out a check and set it on the table in front of her. Abby watched her stand up, adjusting her taupe silk top over a definitely curvy figure, which left Abby feeling just a bit envious for even a little bit more in the chest department.

"See you in a month." Her throaty voice made a simple haircut sound much more intimate and set Abby's teeth on edge.

Abby watched the woman glide out of the shop. "Talk about a barracuda," she commented.

"She's divorced with more money and time than she knows what to do with," he told her, gently pushing her into the chair the woman had just vacated.

"Hey!" She reached up when he pulled the pins out of her hair, the thick strands falling down around her shoulders.

"If the mountain won't come to Muhammad, then Muhammad has to do a little creative maneuvering." He threw a drape around her and turned the chair so she faced the mirror. He cocked his head to one side as he dug his fingers gently into her scalp, pulling her hair away from her face and playing with it.

"You promised me lunch," she reminded him, shifting uneasily in the chair.

"And you'll get it." He frowned as he ran mental pictures through his head and settled on one. For a long time he had wanted to get his hands on her hair, but knew the time would have to be right. This appeared to be it. "But now that I've got you in my clutches I'm not letting you out of here so easy."

"If I didn't know better I'd swear this was planned," she muttered, as he helped her out of the chair and escorted her back to the shampoo sink.

Abby had always decided that leaning back and having her hair shampooed was a sensual experience. Having Zach shampoo her hair transcended even that. She closed her eyes, feeling his fingers massage every inch of her scalp and decided she should have given in to him a long time ago.

Abby knew if there had been any tension in her scalp before, it was now gone thanks to Zach's expert touch. She could feel the pads of his fingers rub firmly along her skin and felt the tingles all the way down to her toes. Funny, she couldn't remember feeling this way the other times someone else had washed her hair.

"Don't fall asleep on me," Zach's low-voiced chuckle intruded.

"Umm, it would be understandable. You certainly have a magic touch," she mumbled, looking all too relaxed in the reclining chair. "If I knew you washed hair this well, I would have been in here every day for this. It certainly beats standing in the shower having shampoo drip down in my eyes, or breaking my back standing over the sink." She silently hoped she was portraying a light enough tone to counteract the dizzying sensation from Zach's magic touch.

Zach sprayed warm water through her hair to rinse the shampoo away before applying a mint-scented conditioner. He used the pads of his fingers to massage the cream into her hair from the roots down to the ends. Funny, it was only when he held her that he realized just how delicate she really was. He was relieved she never knew, because knowing her independent nature, she would probably blast him to hell and back for even considering her delicate.

"Don't you ever take care of your hair?" he scolded, needing to change the focus of his thoughts before they revealed themselves. He once read a book in which a man described a woman's hair as living silk, and he couldn't imagine such a thing until he ran his fingers through Abby's wet hair, which coiled around his hands as if it was alive. "When was the last time you conditioned it?"

"When it was last cut. Let me warn you if you keep that up I will definitely fall asleep."

He chuckled. "Not for long if I have anything to say about it."

There was something in the tone of his voice that brought her eyes open, but she found nothing but light amusement in his eyes.

"Isn't it enough you've finally got me where you've wanted me?"

"Have I?"

Abby then decided it was more prudent to stop the line their conversation was taking. She was surprised at herself for allowing Zach to steamroll her into the haircut he had been threatening her with for years. Actually it had always been a joke between them. And now she knew Carla had hit the nail on the head; letting him work with her hair was an intimate experience. As she was seated in the chair again, he combed out her hair, sectioned it off and began cutting.

"You might want to close your eyes," he suggested as he noticed her unease with every inch he snipped off.

"I don't want short hair." If he was going to do this, she was determined to have some kind of say in it.

"You wouldn't look good in it. Why don't you just sit back, relax and let me do my job. It's not as if I haven't been doing this for years."

"I'm a big girl, I can take it." Abby listened to the soft snip of the shears and imagined she could hear her hair fall to the floor.

"You've got beautiful hair, Abby," Zach spoke in low tones meant to soothe as he moved around the chair. "But you don't show it off to its best advantage. Do you know you have a natural wave? Obviously the weight of the hair kept it straight. Now, what I'm doing will give you plenty of length to put it up for special occasions, but will also give you more ease in taking care of it every day. I suggest you also get in the habit of conditioning it once a month."

"This cut is supposedly easier to care for, and you're already giving me a list of extra chores connected with it," she grumbled good-naturedly, tipping her head to one side when his palm gently pressed down. Abby's eyes widened as Zach stood in front of her, unconsciously giving her a close-up of his belt buckle. Now she had a pretty good idea why so many women came to him. She couldn't keep her eyes away from the gold buckle that really wasn't all that unusual, but it was safer than allowing her eyes to drift lower. Luckily, he moved away before she began to drool. She deliberately kept her eyes away from him as he put the scissors down and picked up the blow dryer. Before turning it on he rotated her chair so she didn't face the mirror.

"I don't want you to see it until I'm finished."

The warm air of the blow dryer caressed her face as he brushed sections of hair with a round brush.

"You must feel very proud of yourself for finally getting me into your chair." Abby could already feel the reduced weight on her head. She knew her hair was thick but she hadn't realized how heavy it was until it was gone. Zach turned off the dryer and spun Abby's chair around to face the mirror. She leaned forward to get a better look because she couldn't believe what she was seeing.

Zach had known exactly what to do. The top and sides were cut shorter than the back, which was shoulder length, and the sides were feathered away from her face in an artful frame.

"No wonder you get forty dollars for a haircut," she breathed.

"I take it you approve." He looked pleased with her reaction. "Actually, all I did was add some fullness to that narrow face of yours and work with the natural wave. Abby, it's a crime what you've done to your hair over the years. I swear if you don't come in to me every six to eight weeks for a trim I'll take my accounting business elsewhere."

Abby laughed at a threat she knew he could never carry out. She also knew she would be coming to him on a regular basis from now on, but she wouldn't admit it to him. Not yet. "You may have shanghaied me into this, but I certainly have no complaints." She laughed. "Are you still taking me to lunch?"

"Right away. I wouldn't want you to faint from hunger."

Carla looked up as they walked out of the salon. "I see you finally gave in," she said slyly in Abby's direction.

"I had no choice," she replied.

"It looks great," she assured her.

"Don't say that around him or his ego will grow even more," Abby warned.

"With you two nearby, I don't need to worry about an ego," he grumbled, placing his hand against Abby's back to guide her out. "Come on, let's get out of here before Carla decides to start announcing all my faults."

"Since I already know them, she doesn't have to worry," Abby assured him with a smile.

Zach muttered something unkind under his breath as they walked toward his car.

"Come on, Zach, you'll feel much better after you've been fed," she crooned, buckling her seat belt.

"I should have shaved one side." He sped out of the parking lot and made a left turn.

"Tell you what, since you gave me the haircut I've been fighting for so many years, I'll pay for lunch," she offered. "Does that make you feel better?"

He sliced her a dark look. "I invited you to lunch, I'll pay. The haircut was pure impulse."

"Did you see me fighting you?"

This time his look was much more dangerous. "No, but it could prove interesting."

"I think when we reach the restaurant you should drink several glasses of very cold water. You'll feel much better."

Twenty minutes later Zach parked near a waterfront restaurant called Nathan's. It wasn't exactly known for its atmosphere, because the owners didn't care to cater to the tourist trade, but it had great food as they both knew from eating there many times.

"My head feels so much lighter that it feels strange," Abby laughed after they ordered their food and relaxed with a carafe of wine and appetizers of calamari.

"Just think, you've probably lost five pounds without doing a thing," he teased.

She wrinkled her nose. "Okay, you were right, I've been wrong all these years and I hope you're happy now."

Zach reached across the table and covered her hand with his. "Abby, I wasn't looking to be right or anything. I guess I just wanted to do something special for you, and giving you a bit of a new sexy image was the only thing I could think of."

She turned her hand around and laced her fingers through his. "Zach, you've done a lot of special things for me. At least, I think they're special," she qualified with a small laugh. "Such as the time Sam and Matt were both sick with that horrible virus, and you came over and spent the night helping me take care of them because Estelle was also sick." She looked down, keeping his hand nestled between her two. "And that first wedding anniversary Jason wasn't there. You took me out dancing because you didn't want me to stay home and feel sorry for myself, which I would have done.''

"Jason took me out and got me drunk the night my divorce became final, and you took care of Beth that night and then took care of us during our hangovers," he mused.

"There was Matt's Boy Scout father-son banquet that he hadn't told anyone about because he didn't want me to feel sad, and you somehow found out and took him," she reminded him. "Don't you realize, Zach, just what kind of a man you really are? For a while you tried to act like a sex-crazed bachelor on the loose, but no matter what, you were always there when Beth needed you and when I needed you. Sorry, but I know too much about you, my friend."

He smiled into her eyes. "Thanks, I like to hear that. I guess it's only fair I sing your praises while we're at it. When Carolyn walked out, I didn't know a thing about changing diapers, feeding a tiny child or even how to relate to her. I'd been so busy with my own work in the beginning that I had no idea what was involved in taking care of a toddler."

"But you were willing to learn," Abby reminded him gently. "You could have very easily hired a housekeeper to do everything, but you didn't. Instead, you took care of Beth as best you could and only used me or someone else to baby-sit while you worked. That says a lot."

He stared down at the table. "I was so bitter when Carolyn left. I couldn't understand why she would want to leave me," he said wryly, "and especially, leave Beth. I mean, the kid slept all night practically from the time she came home from the hospital, and she was never much of a crier. I could never understand Carolyn's reasons, probably because she didn't give any. All she ever said was she didn't want to be married to a struggling hairdresser anymore and she especially didn't want to be a mother. She's certainly proved the last statement, because Beth hardly ever hears from her. The only good thing Carolyn did was remarry quickly, so I didn't have to pay her alimony. And in time my bitterness wore off and I realized I was much better off without her." He stopped speaking and leaned back slightly, but kept hold of her hand as the waitress set their plates in front of them.

Abby's face lit up at the filled plate of scallops. "Just what the doctor ordered." She grabbed the basket of warm sourdough bread before Zach could get to it. "Ah, ah, ah, all mine." She broke off a piece and slathered it with butter. As her teeth broke through the crust and soft center, her eyes closed, the expression on her face could only be described as bliss. "Perfect."

He stared at her face a long time, the finely sculpted cheekbones, lilac-shadowed eyelids and peach-glossed lips. "Yes," he murmured, bringing her captured hand to his lips without even realizing what he was doing.

Abby's eyes snapped open at the warm touch on her fingertips. Something told her the crazy tilt in her stomach had nothing to do with the food. "What are you doing?" she asked in a shaky voice.

He smiled even as he nibbled on her forefinger before returning her hand to the table. "Giving you a compliment regarding your sensual beauty."

Her eyes widened even more, then narrowed in suspicion. "And what brought about this sudden interest in me as a woman with a capital *W*?"

Served with a direct question he knew he could only give her an honest answer. He just wished he had one. "Hell if I know."

"Zach, it doesn't happen overnight, so don't try to say you suddenly woke up one morning and decided I would make good affair material," she informed him. "Just the way you suddenly decided it might be fun for us to start dating and see what happened from there. Come clean, Randolph."

He winced at the mother's tone that said tell the truth or else. "No, it didn't happen overnight," he admitted tersely. "In fact, I think it's been creeping up on me for a long time now, until I couldn't ignore it any longer. I certainly enjoy your company more than the women I've seen in the past and—'' his face reddened ''—this is difficult to admit. I would just rather be with you, and I'm getting tired of our platonic relationship. I want to send you flowers and candy without it having to be a special occasion, and I want us to hold hands in the movies and all sorts of corny things that go with a romance.'' His eyes pleaded with her to understand.

Abby more than understood. ''I'd like that, too,'' she whispered. ''But are you sure? Zach, what you're talking about could turn out to be more than two friends becoming even closer. You've always been wary about commitments. Doesn't that worry you now?''

Zach shook his head. ''Not as long as it doesn't worry you. And as long as you realize this has nothing to with a mid-life crisis.'' He flashed a wolfish grin. ''And as long as I can attack you after the meal.''

She shook her head with a proper show of regret. ''Sorry, I never indulge after meals.'' She ate her scallops with undisguised hunger. ''You're right, let's just pig out and enjoy all this wonderful food.'' She gestured to the waitress. ''Could we have some more bread please?'' She flashed Zach a mock glare. ''And it's all mine, do you understand?''

He shuddered. ''Not when you threaten a person so effectively.''

Except Zach had his ways. When the bread arrived, he withdrew a crusty piece, carefully covered it with butter then fed it to Abby with careful solicitude. If he hadn't looked so serious about this she would have laughed, thinking he was teasing. It was only too clear he wasn't. She had no idea when she finished her food because he started doing the same thing with her scallops. He looked the part of a totally besotted suitor and oddly, the role fit.

"Would you like any dessert?" the waitress asked brightly, after their plates were cleared away and Abby was brought back to the present.

"Yes," Abby said without hesitation. "Cheesecake and coffee please."

The waitress nodded as she noted it on her order pad. "Would you like strawberries or blueberries on that?"

"No, thank you, I'm watching my weight," she said demurely, earning a droll look from Zach.

"And you, sir?" She turned to him with an even brighter smile.

He shook his head. "Just coffee, thanks."

"Usually you give in to Nathan's cheesecake, too," Abby commented.

"Usually, but I prefer to swipe some of yours today."

"Ha! That's what you think. There's a few things I'm stingy with: popcorn when I'm at the movies and cheesecake."

But Abby hadn't counted on Zach's hands-quicker-than-the-eye reflex when her cheesecake was placed before her. Unlike most restaurants that only served a thin sliver of the rich dessert, Nathan's believed in pampering their diners. Abby's slice could have easily fed three people.

"Zach!" she scolded when he swiped a large bite and brought it to his mouth. "Order your own cheesecake and leave mine alone."

"You really should watch all the extra calories, Abby, love," he recommended with the care of a good friend, even as his fork swooped down and stole another slice. "Someday they're going to catch up with you, and you're going to blow up to four hundred pounds overnight."

She glared at him as she protectively circled her plate with her arms. "You know very well quick metabolisms run in my family. All you have to do is look at my mother and father."

"Yep, scrawny."

She adopted an affronted tone. "You just talked your-self out of any more bites of *my* cheesecake. Just sit there and drink your coffee like a good boy."

He leaned back and grinned at her as she quickly fin-ished her dessert before he could have another chance of stealing more.

"Are you sure you're not having a mid-life crisis?" she asked as they later walked through the parking lot to his car.

"Positive. I went through that years ago." He opened the passenger door for her, eyeing her legs with frank admira-tion when she swung them inside and tucked her dress care-fully around her. "How about a drive along the coast? We haven't done that in a long time."

Abby thought for a moment of the errands she still had to run and weighed them against the prospect of a relaxing drive. "Don't you have any appointments this afternoon?" She couldn't believe he had only come in for the one, be-sides her surprise haircut.

"One that canceled," he replied. "I worked in salon number three this morning, so don't worry, I'm not aban-doning my work."

"I'm not, I'm just relieved to know you could afford lunch." She wrinkled her nose at him. "In fact, let's take a drive out to the beach and walk."

"Sounds good to me." He started up the engine and carefully backed out of his parking space. "I'll help you walk off lunch." As he drove he noticed Abby take a com-pact and lip gloss out of her purse and reapply the peach color. How many times had he seen her perform that very same task? Funny how it took on a new meaning now that he saw her as a beautiful woman instead of a good buddy. He noticed her hesitate over the purse-size spray bottle of cologne. "If you feel the need for a touch-up, go ahead."

She shook her head. "The scent will linger in your car."

"I don't mind," he lied glibly, ignoring the silent reminders of the many times he asked his dates not to spray their perfume in his car.

Abby flashed a knowing smile. Her cologne bottle remained in her purse. "Sure you do, but you're sweet to make an exception on my behalf. Now, pick out a semideserted beach where we can run along the waterline and forget all about our responsibilities."

"Is that something you've been thinking about lately?" he asked, sensing something in her tone.

"Sort of," she sighed. "It's called realizing I'm not immortal, and wanting as much security as possible for my family."

Zach frowned. "I thought your business was doing great."

"Oh, it is," she hastened to assure him. "Actually better than great, but being self-employed still means heavy medical-insurance premiums and paying taxes I wish I had a boss paying instead of me. I can't complain since the medical insurance certainly more than paid for itself between Matt's broken bones and Sam's braces."

"Not to mention those few little accidents when you tried to cook," he murmured. "You were the talk of the emergency ward for quite a while back there."

"It was all Estelle's fault for leaving me for two weeks," she defended herself.

"Abby, she had her appendix taken out."

She couldn't help laughing, remembering how Estelle worried more about her kitchen than her own health problems or whether Abby and the family could survive without her. The older woman had even given Abby a list of all the restaurants that had take-out. "I thought baking potatoes in the microwave would be a cinch. I had no idea they could explode if you didn't pierce them with a fork."

"Not to mention the stove catching on fire," he reminded her.

"The stove never caught on fire and you know it."

Zach parked the car facing the beach. "Oh, it must have been the oven."

Abby pushed open the door and climbed out, slamming the door behind her. When she reached the sand she slipped off her shoes and left them near the car. "Nothing happened with the oven, either, Zachary."

He followed her after taking off his shoes and socks. "Are you sure? I'm positive Matt once said something about the oven catching on fire."

Her face tightened as she strode rapidly on the sand. "Zachary Andrew, you are going too far in your fairy tales."

"Maybe there wasn't a fire. Maybe the roast just shrunk to two inches. Was that it?" Laughter ran through his voice. Zach rarely had a chance to tease Abby so unmercifully and some devil inside prompted him further.

Abby ignored him as she walked along the water's edge, with him following swiftly on her heels as he tried to roll up his pant legs so they wouldn't get wet. A faint smile touched her lips as she thought of an appropriate punishment.

"After all these years you should know you and kitchens don't mix." Zach strove to appease her. "Honey, you can't even make instant coffee."

Abby swung around to face him. "And you think that's funny, don't you?" she retorted. "You think the idea of someone who's so capable with the rest of her life and totally useless in the kitchen is a joke, don't you?" She advanced on him, forcing him to back up.

"Of course, I don't," he protested, holding his hands up. "Hey, Abby, don't get mad. We all tease you about this."

"Yes, you do. You think this is some kind of horrible joke, don't you?" She spoke with a calmness that wasn't in the icy glitter of her eyes as she kept walking closer and closer to him. "Well, my dear friend, I do believe the joke is on *you*!" She reached out, pushing him hard enough to unbalance him. To her satisfaction, he landed with an undignified plop in the water.

Chapter Seven

"I hope you're happy," Zach sputtered, making his way to his feet carefully so he wouldn't slip in the water as he stared at her, fit to kill.

"I feel just great." Abby stood back, her arms crossed in front of her chest. Her smile indicated she was very pleased with herself.

"By all rights I should do the same to you," he muttered.

"Then why don't you?" she challenged.

"Because I don't want to ruin your haircut!"

"No problem, I'll just go to Cuts R Us and get it restyled!" she yelled back, dropping her hands to her hips.

That did it for him. Before Abby could react, Zach ran over to her, picked her up and ran back into the ocean.

"Zach!" she shrieked, grabbing on to his neck for fear of falling, although now that would be the least of her worries. "This dress is dry-clean only!"

"So?"

She yelped when the cold water first hit her rear end, and cried even more when Zach dropped her in water deep enough not to drown her, but more than enough to cover her shoulders and splash her face.

"Do you feel better now?" She discovered walking in soaking wet clothing was awkward at best.

"Infinitely."

"I don't care what you're saying, you are in the midst of a mid-life crisis and if you have any brains at all you'll see a doctor as soon as possible." She stalked back up to the car.

"It's amazing how good it feels when you can turn the tables on someone," he called after her.

She spun around. "You deserved it, I didn't."

"Wrong!" He dug his keys out of his pocket along with a sodden wallet. After rummaging through the back of the car he came up with a couple of towels and threw one to Abby.

She wrung out her dress and used the towel to dry her arms and legs before tackling her hair. The more she thought about what had happened during the past fifteen minutes, the funnier she found it. Pretty soon Zach could hear her chuckling.

"What do you find so funny?" he demanded.

"Us." She held out her arms. "Come on, Zach, you have to admit it is pretty funny. I mean, do people our age usually do things like this?"

"People our age? I hadn't realized we were soon ready for the retirement home." His voice was gruff but a smile threatened to curve his mouth.

"My pushing you in was because I got so mad at you teasing me about that oven. I guess it's because while I can work at the most complicated tax problems, I'm completely helpless in the kitchen and there are times it bothers me."

Zach walked over to Abby and took the towel from her hands. He carefully dried her hair, which now lay in tangled waves which he eyed wryly. Acting on impulse, he bent forward and pressed his lips against hers, but instead of it being a quick kiss, he lingered. "You taste salty," he murmured, moving his mouth back and forth over hers.

"So do you." Her voice was shaky. She wasn't sure whether she was growing cold because of her wet clothing or Zach's kiss, but she decided it had to be the latter.

Zach turned her around so she leaned against the warm metal of his car with his body covering her front, sharing his body heat with her. "I think this would be an excellent time for us to kiss and make up." He nibbled on her lower lip.

"Oh? Are you apologizing?" She was rapidly finding any lick of common sense leaving her.

He chuckled as he began nibbling on her ear. "No, I just thought it would be a great excuse to kiss and make up."

Abby tipped her head to one side to allow him better access to her neck. "Zach, we are standing here wearing wet clothing in an ocean breeze. That's a great way to catch pneumonia."

He looked down noticing how the wet cloth had clung to her peaked nipples, and forced his eyes away before his thoughts betrayed him too far. "If I have to catch pneumonia, I can't imagine anyone I would want to share it with more than you."

She smiled. "You do say the most romantic things, Mr. Randolph."

"I try, because I feel like a soppy idiot when I'm with you."

Abby couldn't help giggling. "The correct word for your problem right now is sopping."

And just because he felt she deserved it, Zach began kissing her all over again until she didn't care what term was correct, only that he never stopped. When he lifted his head, she pulled back and stared at him in surprise. "This is something new to me."

"New?" He laughed. "Abby, you've been seeing the wrong guys."

She shook her head, looking very serious. "No, this is something new to me when it's coming from you."

His eyes glowed with a light that was equally new to her. "Then I suggest you get used to it, lady." He reached around her to open the door. "You're right, we better get going."

As soon as the engine was warm enough he switched on the heater adjusting the vents to blow on them directly. "You okay?" he asked, swinging out of the parking lot and heading for the salon.

"Yes, I'm fine." Her brain was still whirling with questions, but that wasn't anything unusual with the way Zach was acting lately. Dating him was one thing, but seeing Zach on a romantic level was something entirely new. A tiny smile touched her lips. It wasn't all that bad either, she decided, relaxing more in the bucket seat.

When Zach parked behind the salon he guided Abby over to her car and waited for her to unlock the door and slide inside.

"I'd be willing to wash your hair and restyle it," he offered.

She shook her head. "I think I would be better off getting home and out of these wet clothes. If nothing else, spending time with you is not normal."

"I'll try to think up something special for this Friday night," he vowed, placing his hand over his heart.

Abby shuddered comically. "Please don't, Zach. I don't know if I can handle it. Thanks for lunch and the swim." As she drove away, she glanced up into her rearview mirror and saw him standing there with a broad smile on his face and couldn't help smiling also, since she knew exactly what he was smiling about.

"DAD WILL BE HOME SOON," Beth commented, glancing at the small clock she had put on the patio table to keep track of the time. She and Matt were relaxing in the spa.

He grimaced. "And I better be out of here before he does."

"Why?" she argued. "It's not as if he doesn't know we're seeing each other."

Matt pulled her into his arms and kissed her soundly. "Yeah, but he's still a father who might be afraid his precious daughter could be compromised if we spend too much time alone around the house."

Beth grinned mischievously. "I could, huh? Personally, I think it sounds wonderful."

"You would." He chuckled, kissing her on the nose and pushing her gently away before pulling himself out of the spa and reaching in for her. "Come on. Time to return to the real world."

"WHAT HAPPENED TO YOU?" Estelle viewed Abby's ruined dress with shocked surprise.

"Zach decided we should take an impromptu swim in the ocean." Abby breezed past, carrying her packages. "Wait until you see the dress I bought. Talk about hot."

"Wait a minute!" Estelle hurried after her, dinner preparations now forgotten. "You're not going to just toss off a blasé statement like that without going into further detail. Not to mention your hair. I could be wrong but it looks a great deal shorter. Or did it happen to shrink during your little swim?"

"All right, I won't mention my hair," she quipped, tossing her bags on the bed and immediately peeling off her dress and slip. "I'm afraid the dress is beyond help. I have got to take a shower. The salt is making my skin itch. No wonder I don't care to go to the beach anymore."

Estelle grasped her arm to halt her escape into the bathroom. "Now, what is this about Zach pulling you into the ocean? I thought all you were doing today was getting your nails done and some shopping. Where did he come into the act?"

"He came in to do someone's hair just as I was leaving. He asked if I wanted to go to lunch when he was finished. I said yes, did some shopping while waiting, then went to lunch at Nathan's, and went for a drive along the coast and walked on the beach. We horsed around a bit too much and we ended up in the water.'' She deliberately left out the reason for horsing around and the kiss afterward. After all, some things weren't meant to be shared.

Estelle walked into the bathroom and ran hot water into the tub, adding scented bath oil. "I like your hair,'' she told her, grabbing a robe out of the closet and handing it to Abby. "Makes you look sexier.''

She turned to look at herself in the mirror. "Really?'' Abby wouldn't ignore a compliment like that. What woman could? "I still have to get used to the shorter length although it's still long enough to put up. I'll have to have Beth teach me some of the fancy braids she does. I admit I won't miss the extra weight it caused during hot weather.''

"Take your bath. We'll talk about this wet luncheon later, and I want to hear all the gory details.'' Estelle picked up the wet clothing and carried it out of the room.

Abby spent the better part of an hour luxuriating in the hot bath with a big smile on her face as she recalled Zach's kiss. She had certainly been kissed more than a few times over the years and by men who had a great deal of experience in that department, but she couldn't recall one that made her feel the way his did. "The man has a touch,'' she sighed, reaching for a loofah sponge. "Okay, calm down, Abby, or you're going to have to follow this up with a cold shower.'' With that in mind she quickly finished her bath and climbed out, wrapping a sheet around her. Dressed warmly in her robe, she took the time to put away her purchases before choosing a periwinkle-cotton short jumpsuit to wear.

"So what happened?'' Estelle asked when Abby entered the kitchen. Abby winced when the older woman opened the oven door to check the roast. Right now she didn't want any kind of reminder of the oven.

"When I returned to the salon to meet Zach for lunch he sort of shanghaied me into his chair and cut my hair," she explained, looking through the mail sitting on the kitchen table.

"I gather you didn't put up much of a struggle," Estelle said dryly.

"Why should I when I turn out looking sexier," Abby said airily, looking up when Samantha burst through the back door.

"Hi!" She stopped short in front of her mother. "Mom, you got your hair cut."

"Thanks to Zach."

Samantha cocked her head from one side to the other, studying her carefully. "It looks pretty okay."

"I'm sure Zach would appreciate your candor."

"Well, I mean, he can do something good with anyone's hair, no matter how bad it is," she said brightly, accepting the letter Abby handed her.

Abby sighed. "Why doesn't that make me feel better?"

Samantha giggled as she left the kitchen. "I bet Zach is gloating that he finally got to do something with your hair."

"With a daughter like her I don't need enemies," she muttered, grabbing a mug and pouring herself a cup of coffee.

"You've been putting Zach off for more years than I can remember, and all of a sudden you waltz in with a new hairdo that's more than a trim. What can you expect?" Estelle said.

Abby groaned. "So I got a haircut. I've gotten them before and no one ever said a word."

"That's because it usually doesn't change your appearance so radically." Estelle mixed up batter for corn muffins.

"Are we having all this for dinner?" Abby looked at the food with dismay.

"You said it sounded fine this morning."

"Yes, but I had a large lunch."

Estelle turned and looked at her with surprise. "That never stopped you before."

Abby fidgeted with her mug under the housekeeper's knowing gaze. "I had a large lunch and an even larger slice of cheesecake."

"Oh, yes, that would cause it, wouldn't it?" Her light sarcasm wasn't lost on Abby.

"Yes, it would," she retorted, carrying her part of the mail out of the room.

Abby hoped the subject would drop but should have known better. During dinner Matt smirked at her.

"Beth said Zach came home with wet clothes and Estelle said you did, too. Something about falling in the water while walking on the beach? Not too cool, Mom." He selected a slice of meat and placed it on his plate. "Oh, your hair looks pretty good. I knew Zach would finally get his way."

"Now that everyone has gotten their two cents in, could we please finish this meal in peace?" Abby requested frostily, by now tired with everyone's teasing.

Matt raised his eyebrows in surprise. "Okay," he murmured.

After dinner Abby retired to the den with Max, whom she knew wouldn't tease her. The macaw sat on a towel draped over the back of the couch and kept bumping her ear with his beak in an effort to gain her attention.

"Why don't you just watch the movie," she said absently, handing him a walnut.

"Umm, good," he crooned to the walnut before cracking it open, gobbling up the contents and immediately asking for more, this time receiving a Brazil nut.

"He gets treated better than I do," Samantha complained, walking in and plopping herself in an easy chair.

"Is your homework all done?"

"Yes. He doesn't have to do any homework, either."

"My, aren't we glum all of a sudden." Abby looked at her daughter's grumpy features.

"It's allowed, isn't it?"

Abby raised her eyebrows—the same expression her son obviously picked up from her. "Only if there's a good reason."

"I do have one." She stared down at her lap. "I have cramps."

Abby's face softened. "Did you take anything for them?"

Samantha nodded. "Just a little while ago. I don't see why we have to suffer like this and guys don't get anything similar."

Abby chuckled. "I always felt that way, too. When I went through my first few bouts of morning sickness when I was pregnant with Matt, your father and my obstetrician used to tell me it would get better soon. As they were both men, I told them they were much safer not offering advice about something they had no idea about. It wasn't much later your father got the worst case of flu he'd ever had. He couldn't keep anything down for a couple days. I waited until he was better before I told him now he knew what it was like. He was so horrified that I guess it could be considered a miracle you were ever born."

Samantha smiled faintly but her expression remained serious. "Did it bother you having to get married?"

Abby shook her head. "We loved each other and we didn't look at it as the thing to do. We had created a baby with that love and we knew we wanted to be together always."

"But it still bothers Granddad, doesn't it?"

Abby grimaced at the memory of her father's features when he first heard of her pregnancy. "Let's just say he wasn't all that pleased. He felt we were too young, and he spouted statistics about teenage divorces and how we had our lives ahead of us. He gave us a very rough time, but all it did was make us more determined to make it work. And

I'm pleased to say that it did and to this day, your grand-father hates to admit he just might have been wrong.

Samantha studied her fingernails. "If the baby had lived, do you think he would have grown up to be more like me or Matt?"

She licked her lips. "He would have grown up like himself," she whispered, thinking of the tiny baby that had died. Jason Townsend Jr. had lived only six months, but he was never forgotten in Abby's heart. She struggled to bring the conversation onto a happier note. "What brought all this about?"

Samantha shrugged. "Oh, I guess because word is that Jennifer Simpson is pregnant."

"Jennifer Simpson?" Abby choked, picturing a gangly girl wearing braces. But then, she hadn't seen her since the beginning of summer. She could have blossomed the way Samantha had during the past few months. She quickly composed herself. "Well, just remember that rumors are just that. Don't believe anything you haven't seen." *She's three months younger than Sam,* Abby thought wildly. *My God, I can't handle this.*

"Yeah, maybe someone is just saying it because they want her to look bad. It happens all the time. Just like when someone said that Tiffany puts out to anyone, and she's vowed to die a virgin."

Abby closed her eyes. Now she knew she couldn't handle it. "Whatever happened to rumors that so and so was caught smoking in the girls bathroom?"

"Sorry, Mom, you're back in the old days. If they're caught smoking now it's pot, not cigarettes." Samantha levered herself up. "Can I borrow your heating pad?"

"Sure, honey, you know where it is. And don't forget to raise your knees, that usually helps." Abby collapsed back when she was left alone. "Damn you, Jason, for leaving me to go through this alone," she muttered. "I hope you're having a good laugh up there. Because I'm sure as hell not laughing down here.''

"Walnut," Max croaked, butting Abby's head again with his beak.

"I'm so glad life is simple with you, Max." She complied with his request. "Because the day you ask for a female companion is the day you leave this house."

ABBY WAS GRATEFUL to return to her accounting work the next day because she felt it was the only normal thing she had in her life. When she received a call from an old classmate inviting her to lunch that day she happily accepted.

"Abby, you look great," Jerry Harkness greeted her with a kiss on the cheek when she entered the restaurant. He eyed her, in her peach silk dress with the slim torso and dropped waist, with frank male admiration.

"Well, thank you, sir." She inclined her head. "So why the visit south? I always thought Las Vegas or Tahoe was more your idea of a vacation?"

"Actually, I came down here to see you," Jerry explained.

"Me?" she laughed. "Why me?"

Jerry held up a finger when the waiter brought their drinks and took their orders. "After we eat. First of all, tell me about yourself. How is your business doing? And those kids? The last time we talked, Matt was considering law school."

She nodded. "Yes, just as soon as he finishes college here, he'll be moving up to L.A. for law school. With his grades he shouldn't have any problem. Thank goodness Jason's trust fund will cover the school fees, so he'll only need a part-time job for his personal expenses. As for me, I'm pleased to say my work load is more than sufficient to keep the wolf from the door."

Jerry smiled. "I'm sure you're having no problems at all. You were always a great accountant. I just wish we had kept in touch more often than we have. Let's compare notes so we can catch up on all the changes."

As they ate, Abby couldn't help but notice Jerry asked her more questions about her work than answering her questions about his, and wondered what was going on. It wasn't until they were relaxing with their wine after lunch that she finally was able to pin him down.

"Okay, enough trivialities. What exactly are you doing down here?" she demanded.

He nodded. "It's very simple. Our firm is expanding and along with that expansion comes the desire to expand our client list. And some of the partners in the office have decided the best direction is with small businesses. There are more and more of them out there every day."

"And most of them fail," Abby interjected.

He nodded. "True, but those with the savvy don't. Our firm has enough experience to keep the savvy ones going and help them expand when the time is right. The thing is we don't have anyone with the knowledge of working with the small businessman or woman. That's where someone like you would come in."

The wineglass Abby had just lifted to her lips was carefully replaced on the table. She had a feeling what was coming next.

"Me?"

He grinned. "Sure, why not? You've certainly had the experience, and judging by the business you're doing, you certainly know how to treat your clients. No matter what, it's a different ballpark from dealing with big business and you know it. When we discussed this idea, I brought you up because I knew you'd be perfect for something like this. Matt will be going to school in L.A. and you'd be closer to him. Sam's young enough to change schools without too much trauma."

"Sam is fifteen. Right now the entire world is a trauma to her," Abby said dryly. "Jerry, this is all crazy."

He named a figure that left her gasping. "Does that sound crazy? Along with excellent company-paid benefits, a pension plan you wouldn't believe and a yearly bonus. I'll be honest with you, Abby. It's not an offer you'd get every day."

"No kidding," she muttered, quickly polishing off her wine. "Jerry, this is very sudden and I'd like to think about it."

He nodded in understanding. "Sure, but don't take too long. We'd like to get this going within the next few months."

"Just in time to begin preparing for tax season."

"You got it."

Abby shook her head. "Most small businesses don't feel comfortable changing accountants before tax season, Jerry."

"They will if you're the accountant. Think of it, an office overlooking the city, a secretary to field all your calls and do your typing. I'll be honest with you, babe, you'd be a fool to turn it down."

"I'd be a fool to give in to impulse," she corrected. "Just give me the time to think it over. I'll call you in about a week, okay?" He didn't appear happy that she hadn't jumped at the chance, as he obviously thought she would. "All right, one week, but no longer."

Abby's eyes grew cold. "Jerry, I know all your hard-sell techniques, so don't try any on me. You're asking me to make a sudden decision on a matter that not only affects me, but my family and my clients. That involves a lot of consideration I don't intend to do lightly. Understood?"

"Loud and clear." He gave the waiter his credit card. "You never could be pushed, Abby. I don't think even Jason ever tried."

They walked outside, waiting for the parking valet to retrieve their cars. Abby's arrived first and before she got in, she turned to Jerry. "You know, I don't think you'll ever change," she told him. "In fact, I'm very surprised you don't own a fleet of used-car dealerships and advertise during the late-night movies. It's what you were really meant to do."

"You just phone me with a yes and we'll all be happy," he called after her.

When Abby arrived home, she found Estelle polishing the living room furniture.

"How was your lunch?" the housekeeper asked.

Abby dropped her purse on a table.

"That depends on how you look at it," she replied. "How would you feel about my taking a job with Jerry's firm and we all move to L.A.?"

Estelle dropped her dust cloth. "Abigail, this is the last time I allow you out of this house for a luncheon date with old school friends."

Chapter Eight

"Why would you want to move up to L.A. when all your friends and work are here?" Zach demanded, after Abby told him about her day. "*I'm* here."

"Zach, I'm not picking up and moving tomorrow," she protested laughing. "I told him I would think about his generous offer." His reply was muttered under his breath. "What did you say?"

"Just that I'd miss you." He drew in a deep breath. "Abby, I'm just thinking about you. Sam's happy in her school, you've picked up quite a few new clients lately, not to mention everything you know is down here." He didn't want to discuss the sudden drop in his stomach when she first told him about the job offer. Abby move away? Sure, L.A. was only about a two- or three-hour drive away, but he wouldn't see her as much as he was used to. While they talked a great deal on the phone, it would be different when he had to tack on an area code to her number. Damn it, he didn't want her to move away!

"I wish I hadn't even told you about this so soon," she sighed, twisting the phone cord between her fingers. She knew what bothered the most was his admission that he'd miss her, because she already knew how much she would miss him.

"It wouldn't have done you any good because Estelle already told me the situation when she answered the phone."

"Estelle has a big mouth."

"Estelle has a sense of togetherness." That silenced Abby effectively, which Zach fully intended it to do.

"We are a family, Abby," he said quietly. "We may not be blood relatives, but the six of us have gone through more than most families do. And I hope you notice that I included Estelle in this particular family, because she's certainly a good part of it. I understand you've been feeling a bit nervous about any added expenses Matt might come up with while at law school, since it's doubtful his scholarship will cover everything. You forget I was there when he announced he was going to be a lawyer and I remember what you said."

"That he wasn't going to have to work the extra jobs the way his father did. I wanted him to have the luxury of studying," she whispered. "I didn't want him to worry about anything heavier than the next day's classes. And I was going to do everything in my power to see that happened. The next day Jason set up the trust fund for Matt's education."

"And hasn't Sam expressed a recent interest in medicine?"

Abby groaned. "Which is just as expensive, if not more. Zach, let me warn you that you're putting up a wonderful argument for me to seriously consider taking that job if the other partners want me."

"And last but not least, what about us?"

She fidgeted in her chair. "Zach, we haven't discussed—"

"And we need to. Abby, we've started something that can be wonderful if given the chance. Allow it to grow. Okay?"

"I thought we were going to take this slow and easy," she retorted.

"That was before you started talking about moving to L.A.," he spoke harshly. "Besides I'm not talking about jumping into something we're not ready for. I'm talking about us nurturing something special. Is that so bad?"

"Of course not, but there are so many factors," she argued. "After Jason's death, I was left to work out a lot of problems. I may have been on my own for ten years but it still doesn't get any easier. And you've been a wonderful help. I honestly don't know what I would have done if you hadn't been here to help me over the rough spots."

"I don't want your gratitude," he said roughly.

She rubbed her forehead with her fingertips. "That's not what I mean. I promise no decision will be made in haste, and right now I can think of one reason to stay, and that's you."

Zach was silent. "Would we be better off to leave it on that note?"

"For the time being."

By silent consent they each hung up. After listening to the dial tone for a few seconds, Zach replaced the receiver in the cradle. He walked outside and sat by the pool, while telling the night air exactly what he thought of Abby's new job offer.

"Mr. Randolph!" A scandalized voice sounded from the other side of the block wall.

"Oh great," he muttered, slouching down in his chair. He didn't have to see the tiny figure to know who was speaking.

"Mr. Randolph, I have always believed in allowing people their privacy, but when others can hear the filthy language you are presently indulging in, I feel I must speak up." The cultured tones easily reached his ears without her having to resort to raising her voice.

"I apologize, Miss Howard." He forced himself to keep his voice even. "I'm afraid I wasn't thinking."

"Then I suggest you do so in the future before you open your mouth. After all, you do have your daughter to consider and you should set a better example for her, so she will grow into a proper young lady."

A moment later he could hear her back door close.

"It's amazing how she can read someone the riot act without raising her voice." Zach turned his head and saw his daughter standing in the doorway. "She's a retired teacher. It must be in the genes or something. I said one damn and she's going to make me stay after school for the rest of my life." He sighed heavily but brightened up when Beth handed him a frosty bottle of beer. "Ah, I knew I brought you up right. Thanks, honey. I thought you and Matt were going out."

Beth took the chair next to him. "We did, but since I have an early class tomorrow, we decided it wouldn't be a good idea. Besides, I'll be going over there for dinner tomorrow night and we're going out then. Now, don't change the subject from what I really want to talk about. What is it with you and Abby lately?"

"*Hell* if I know." He looked at her with a rakish grin. "I heard Miss Howard go inside so I know I'm safe."

Beth adjusted her body so she could curl her legs under her. "But you two are dating now. And I don't mean the way you used to go out together, but really dating."

"We're trying to. It hasn't exactly been easy."

"Why?"

Zach pulled on his beer and brought the bottle down as he considered her question. "Because she's always been the most interesting woman I've known and I finally realized that I'd like to know more about that person, and not just Abby the friend or Matt and Sam's mom and Jason's widow. The trouble is she doesn't look at it that way and she's leading me a merry chase."

Beth's face brightened. "You're in love with her."

He shook his head. "Hey, wait, it's much too soon for a weighty decision like that. I've seen her in one light for so long that it's a little difficult to shift gears. But I'm trying my damnedest to do it."

She smiled. "Then I have only one thing to say, Father, dear."

"What's that?" He lifted the bottle to his lips to finish the cold brew.

"That you have my blessing. I always thought you would be better off marrying again." She rose from her chair and stopped long enough to slap her father on the back to stop his choking and sauntered into the house. "Good night."

ABBY'S RESTLESS NIGHT did nothing but make her feel even more disoriented. The only bright spot was Zach's admission that he'd miss her if she moved away. With a decidedly silly smile on her face, she brushed her hair back into a loose ponytail and threw on a robe before going in search of coffee.

"Good morning," Zach greeted her, sitting at the kitchen table as if he sat there every morning enjoying Estelle's buttermilk waffles.

She stepped back a pace, unsure what she was seeing. Realizing he wasn't a figment of her imagination, she said nothing, but headed for the coffeepot and filled a mug to the brim, drinking deeply.

"She never gets up in a good mood," Estelle informed Zach. "You're best off not talking to her until she's had her coffee. It's just safer."

"I wake up in a wonderful mood. It's just hard to verbalize before I have my caffeine fix," Abby mumbled, looking at Zach over the rim of her mug, a shy smile on her lips. She took a seat next to her daughter.

Samantha eyed the two adults with a curious gaze.

"Is there something I should know about?" she asked, pushing her school books to one side.

"No," Abby said succinctly. "And if that blouse came from my closet, I suggest you change before leaving for school or I'm putting a dead bolt on my bedroom door today."

"You said I could borrow it if I was careful," Samantha reminded her mother as she finished her milk and escaped from the room.

Matt sat back in the other chair watching the proceedings with an amusement Abby didn't find the least bit funny. "Shouldn't you leave for school soon?" she demanded of her son.

He shook his head, clearly enjoying his mother's discomfort. "I don't have a class until eleven." He rose from his chair, poured himself another cup of coffee and snared another waffle from Estelle, who had just set one in front of Abby, along with butter and warmed syrup. "You know, this is better than daytime television."

Abby fixed him with a look to kill. "You'd be safer watching some right about now."

"I think I should remain in case Zach needs some assistance. After all, Mom, he doesn't know how grumpy you can be in the mornings when you haven't had all your sleep." He smilingly dug his hole a little deeper.

Zach watched her teal eyes growing stormier by the moment and the tight line of her mouth that he whimsically thought a kiss might soften. "Maybe you'd be safer out of the line of fire, Matt," he advised. "If I need any help I'll holler, okay?"

Matt grinned and nodded. He picked up his plate and coffee cup and headed for the den. Estelle had also magically disappeared from the kitchen.

Abby poured syrup over her waffle and cut it into neat squares. She took several bites before speaking. "Is there a special reason why you're gracing us with your presence this morning? After all, this isn't one of your usual habits. You should be careful, Zach, people might talk."

"The only one to talk is Miss Howard. It appears she was outside while I paced the patio casting aspersions on your ancestors, and I gave her a pretty good shock. She coldly informed me I was setting a very bad example for my daughter and I should watch my language in the future." He momentarily thought about shocking Abby by relating interesting tidbits from the conversation he and Beth had shared last night.

Abby didn't mean to let the smile slip out, but was powerless to stop it. "She did, huh? I just bet she had her virginal ear pinned to the window screen so she didn't miss one word. That will also teach you in the future to stay inside and have your windows closed when you intend to bawl someone out."

He chuckled, relaxing now that he saw she wasn't going to throw him out. "I don't know, with all her prim and proper ways she does make life interesting."

Abby continued nibbling on her waffle. "Zach, I feel as if you're taking all of this personally."

"If the positions were reversed wouldn't you?"

She held up a hand to silence him. "To be honest, I probably would. I received a flattering offer, nothing more. But this isn't the time to even consider it. Before I know it, I'll be engrossed in tax season and won't have time to think of anything other than my clients. So please don't worry about it? I don't intend to."

He nodded. "So you won't turn down a dinner date for Friday night?" he asked lightly.

Abby considered. "Dress up, adult time, put on our best table manners, a restaurant with waiters and real cloth napkins and candles on the table?"

"Dress up, adult time, best table manners." He held his fingers up with the Boy Scout salute. "I promise I'll even take a shower."

Abby laughed, instantly forgiving him. "Zach, you were never a Boy Scout."

"No, but it makes people feel safer if they think you were."

"That's because they don't know you as well as I do," she teased.

"I'll take you dancing," he tempted.

Abby's face lit up. Zach wasn't fond of dancing and for him to suggest it was an offer she couldn't refuse. "What time?"

"Seven?"

Abby nodded. "I'll be ready." She sat back and eyed him more thoroughly. The green knit shirt he wore matched his eyes, and his jeans were the soft and faded kind meant to cling to the body. Although he hadn't stood up yet, she knew just what the effect would be. "I gather we're working at Punks Anonymous today."

Zach grimaced at her nickname for his third salon situated near the university, catering to a younger clientele. Abby had only been there once, for the opening, and after viewing the ultrabright colors, loud rock music and equally colorful characters, she dubbed it the new name. She told him she knew he would have a successful salon but it wasn't her type. Samantha usually worked in that one on the weekends.

"Zach's Three does very well, thank you," he pointed out.

"How many heads can you shave in an hour?" She couldn't resist teasing him.

"I leave that to some of the other stylists. I like something to work with." He stared pointedly at her ponytail. "That's all you could do with it this morning?"

"That's all I wanted to do with it this morning," she smiled winningly. "Don't press your luck, Zach."

He glanced down at his watch and stood up. He began to leave the table when he caught himself and hurriedly retrieved his cup and plate. "No use having Estelle gunning after me." He placed them on the counter before returning to Abby. He pulled her out of her chair and into his arms with one smooth motion and finished it with a kiss guaranteed to wake the dead. His lips nibbled their way around her mouth until it parted on its own, anxious for the soft invasion of his tongue. Even then he wasn't ready to stop until he coaxed a response from her, which was easily won as Abby's arms circled his neck and brought him back for more, as her tongue traced his mouth's outline and dipped past the crease to taste the smooth flavor of coffee and maple syrup.

"If you think you're going to stop there, you have another think coming," she murmured against his mouth.

"Do you hear any arguments on my part? In fact, this could grow into a very nice habit," he murmured back. "See you Friday at seven. Dress sexy."

"You can count on it."

After releasing Abby with an obvious show of reluctance, Zach walked out the back door calling out, "Thanks for the breakfast, Estelle."

"Anytime." The housekeeper appeared in the doorway.

Abby reached for her coffee cup and downed the contents in one gulp. She desperately needed the rush of caffeine to clear her muddled brain.

"I gather he knocked your socks off." Estelle began stacking the dirty dishes in the sink.

Abby gathered up the remnants of her dignity. "He certainly did not."

The housekeeper eyed her skeptically. "Is that why you look well kissed? I'm just glad the children weren't present to view something that was probably midline between an R and X rating."

"Those children of mine probably know more than I do," Abby muttered, straightening the tie on her robe. She hadn't even realized the neckline was gaping and had a pretty good idea who was to blame for that!

Matt entered the kitchen and placed his dishes on the counter. He leaned toward his mother, saying under his breath. "Things are sure changing around here. If this keeps up, I'm going to have a talk with that guy about his intentions."

"If you say one word to Zach or another to me, you will be locked in your room until your fiftieth birthday," Abby said softly, her threat more than obvious.

"Gotcha. 'Bye, see you tonight."

"Is Beth still coming over for dinner?" Estelle spoke up.

"Yep."

Now that the house was quiet again, Abby announced she was getting dressed and holing up in her office to begin her own work.

"Zach should stop by for breakfast more often," Estelle announced.

Abby spun around. "What?"

The housekeeper smirked. "He sure snapped you out of your Wicked Witch of the West mood fast."

"Just remember it can return just as quickly."

Estelle laughed. She never worried about Abby's moods and told her so.

DINNER THAT EVENING was calmer than breakfast. Abby knew it had to do with Zach's absence. Since he always worked that particular evening they hadn't bothered inviting him.

"How are you finding your classes, Beth?" Abby asked, as they lingered over dessert.

She wrinkled her nose. "A lot more difficult than I thought. My one science lab demands constant studying. Sometimes I wonder if I really want to be a physical therapist."

Abby's lips curved in a smile. "How long do you wonder?"

Beth looked sheepish. "About five minutes."

"Don't let her fool you," Matt spoke up. "She got an A on her last quiz in that lab."

She blushed under his loving regard. "I guess I do better than I think I do."

"That's better than the other way around," Abby replied. "And better than someone else I know." She fixed her daughter with a knowing eye.

Samantha fidgeted, aware her mother learned about her last test grade in Life Science. "Okay, so I won't be a doctor. How did I know dissecting could be so gross?"

"Good idea. You'd be slapped with a malpractice suit first time around, and you'd probably expect me to defend you," Matt joked.

"If you even make it through law school."

Abby held up her hands. "Okay, no battles at the table, if you please. What are you two planning on doing tonight?"

"We thought we'd go to the movies," Matt answered, stealing another piece of pie.

"If it wasn't for your inheriting your mother's metabolism, you'd weigh five hundred pounds," Estelle predicted.

"At least I'd enjoy gaining every pound." He polished the slice off in record time and looked at Beth. "Ready?"

She nodded. "Although I should help with the dishes," adding slyly, "and you could help, too."

"No, thank you, I would like to keep all these dishes intact," Estelle said. "You two go on. Sam can help tonight."

"I have homework."

"You finished it this afternoon. At least, that was what you told me."

Samantha stood up and began stacking plates. "I guess I should be grateful Max isn't in here ruining my evening even more."

Matt tousled her hair. "Be careful, kid, that can easily be arranged." He disappeared for a moment and returned carrying Beth's sweater and a lightweight jacket for himself.

"Thanks for dinner," Beth said before they left. "And Abby, I really do like your hair. It just goes to show what good work Dad does. You have to keep it that way. It gives you an entirely different look, and for the better."

"Thank you. I admit it took a little getting used to, but I'm certainly not unhappy with it. I guess I'll have to learn how to do some of those fancy braids you do." Abby smiled. "Now that I don't have as much hair, I should have an easier time attempting them."

"They're easy. I can teach you how to do some of them in no time. In fact, I have a book that shows all kinds of braids. I'll bring it by sometime and we'll practice," she promised. "Good night."

"How come Beth gets to go out on a school night and I don't?" Samantha asked, while stacking the dishes in the dishwasher after Estelle rinsed them off.

"She's older," Abby answered. "And I'm sure her homework is done the minute she gets home."

"Sure, she has plenty of time since she gets home at noon."

Abby frowned. "Noon? I thought she had classes all day today."

Samantha shook her head. "I asked her what her class schedule was like and she said she arranged it so her last class was at eleven two days a week, but her first class is at seven. Ugh!" She began arranging the glasses in the top shelf. "Why would anyone want to get up so early just to go to school is beyond me. When I go to college, I'm not going to have my first class until ten or eleven."

Abby murmured she was going into the den. When she reached the room she turned on the radio and let Max out of his cage. He immediately climbed to the top of the dome and flapped his wings in happiness of being out.

For a moment she stood there tempted to call Zach at the salon and casually bring up Beth's class schedule and find out what he might know about it. Why it bothered her she wasn't sure, but she couldn't understand why the girl would say one thing to Samantha and another to her.

"This is crazy," she scolded herself. "I'm worrying about her and Matt when I know very well he has classes all day, every day. I've got to do something about this crazy imagination of mine before I conjure up something totally unbelievable."

Chapter Nine

Abby stood back and studied her reflection in the mirrored closet door. The effect she was looking for was perfect. The bronze dress was definitely sexy and her upswept hairstyle served to accent it. Perfume in all the right pulse points, and she was ready to go.

Matt walked past the open door, did a double take and backed up. Leaning against the doorway, he issued a low, drawn-out wolf whistle. "Mom, you're going to knock him dead in that dress," he predicted.

She inclined her head. "Thank you. It's always nice to know your children don't think of you as an old hag."

He grinned. "I wouldn't worry. If the restaurant is dim enough no one will even notice those wrinkles around your eyes."

"Go away, Matt."

"Just kidding, Mom. You look great." He laughed as he walked away.

Abby still went into the bathroom where the light was stronger and looked closely into the mirror. She knew she wouldn't see the image of a twenty-year-old but she hoped she wouldn't see an old crone, either. Luckily, the aqua-tinted concealer she used under her eyes before applying base makeup did the trick. The lines were there but at least they didn't look as if they had been etched in stone.

"Zach is here." Estelle stood in the bathroom doorway.

Abby hurriedly applied lip liner and a copper gloss and returned to the bedroom to slip the lipstick into her evening bag. "Why is it men age gracefully and women just age?"

"It probably has to do with Eve causing all that trouble in the beginning. But I wouldn't worry if I were you. Men are going to take one look at you in that dress and Zach might get run over in the stampede."

"Maybe he'll head it," Abby said whimsically, leaving the room.

She found Zach seated on the couch in the den talking to Samantha. When he heard her enter the room, he turned his head to greet her. On first glance, his eyes widened and he stood up, looking handsome in a dark blue suit and pearl-gray shirt with striped tie.

"When I asked you to wear something sexy, I didn't realize you'd more than take me at my word," he murmured, noticing the way the bronze silk outlined every curve. "Shall we go?"

She looked down at Samantha. "Don't bother waiting up for me."

"Does this mean when I begin dating you won't wait up for me?" she asked hopefully.

"No, this means when you begin dating I'll be standing at the door with Matt's baseball bat when the clock strikes eleven." She dropped a kiss on her daughter's forehead. "Good night, sweetie."

"You're a tough mom," Zach kidded her as they walked outside to his car. "I'm sure glad you weren't any of my dates' mothers."

Abby waited until they drove down the street before asking a question that had been niggling the back of her mind for a while. "Why didn't you ever ask me out when we were in school?"

His lips twitched. "If you remember correctly, you only had eyes for Jason, even in the beginning. I doubt you saw me as anyone other than his friend. Besides, I was into older women back then.''

She remembered only too well. ''Ah yes, that sophomore at the university who was a language major. The girl only talked about her love for dead languages, and I was so naive then I couldn't understand why she would want to study a language no one spoke anymore.'' She gave him a sly look. ''Of course, I should have realized you were more interested in the dimensions of her chest instead of her IQ.''

''All young men think with their hormones.''

''Please, I have a young man in my house. That thought can be a bit unsettling.''

''And I have the girl that young man is dating. Who do you think is more worried about those hormones?''

''Only because you know what happens to a young man's hormones.''

''Both of us do,'' he added quietly. ''I think that's why we might worry more than most.'' His voice grew stronger and more lively. ''But that's enough of that. This is our evening out and the kids aren't going to intrude.''

''Maybe that's why it's so difficult for us to see each other in a male-female role,'' Abby suggested. ''We're too used to the parental role.''

Zach looked over at her sitting in the shimmering silk and the enticing length of stockinged leg. ''Tonight I doubt very much I'll view you as the parent of two children.''

''Like my dress, do you?'' she asked archly.

''Yes, and you know it. That's the kind of dress to raise a man's blood pressure.''

She sat back, fully satisfied with his reply. ''I'm glad to know I didn't waste my money. Now, do I receive any hints as to our destination?''

''Not a one, but I'm sure you'll be pleased with my choice.'' He headed toward La Jolla.

''How are all your adoring little heads of hair?'' Abby asked.

"Keeping me busy, as usual." Zach grimaced. "Today turned out to be almost more than any sane person could stand. One of my oldest clients was going on about her husband's affair with one of his associates, and she was calling him and the girlfriend every name in the book. The more she talked about it the angrier she got, and for a moment I thought I would have to throw cold water on her. Wouldn't you know said co-worker was in there getting her hair done at the next station! Needless to say she stood up and informed the wife she didn't appreciate being called a bimbo, and that was the politest term used. I thought we were going to see some blood flowing."

Abby was intrigued. "What happened?"

He chuckled. "After a great deal of shouting at each other, they calmed down and decided to have a liquid lunch and plot revenge on the poor guy for lying to both of them."

"Poor guy!" She was indignant. "That man cheated on his wife and lied to his girlfriend. He deserves everything they do to him."

"I'm sure between the two of them they'll come up with something quite suitable." Zach pulled in front of a three-story Victorian house that was a well-known restaurant.

"How lovely," she breathed, looking up at the eaves and gingerbread trim.

"It hasn't been open long, and I've heard nothing but raves about their food." Zach guided her inside with his hand against the small of her back. "They don't have a menu, instead they serve a different meal every night. So we'll be in for a surprise."

Abby looked up at him and smiled. "I love surprises."

He found himself tempted to kiss that smile but the maître d' approached him and he had to quash the thought; for now.

Abby looked around with interest at the opulent furniture, plush carpeting and bric-a-brac of that period. She was equally enchanted with the rose garden where they were seated at a candle-lit table. With only three other tables in the area, the diners were given the feeling of intimacy.

"I feel elegant," Abby confessed after the waiter had stopped by to ask if they wished wine with their meal and inform them what the menu for that evening was.

Zach reached across, grasping her hand and bringing it to his lips. "You deserve elegance."

As before, Abby felt the light touch all the way to her toes. "How do you do it?"

He smiled, guessing the direction of her thoughts. "Do what?" He continued nibbling on her fingertips.

"Get away with acting so seductive and treating a woman as if she were the only one in the world?"

His expression was perfectly serious. "It's no act, and as far as I'm concerned you are the only woman in the world for me. It appears I'm going to have to convince you of that." His fingers fiddled with her smoky-topaz ring. He remembered giving it to Abby for her thirty-fifth birthday.

"I'm not older than you are," she reminded him. "Nor have I ever studied a dead language."

His raised eyebrow gave him a rakish air. "Maybe I'm finally realizing that younger women who aren't bilingual are sexier." His tone may have been light but there was something much more elemental in his eyes.

She smiled. "I'm glad you finally came to your senses."

"So am I."

Abby soon decided the restaurant was only part of a perfect evening. While the food was more than excellent, Zach's company was the best part.

"These crepes are delicious," Abby sighed, sampling another bite of the dessert filled with lemon-scented farmer cheese and raisins. "Oh, Zach, we have to come back here again."

"We will," he promised, glad he had pleased her. "As much as you like. Think you'll have the energy to dance?"

"Have I ever turned down the opportunity to dance?"

The club they went to after dinner was packed with its usual crowd, but Abby didn't mind. Not as long as she could keep Zach on the dance floor. The club specialized in playing music from the fifties and sixties and Abby was happiest when she was on the floor dancing the bugaloo or swim.

"This is so much fun. We should do it more often," she told him when they finally returned to the table for drinks.

"Fine with me."

Abby laughed as she sipped her amaretto and soda. "You are definitely mellowing. Come on, Zach. I was surprised when you suggested this because you don't even like to dance. Usually it's like pulling teeth to get you on the dance floor."

He looked hurt at her assumption. "I may not be the world's best dancer but I'm not that difficult to get out there."

"Yes, you are!"

"Listen to this, will you?" Donna and her husband, Steven, appeared next to their table. "I swear you two are sounding like an old married couple." Her eyes were full of speculation. "Is there something going on you haven't told us?"

"Not a thing unless you count that Zach is trying to claim he loves to dance," Abby replied. "How are you two doing?"

"Fine. I love your hair. I see Zach finally had his way." Donna took the chair Zach offered her.

"Not yet," he murmured so that only Abby could hear, but she pointedly ignored him.

"You know Zach. He's determined." She changed the subject. "You two out painting the town?" Abby looked at Steven.

"Donna isn't happy unless I take her out to dinner and dancing at least ten times a month," he joked.

"If you haven't been there you should try the Victorian Garden," Abby told them. "We went there tonight and it was just lovely."

Steven stared at Zach with horror. "You took Abby to the most expensive restaurant in town? How many extra heads of hair are you going to have to cut to pay for it?"

"Maybe I'll just count it as a business expense."

Abby glared at him. "Over my dead body." She stood up and pulled him out of his chair. "Come on. For a remark like that I'm going to make you suffer and force you to dance with me again." She cocked her head listening to the beginning strains of the Doors' "Light my Fire."

"The woman is a sadist," he told their friends before she dragged him through the people.

But Zach got even when the Association's "Cherish" began. He always thought of it as slow and sexy. He drew Abby into his arms, linking her arms around his neck and his hands braced on her hips. "Now this is the way to dance," he announced in her ear as he tickled it with his tongue.

Abby closed her eyes allowing the warm sensation to wash over her. "Dancing is done with one's feet," she reminded him in a husky voice inhaling the warm scent of his cologne. She recalled the ads for the cologne were sexy; perhaps that was part of the reason she bought it for Zach last Christmas.

He gently bumped his pelvis against hers. "Call this something extra," he said huskily.

Abby tipped her head back, looking up at him with heavy-lidded eyes. "I'm learning a lot of new things about you, Mr. Randolph."

"Oh? Such as what?" He brought one of her hands to his lips and softly mouthed the fingers.

"You're a class-A kisser, a top-notch gentleman, good-looking and you're also not a party animal—thank goodness. Not to mention that you're a wonderful father. Of course, you do have many more pluses but I don't want you to get conceited."

He inclined his head in silent thanks as he dropped a light kiss on her lips then lingered over them to whisper, "That's one thing I've always liked about you, Abby. You know how to make a guy feel good." They halted when the music stopped. "Think we could sit a few out?"

She couldn't resist grinning. "I guess you deserve a reward for dancing with me as long as you did. Usually I'm lucky to keep you dancing through half a song." She turned away and walked toward their table where Donna and Steven were already seated.

"Zach, if you're in the mood, I'm claiming the next number," Donna teased, aware of his dislike of dancing.

He grimaced, looking as if he had just swallowed a nasty-tasting medicine. "Okay." The other three laughed.

"Then I'm grabbing hold of Abby," Steven announced, standing up and pulling her out of her seat before she could reply. "I know for sure this lady loves to trip the light fantastic."

"The trouble is you're not Fred Astaire," Abby retorted, laughing as he pulled her back onto the dance floor.

Donna sipped her drink watching Zach watch Abby dancing energetically. "I'm glad to see you two are finally doing more together," she commented with a sly smile.

He chuckled. "Donna, Abby and I have always done things together."

"There's together and there's *together*. I'm sure you know very well which version I'm talking about." She used the small straw to stir her drink. "You two have always made a great couple and yet you seemed to persist in only being with each other if it was some kind of family get-together or if one of you was in need of an escort. I'm just glad you two finally put aside the kids and social obligations and went out to just have fun. Or whatever."

Zach frowned at Donna's raised eyebrows. "You have a dirty mind."

"I'm allowed to. A woman is in her sexual prime when she reaches her thirties so it's natural that all I would think about is sex." She finished her drink and stood up when another song came on over the speakers and it was obvious Steven was going to keep Abby on the dance floor. "Come on, the least you can do is dance with me."

Looking long-suffering, Zach allowed her to pull him out of his chair and into the crowd. Halfway through the song he steered Donna toward Abby and Steven and maneuvered a change in partners.

"I should be jealous," she teased. "For one who hates to dance I'm surprised Donna got you out here."

"Donna refuses to hear any arguments or laments about old war injuries." He enjoyed watching Abby's sensuous movements as she twisted and turned to the loud beat.

"You came back without a scratch," she laughed, then took pity on him. "Come on, old man, let's go."

"I thought you'd never ask," he sighed, as they left the loud, smoky confines of the club. "How about a detour by my place for a brandy?"

"After all the alcohol I've consumed I'd really prefer coffee."

"All right, coffee then." He started up the engine.

Abby leaned her head back against the soft leather seat. "You know what? I think I like grown-up dinners. It certainly beats cheeseburgers at Carl Jr.'s."

Zach nodded. "Yes, but at least if we all go, there aren't any French fry fights between the kids."

She groaned. "The last time it happened you said there would come a time we would laugh at the memory. I don't think it's happened yet."

"Just be thankful their employee turnover is fairly often so we can go in without receiving dirty looks."

"As if we have the only kids with lousy manners," she grumbled. "At least they never sprayed their colas over people like I've seen other kids do."

"Yes, but there's something about our crew that's always remembered," Zach pointed out.

When they arrived at Zach's house and got out of his car, they both noticed the curtains at the front window next door fluttered.

"Good evening, Miss Howard," Abby called out as she strolled up the walk to Zach's door.

"Bad form, Abigail," he said under his breath, reaching around her to unlock the door and usher her inside.

"She deserves it. She may be harmless most of the time, but her constant spying on you must be grating on the nerves." Abby walked toward the living room. She stopped and spun around. "On second thought, I bet if I asked the right questions, I could learn a great deal about your former lady friends."

He advanced on her rapidly. "I wouldn't advise it," he said darkly, all the while wondering, and worrying, just how much the little white-haired lady had seen in the past.

Abby's eyes twinkled at the sight of throwing Zach off balance. "I can imagine she would be only too happy to tell me all, so I won't fall into the same trap as those other sweet women."

He didn't look happy. "That isn't exactly what she called most of them. I'll make the coffee." He took off his suit coat and laid it over the back of a chair.

Taking pity on him, she stayed behind so she wouldn't be tempted to tease him further. Abby settled herself on the white couch and kicked her shoes off while looking outside. She gazed over at the lit pool with its tropical waterfall at one end. The perfect scene for a seduction, she decided. It wasn't long before the fragrant aroma of brewing coffee trailed into the room just before Zach returned carrying a tray.

"Knowing how dancing works up your appetite I thought I should add a snack with the coffee," he explained, setting the tray on the coffee table and sitting down next to her. He handed her one cup and picked up the other.

Abby's eyes lit up at the sight of the delicately iced petit fours she knew from past experience to be liquor filled. "You do know me well," she agreed, picking up one cake and biting into it, savoring the subtle Irish cream flavor. She sipped her coffee, watching Zach over the lip of her cup. "Why didn't I notice sooner how good-looking you are?"

"Probably because we were both used to seeing each other in the worst possible lights," he said lightly. "I've seen you without makeup and wearing a ratty robe looking like hell after staying up all night with a sick kid. You've seen me with red eyes, unshaven and feeling lousy because of the flu." He stared into his own cup. "And we've known each other through double dating, marriages, a divorce, a death and childhood calamities. We hold no mystery to each other."

Abby disagreed. "No matter how long two people know each other there is always a bit of a mystery. That's what makes life so interesting."

Zach half turned to face her. He set his coffee cup down and braced his arm along the back of the couch. "You're seriously thinking about that L.A. job, aren't you?"

She exhaled a deep breath, hoping this discussion wouldn't escalate into another argument. "I drew up a list of the pros and cons, and the pros are tempting."

He nodded, not trusting himself to say anything for the moment.

"I meant what I said before, Zach. I'm not going to make a spur-of-the-moment decision on something this important. I'll think all of this over very carefully, because I want the best for everyone," she assured him.

Zach thought of telling her that he wanted the best for everyone, too—and that meant Abby not moving to Los

Angeles before they had a chance to find out what they had between them—but knew that would only begin an argument. And he didn't want that, not tonight. "Beth said that Jason's old law firm might hire Matt on a part-time basis." He decided to bring up a safe subject.

She nodded. "I think it would be a good idea because he'd have a chance to decide if he wants to specialize in corporate law like his father or try something else. Lately, I've had the idea that he wouldn't mind seeing if he could be another Perry Mason. Beth seems to keep busy with her schoolwork," she brought up.

"She stays up pretty late most nights studying," he replied. "I don't know how she can manage such a heavy work load, what with not finishing until late afternoon four days a week."

Abby drank her coffee so Zach couldn't see the surprise in her eyes at his statement. "Yes, she mentioned that the last time she was over for dinner," she murmured. "I guess she's learning there's more to college than guidance counselors tell you." Now she wasn't sure what to believe. Either Beth was lying to her father, too, for some reason, or Samantha had gotten her facts wrong. And no matter how much Samantha could act scatterbrained at times, Abby knew her daughter had a memory that could equal any elephant. She decided it wouldn't be a good idea to bring up her suppositions until she had a better idea of what was going on. One fear was steadily burning in the pit of her stomach and she didn't like it one bit.

As Zach listened to Abby talk about Matt's job and Samantha's problems with school he felt there was something more she wanted to say, but every time he tried to steer the conversation to any more personal subject she avoided it. "Enough talk," he ordered quietly, taking the cup out of her hand and placing it on the tray. He moved closer until his knee bumped gently against her thigh.

He caressed her face with his hands and slowly lowered his mouth to hers. Once, twice, three times his lips moved teasingly over hers. Abby's lips parted slightly as his tongue followed the same path. Without missing a beat, Zach pulled Abby over onto his lap and began kissing her in earnest. His mouth moved over hers with a single-minded purpose before placing a wicked kiss just behind her ear.

She turned her head in the direction of his mouth, feeling it slide along her skin, soft sounds leaving her throat as his teeth grazed the silky skin before moving up to cover her mouth again.

"Do you have any idea how good you taste?"

"Probably as good as you taste. Although I'm infinitely sweeter." She laughed against the slightly rough skin of his throat. He trailed a path over her ear and back to her mouth with a finesse that effectively destroyed Abby's thought processes. She nibbled back, delighted to discover his ear was just as sensitive as hers.

"Lady, you have talents I never dreamed of," he laughed huskily, circling her nipple with the tip of his finger before encasing her breast with his warm palm and kneading gently. "And I like them very much. We should do this more often."

Abby's slim skirt was hiked up above her knees, and if her seat on Zach's lap was awkward she didn't feel it. She was too busy discovering how his hair curled just a little bit around his ears and she murmured how sexy she found it. Feeling more reckless than she had in a long time, she began a trail of kisses at the middle of his chin and ended with a nibble on his earlobe that she found equally sexy.

"Men's earlobes aren't sexy," Zach said in a hazy voice. When he had decided to indulge in some old-fashioned necking that evening, he hadn't realized Abby would throw her all into it! And he had to admit he was enjoying it immensely. "Abby, you're driving me crazy. If I didn't think Beth would be coming home in about an hour I'd consider something else a great deal more pleasurable for the two of us."

Whatever Abby was about to say was halted when they heard the front door open and close. Her eyes flew open and she looked at Zach with shocked surprise. His answer was to curse softly.

"Beth?" he called out, then saying under his breath, "Just because I said she was due home soon didn't mean she had to appear on cue. She was never this well behaved as a child."

"Dad?" Her footsteps on the entryway sounded as if they were headed for the living room.

Abby tried to move away from Zach's firm grip but he refused to let her up. She glared at him, furious that she appeared well kissed to the naked eye while he looked not the least bit ruffled. She again tried to move away but he held on to her tightly.

"Stay close or Beth will get an addendum to her sex education I sincerely hope she isn't aware of yet," he whispered fiercely.

Abby's eyes drifted downward and she couldn't keep her smile back. Obviously, Zach was more than a bit ruffled! She adjusted her dress but the skirt was too slim to drape over his lap. "Cross one leg over the other," she ordered softly just as a mussed-looking Beth appeared. The young girl didn't look happy.

"Hi, I'm tired so I think I'll go to bed," she mumbled, turning away.

"Honey, is something wrong?" Zach asked, halting his daughter's escape. She didn't turn around, just shaking her head in answer.

"Perhaps she and Matt had an argument," Abby suggested. "There's been a lot of tension between them because of his going away to law school after the first of the year. I'm sure everything will be fine once they talk things out. And I think this is an excellent time for you to take me home.''

Zach would have liked to argue differently, but his curiosity about Beth's manner was aroused. He helped Abby up from the couch and guided her outside where they noticed the neighboring house's curtains fluttered.

''I'll talk to her tomorrow. She probably knows all about this,'' he said sardonically.

When they reached Abby's house Zach walked her to the porch and stood to one side as she unlocked the front door. He leaned around her to switch off the porch light and drew her into his arms in one smooth motion. His mouth covered hers and his tongue thrust between her parted lips. This time his kiss was meant to draw her into something dark and compelling, and it more than accomplished its purpose. When he pulled away both were breathing heavily.

''When you think about that job offer you think about this, too,'' he rasped, just before walking away without looking back.

Chapter Ten

"We're going to what?" Abby wasn't sure she heard correctly.

"Come on, Abby, you're not deaf and we have an excellent connection here. We should with what I pay the phone company every month," Zach countered. "I said I made reservations for a cozy little inn and we're going up there next Saturday. Sound good to you?"

"Yes, but what brought this about?"

He was silent for a moment. "We need some time for ourselves without any kind of outside interference, namely our kids. First of all, I want you to know I reserved two rooms. I just want us to be together." There was a pleading tone in his voice Abby couldn't remember ever hearing before.

"What time shall we leave?"

"YOU AND ZACH are going away for the weekend?" Estelle crowed, looking extremely pleased.

"We are," Abby confirmed, mentally going through her closet trying to decide what to take with her.

"I think it's wonderful." She finished folding the clean towels and picking the stack up to put them away in the linen closet. "So where are you going?"

Abby shrugged. "He made reservations for us at an out-of-the-way inn."

"It will be good for the two of you. Give you a chance to really be together. Stop chewing on that nail or Carla will have a fit."

Abby picked up one of the stacks of towels and followed Estelle down the hall. "I called Jerry this morning and told him I wouldn't be interested in the job."

Estelle turned her head. "How do you feel about it?"

She managed a wan smile. "Relieved."

The older woman smiled back as she opened the closet door and began putting the towels away. "Then that's what counts. Now, you only have five days before you and Zach go away. Don't you think you should decide what to take with you?"

Abby flushed, since that was exactly what she had been doing. "I think I have plenty of time to figure that out."

Estelle smiled knowingly. "Of course you do."

Abby should have known the rest of the week wouldn't be idyllic. By the time Zach arrived to pick her up, she grabbed his arm and practically dragged him out of the house before he could greet Estelle, a broadly grinning Matt and Samantha.

"What is going on?" he demanded once he'd tossed her weekend tote in the back of the car and settled her in the passenger seat.

"After this week, I want to get as far away from here as possible." She quickly fastened her seat belt.

They sped off in record time. "What happened?"

Abby sighed. "Let's see, where shall I begin? One of my clients had an attack of conscience and confessed that most of his business receipts for the past two years were falsified. That means I have the wonderful, time-consuming task of going back through his records and filing amended tax returns. The only consolation is he is going to be hit with a heavy bill from me and an even heavier one from the IRS."

Zach shook his head. "That's a winner all right."

"Oh, but that isn't all of it. Samantha has been asked to the fall dance and immediately begged me to take her on a shopping trip for a dress, shoes and whatever else was necessary to give her the perfect image. With luck, that client's fees will pay the bill." She half turned in her seat so she could face him.

"I still remember the cost of Beth's first formal and the accessories that she felt had to go with it. In fact, I think the cost is engraved on my brain. They never pick anything cheap, do they?" he chuckled. "I gather this isn't the end of it."

"Not by any means. Matt's car needs new shocks and brakes, but he doesn't have enough money to pay for them right now although he did explain he could pay for two-thirds of the bill. That was when I sincerely considered running away from home. Then Estelle came to me with the joyful news that the dishwasher died and the repairman advised it would be cheaper to replace it than have it repaired."

He reached out with one hand and grabbed hers in a warm grip. "Poor baby," he commiserated. "You really need this time, don't you?"

She nodded. "The moment Sam heard she would be expected to wash dishes for a little while, you would have thought I had sent her to a workhouse. So, tell me something cheerful. What is Beth going to do this weekend?"

"She said something about inviting one of her friends to stay with her," he replied. "And I guess they're driving down to Tijuana tomorrow."

"Matt did say something about that." Abby was content to just sit back and relax.

"Considering the week you've had I suggest you close your eyes and rest. We've got about an hour's drive ahead of us."

She did just that. "I like your ideas."

Abby didn't fall asleep but she did enjoy the sensation of the moving car and allowing the week's tensions to flow out of her body. Zach kept hold of her hand except when he needed to shift gears and every once in a while squeezed her fingers lightly.

"You haven't said anything about your week," Abby murmured.

"Probably because it wasn't as exciting as yours," he replied. "In fact, it was too bland. I don't like that because I see it as the calm before the storm."

"No, you were just lucky." Zach had turned the car inland. "You never did say where we were going." Abby squinted to read the rapidly passing road signs.

"It's a surprise. Susan mentioned this place once so I thought we would give it a try. It's sort of one of those bed-and-breakfast places that believes in peace and quiet for the guests. They do have hiking trails and horseback riding for the more energetic and a pool and spa and even a large library for those who prefer to play lazy."

"I like the lazy part."

Zach grinned. "There's one part you'll like even more. No phones."

"You're right, that part I *love*." Abby laughed. "Hurry up! I want our weekend to begin as soon as possible!"

"As you wish."

A little over an hour later Zach slowed in front of what looked like a large farmhouse. A couple in their fifties walked out to greet them and introduced themselves as Ben and Julia Matthews, the owners of the inn.

"I'm sure you must be tired from your drive and might like your dinner in your rooms," Julia told Abby.

"That sounds heavenly," she agreed. "Would I have time for a bath first?"

"Of course." The older woman smiled, leading them down a long hallway in the rear of the house to two adjoining rooms. "You share a private patio where you can have breakfast if you wish." She handed one key to Zach and another to Abby. "If you need anything, use the bellpull by the bed. Just pull it once when you wish your dinner served. There's no menu to choose from."

"Right now it's just wonderful to leave something up to someone else." Abby smiled. "Thank you." She glanced at Zach. "Twenty minutes?"

"I'll give you ten extra. We can meet on the patio then."

She nodded and entered her room to find it furnished in antiques with a beautiful four-poster bed dominating the area. Abby was tempted to fall back and test the mattress, but she was afraid that would only lead to her falling asleep. After rummaging in her bag for clean clothing, she headed for the bathroom, delighted to find a deep old-fashioned claw-foot tub with apothecary jars filled with a variety of bath salts sitting on an overhead shelf. She chose one giving out an exotic honey-and-almond fragrance, sprinkling the salts liberally in the hot water. While she would have liked to linger in the water, she settled for a quick soak and freshened her makeup before changing into silk deep gold pants and matching tunic top that was belted with a dark green, bronze and gold braided belt. She brushed her hair out loose and walked outside to find Zach already sitting at a black wrought-iron table sipping a glass of wine. When he noticed her walking toward him, he immediately stood up as Abby approached the table.

He ran his fingers through his hair in an uncharacteristically nervous gesture. "You look beautiful."

Abby felt a little shy herself. "Thank you."

Zach turned to pick up a bottle of wine from an ice bucket and gestured toward a glass. "Would you care for some?"

She sat in the cushioned chair to his left. "Yes, thank you." Abby looked around the brick patio brightened with flower boxes on the edge, planters hanging from the roof and a hummingbird feeder being used by several of the tiny birds. She breathed in the clean-scented air and felt her earlier tensions disappear. "This is beautiful," she pronounced. "I feel as if we're in another world."

"We are." Zach handed her the glass of white wine. "The way the rooms are fixed, each guest has as much privacy as they wish and children aren't allowed, so it's the perfect getaway. Abby, look at me," he commanded softly. When her eyes met his, he went on to say, "This is our time."

Her lips curved. "Is the pool heated?"

"Naturally."

"The hiking trails not too arduous for a tenderfoot?"

"There are some for the novice." He was now grinning broadly.

"The last thing I want to do is play any tennis or do anything that requires a great deal of energy," she told him in a light tone.

"Swimming requires energy," he reminded her.

"Swimming, yes. Floating, no." Abby sipped her wine, closing her eyes in bliss as the cool liquid slid down her throat. "If the dinner is anything like this wine I may not leave."

It turned out be just as excellent, and Zach and Abby took their time with their meal. When they'd finished they decided to walk around the grounds. During their travels they met two other couples with the same idea. Each time they nodded and smiled but no one cared to initiate a conversation. It was as if the others had the same idea about privacy.

"Zach, look!" Abby pulled on his hand, dragging him toward a tree with a large outflung branch that held a large swing. "Oh, please, you have to push me." She settled herself on the smooth wooden seat.

Zach moved around behind her and grabbed hold of the chains, pulling her back toward him. "Do I get payment for this?"

She turned her face smiling up at him. "My sincere thanks."

"Not enough."

"Then my heartfelt thanks."

He shook his head. "Nope, try again."

Abby tipped her head back, aware the top of her head just brushed his shirt front. "Ah, let me see," she mused, but her eyes sparkled with laughter as if she knew exactly what he wanted. "How about a . . . kiss."

Zach dipped his head down, allowing his mouth to rest lightly upon hers. "What an excellent idea." His voice was teasing. "Now why didn't I think of that?"

"Probably because you aren't as clever as I am." Abby's smile was outlined with the tip of his tongue. When his mouth covered hers fully, she released one chain to encircle his neck with one arm, but just as suddenly Zach freed her and stepped back a pace. Abby squealed with laughter as the swing flew upward. She quickly straightened her legs and pointed her toes to allow her to go as high as possible. She laughed with glee as the wind tore through her hair and clothing, letting her feel as free as a bird even as the swing just as swiftly returned to earth. When the swing soared back, Zach grabbed hold of the chains and held them fast.

"This is a toll swing, madam. Payment is required each time," he informed her in an officious voice.

"Of course." Abby barely tipped her head back before Zach captured her mouth, this time with a kiss that warmed her to her toes as his teeth nibbled her lower lip and gently tugged on it. As before, she was freed and pushed forward and each time she returned she gladly paid the toll. Abby had no idea how long this went on, in fact, she could have cared less as long as she returned to Zach's loving touch.

He soon nudged her over until she shifted her position to straddle the swing and he sat facing her. From there it was easy for her to cuddle against him. "I never knew swinging could be so fun," Abby murmured, trailing her fingertips across Zach's jaw and finding the skin barely rough, showing he must have shaved earlier in the evening. "I always enjoyed the swings as a child but never quite like this."

"Probably because you didn't have the right person pushing you." He was clearly enjoying himself in the sensual exploration of her throat and finding it lightly scented. "You smell exotic."

"It was the bath salts. They always make me think of caliphs and harems." It may have been dark but she had no problem finding the open collar of Zach's shirt and discovering the crisp hair peeking out of it. She lightly pulled on several strands.

"Hmm, all I need is a black patch and saber to play the pirate needed to kidnap you." He bit gently on her earlobe.

"I think you already did." Her whisper was swallowed up from the hard-driving kiss he gave her as they moved as close together as possible on the slightly rocking swing.

Zach's hand found its way under her tunic to find her breast covered with a brief strip of lace. He groaned into her mouth as her nipple hardened under his touch.

Abby pulled his shirt out of his jeans waistband and moved her hands upward over his back and around to his chest. At first, his skin was cool to the touch, then quickly warmed.

"Even in the dark you're beautiful," he muttered.

"Probably because you can't see me very well," she teased, running a fingertip over one of his nipples and feeling it respond to her.

With a deep-throated groan, Zach gathered her into his arms and pulled her hard up against him. Their mouths met in a hungry kiss, each wanting as much as the other would give them. The more their bodies strained against each other, the more the swing moved until it suddenly tipped under their movements and they almost fell off. They quickly gained their balance and stared at each other in the darkness trying not to snicker, but Abby couldn't hold it in.

She put her arms around Zach, laughing hard. "I think this is a hint," she giggled.

Zach sighed. "You're probably right." He stood up and held out his hand to help her up. Keeping hold of her hand they walked back to their rooms.

In front of Abby's door Zach stopped her long enough to place a light kiss on the tip of her nose. "Sleep as late as you want," he told her. "We can have brunch whenever you like."

"All right." She smiled. "Good night, Zach." She inserted her key in the lock but before turning it looked up at him. "I turned the job down." Even in the dim light she could see his features relax.

"I'm glad."

Without saying any more Abby unlocked her door and slipped inside.

When Zach entered his room he didn't bother with any lights. He could see well enough in the dark to strip down to his briefs and left the drapes covering the sliding glass door open to allow the faint moonlight in.

He stretched out on the bed, his hands laced behind his head as he thought over the events of the evening. He was right, this was exactly what they needed.

Zach had always enjoyed being with Abby and deep down he must have known he felt more for her than just as a good friend. Too bad he had left it buried for so long. Perhaps that was why he thought if they got away for a weekend they would have time to explore each other as two people attracted to each other, without any outside interruptions. He suddenly grinned. Of course, he hadn't expected a swing to do just that. He'd make sure to stay away from there tomorrow night.

Zach strained his ears but couldn't hear anything from Abby's room, which showed just how well insulated each room was. But it didn't matter. He knew she was there and that was what really counted. Before he knew it he fell into a deep sleep.

"NO WONDER PEOPLE LOVE country living," Abby enthused, as she and Zach followed a well-marked trail. Dressed in a cream-colored sweater over a plaid shirt, jeans and running shoes, she didn't have too much trouble walking up the slight incline although they had been walking for more than an hour. Zach followed, carrying a small knapsack the proprietors provided. "Look at all this clean air!"

"You've been living in the smog too much. You can't see clean air," Zach pointed out.

"A minor point," she dismissed with a wave of the hand. "All I'm saying is it's so beautiful and peaceful around here. Anyone with a lick of sense could easily relax here. I couldn't believe how well I slept last night. Of course, if I stayed here too long and ate the way I did for breakfast I'd end up looking like the Goodyear blimp."

"What are you talking about? You eat like that all the time."

She glared at him. "If I remember correctly, you were the one to snatch the last blueberry muffin."

"That's because I was trying to save you."

Abby picked up the pace. "Sure you were."

What she hadn't realized was that the quickened pace would affect her more than Zach. All too soon she was breathing heavily, while she heard no complaints from the rear. "You need to rest?" she managed to ask without panting.

"No, I'm fine, but if you need to."

"No, not at all." She forced her feet forward, wincing as the needles shot up her legs. She vowed to join a health club the minute they got back to San Diego.

Less than five minutes later, Zach grabbed her arm and pulled her back. "Slow down, you've shown you're tough," he rumbled, leading her toward a rock large enough for them to sit on. He pulled a canteen from the knapsack and handed it to Abby.

"Did you know Ben and Julia opened the inn right after Ben retired?" Abby remarked, after taking a sip of water. She pulled herself up on the rock and drew her legs up against her chest, linking her arms around them. "She told me they got tired of the rat race and thought of this. They've been here for three years and never regretted their decision for getting away from it all."

"Something like this would be nice." Zach leaned against Abby's legs. With his head resting against her knees she had the freedom to play with his hair, running her fingers through the thick strands, lifting them up and watching the slight breeze play with them.

"The way the light shines you can't tell which is silver and which is blond. That is not fair." She dug her fingertips lightly into his scalp massaging the rough skin.

"Your gray isn't all that apparent, either, except to you," he said lazily, dropping his head back even farther under her attentions. "Umm, that feels good. Don't stop."

Encouraged, Abby continued her massage down his neck and rubbing any lingering tightness from his nape before moving to his shoulders. When finished, she linked her arms around his shoulders and kept him back against her as they drank in the beauty around them.

"You can hear the birds and even the insects," she whispered, leaning forward to whisper in his ear.

He nodded, covering her hands with his own. For the moment all they wanted to do was gaze upward at the surrounding mountains and listen to nature's sounds while sharing each other's company.

"Abby."

"Hmm?" She leaned forward resting her chin on top of his head.

"I love you."

Abby smiled, feeling the warmth steal through her body beginning at her toes and coursing upward to her heart. "I love you, too," she whispered.

Zach's hands on hers tightened at her admission. They remained in their position for a long time until he noticed the afternoon beginning to wane. He glanced down at his watch and announced they should think about getting back since they still had a long drive home. As they walked down the trail holding hands they felt more than a little sorrow at the end of their weekend but happy they had finally admitted to each other what they had felt inside for a long time. Just before they reached their rooms, Zach pulled Abby to a stop. "Think you'd like to come out here again?"

She smiled, banishing any doubts he might have had. "You make the reservations and I'll be packed before you know it."

THEIR DRIVE HOME was silent as if they preferred to preserve the quiet contentment of the past twenty-four hours. When Zach pulled into Abby's driveway, they both felt the abrupt change back to the present.

"I enjoyed this time so much," she said in a soft voice.

"I just wish it could have been longer," Zach replied. "Next time."

"Yes, next time."

When Abby entered the house she felt more relaxed than she had in a long time and had a broad smile on her face that faltered when she heard raised voices coming from the den.

"We don't have a lot of time to waste!" Matt's voice was taut with tension.

"Don't you think I know that?" Beth sounded equally upset. "But I don't know how to handle this, do you?"

"Handle what?" Abby stood in the doorway.

"Hi." Matt looked up from his standing position over Beth curled up on the couch. His face was pale and drawn and his Adam's apple bobbed up and down nervously. "Did you have a good time?"

"Yes, it was very relaxing. Hi Beth." Abby was surprised to see them together, considering the late hour, and would have assumed Beth would have been home. "Did you leave a note for your father so he won't worry about not finding you home?"

"Yes," her voice was barely above a whisper.

"So what is going on here?" Abby walked into the room and sat in a chair facing them. Matt had already sat down next to Beth, taking hold of her hands in his. Both looked very young and very scared.

"Mom, Beth and I want to get married," Matt began, his voice sounding unnaturally high before he could bring it back to its normal register. He looked down at Beth's hand, fiddling with her fingertips.

Abby didn't miss Beth's look of surprise. So, this wasn't what they were discussing when she walked in. A funny feeling began in the pit of her stomach and she began to anticipate the worst. "Are you sure this is a good time to discuss this. Oh, I know only too well how the two of you feel about each other, but—"

"We are in love," Beth interrupted, her voice quavering, but as she looked up at Matt her voice grew stronger. "Abby, you, of all people, should know that. Matt and I don't even want to think about a future without each other. I realize this may not be a good time what with school and all..." Her voice dropped off and she could only look at Matt as if she was about to burst into tears at any second.

Abby held up her hands to halt further discussion. "All right, you are in love, and you're right, there's a lot ahead of you two. Matt, you have law school to attend, which will be a heavy load for a single person, much less a married one. And Beth, you want to study physical therapy, which won't be easy, either. Can't you two consider waiting a few years until you have school out of the way? All I ask is that Matt graduate from law school and gets settled before we begin to plan a wedding. At that time we'll throw one to rival both royal weddings. I promise you." She sat back, pleased she had spoken so rationally. Still, that nagging feeling wouldn't leave her and she had the sinking sensation she had walked into something that couldn't be so simply rearranged just by saying the proper words.

Matt's face reddened. He sat forward, releasing Beth's hand so he could gesture with his hands as he spoke. He kept shifting his weight as if he couldn't get comfortable. "Mom, you're not listening, we don't want to wait a few years."

Abby didn't like the tone of his voice and her attitude more than showed it. "Matthew, as long as you love Beth so much there is no reason why the two of you can't wait." Is there? No, her brain cried out. Oh, no. She should have listened to that sinking feeling.

He jumped to his feet, his fists bunched at his sides as he shouted at her. "Damn it, we can't wait, because Beth is pregnant!"

Chapter Eleven

Abby's half smile froze. If she hadn't been sitting down she probably would have collapsed. She wondered if the rapid pounding in her chest and roaring in her ears wasn't a warning for a heart attack. No, she couldn't be that lucky.

Why couldn't Donna Reed and Jane Wyatt have prepared her for this? she asked herself. "How far along are you?" she forced her lips to move.

"Nine weeks." Beth looked utterly miserable.

Abby nodded. "I, ah, I won't ask how this happened because the answer is only too obvious. But I do recall talking to Matt about birth control when he first started dating and I also recall talking to you about the very same thing."

"I'm on the pill," Beth spoke up, looking on the verge of tears. "The doctor explained it's rare but it sometimes happens."

Abby nodded again, moving her head carefully so it wouldn't break into a thousand pieces. "Does your father know?"

Beth finally broke down in tears. Matt put his arm around her and pulled her close to his side.

"She's afraid to tell him," he confessed. "Mom, Zach is going to have a fit."

"And you thought I wouldn't?" Abby thought seriously about breaking down into tears herself.

"You're just more flexible on these things." He tried hard to sound lighthearted, but it didn't come off.

Abby jumped up. "Flexible? You come in here telling me you got your girlfriend pregnant, so you plan on marrying before you enter law school. What in the hell am I supposed to be flexible about? The idea that neither one of you might finish school because of the baby?" she choked. "If it wasn't for the fact that the pill isn't infallible, I swear I'd murder one of you. That is, as long as you didn't forget to take a few of them?" She looked at Beth who shook her head.

"You make it sound like some kind of preplanned event!" Matt shouted back.

"I won't have an abortion!" Beth wailed. "And I won't give the baby up for adoption, either."

Abby turned away taking several deep breaths in hopes of calming down. She knew immediately it didn't help. "No one spoke about abortion or adoption," she said quietly, once she regained her temper. "I just wish you two could realize the magnitude of all this. That as of this time your future will never be the same."

"You, of all people, should understand. You had to marry Dad because you were pregnant," Matt blew up. "And you were the same age as Beth. So don't put on some outraged parent act for us, okay?"

She blanched at her son's deliberate attack, then fury took over. Before Abby could reconsider her action, her hand shot out and she struck him across the face. Matt stepped back, his hand covering his cheek. He looked shocked by her unexpected, but deserved attack.

"I won't apologize for hitting you," Abby said in a deadly tone. "But I will apologize for doing it in front of Beth. She has enough worries without us creating a scene in front of her. But what you said to me was unconscionable, Matt. As a prospective attorney I want you to remember that a person's past cannot be brought up."

He had the grace to look shamefaced. "It's just that I thought you would understand more than Zach."

"Zach will be furious," she predicted. "He will rant and rave and he will rake you over the coals, but in the end he will calm down and inform you to take care of his baby girl or he'll hang you by your heels. I suggest you tell him as soon as possible, before he finds out on his own." She turned to Beth who sat huddled on the couch. "Are you suffering from morning sickness?"

She nodded. "The doctor gave me medication for it, but I'm afraid to take any medicine."

"If the doctor prescribed it, it's more than safe. Take it starting tomorrow and keep a package of Saltines by your bed," she suggested, feeling the tears fill her eyes that she saw on Beth's cheeks. "Beth, honey, you're going to be going through a lot of changes in the next seven months, but we're all here to help you. And it appears we will be planning a wedding, but only on one condition." Her tone turned to steel as she gazed at the young couple. Matt glared back at her as if he feared the worst and was prepared to battle her. "I want both of you to be absolutely sure you love each other enough to go through this pregnancy, not to mention a heavy class load for Matt."

"I could put off going to law school for a year," he suggested.

"No, the expenses are taken care of and you won't put it off any longer. The rest we can work out." Abby paced back and forth, rubbing her fingertips across her temples. She had an idea this tension headache wasn't going to disappear with just plain aspirin.

"Daddy has always talked about trusting me. He's going to feel I let him down. He's going to be so upset," Beth whispered.

Abby squatted down in front of her, holding onto her ice-cold hands. "Do you love Matt?"

Her eyes shone. "Yes." There was no hesitation and Abby saw the answer in her face just as strongly as her verbal reply.

"That will certainly help," she said quietly, finding the strength to manage a smile. "I suggest Matt take you home so you can get a good night's sleep and we'll come up with something about announcing it to the rest of the family. Perhaps we can have a family dinner here Saturday night."

"You'll help us then?" Matt asked.

She shook her head as she straightened up. "No, but I will be here to bind up the wounds after Zach finishes taking you apart. Now, take Beth home. I'll call Zach in the morning and invite him over for dinner."

Matt pulled Beth to her feet. She faced Abby with a tremulous smile. "You know, it's funny, but when I was a little girl I used to wish you were my mother. The times we went to mother-daughter banquets I'd pretend that you were," she said softly, kissing her on the cheek. "Thank you."

Matt flashed Abby a tight smile and the two walked out.

Assured she was alone, Abby finally collapsed on the couch feeling as if she'd aged one hundred years in the past few minutes. It didn't take long for the tears to begin falling. She saw bits and pieces of her own teenage past flash before her eyes, which only added to the crying jag she had started on with a vengeance. She wiped her nose with the back of her hand, feeling more upset the more she thought about it.

"Oh, my God, I'm going to become a grandmother," she moaned. Which set her tears off again.

Abby waited for Matt to return because she had a lot more to say to him that she hadn't wanted said in front of Beth. The girl was upset enough without worrying her further. It was more than an hour before he walked in the door. She could tell by his footsteps he was going to bypass the den, but she wasn't about to allow him to evade her. "Matt, would you come in here please?'' As far as she was concerned it was an order, not a request.

His footsteps stilled for a moment, then walked slowly in her direction. He halted in the doorway looking uncertain.

"Sit down." She nodded her head toward one of the chairs and waited for him to be seated. "I think we have some talking to do."

"Isn't that what we did before?"

Abby's eyes glittered. "Not by any means, but I love Beth and the last thing she needs is to be upset right now. Unfortunately, you inherited my temper so if we're going to have a battle, which I have an idea we are, then it will be without witnesses."

His head snapped up. "Damn it, Mom, I love Beth. I've loved her ever since I can remember. Okay, maybe this is a bad time to get married, but I'm not doing it because I feel it's the right thing. I'm doing it because I love her and I don't want her to go through this alone."

Abby drew a shuddering breath. "You sounded very much like your father just then. What I resent is the fact that I was lied to, even if it was by omission. Beth mentioned she has late classes every day. I found out, purely by accident, that she doesn't. Were the two of you together then?" Matt's red face was his reply. "And the time you had car trouble and you came home so agitated? Were you lovers then?"

"Yes," he mumbled.

Abby gnawed on one of her nails, not caring that Carla would have a fit when she saw them next time. "Matt, you seem to think your father and I married and lived happily ever after, but we didn't. We had a lot of problems because we were so young. I was no longer a carefree teenager, I was a wife and prospective mother. My parents were furious with us and it took a good many years before the bitterness began to dissipate. Your father was sent overseas before I barely knew what it was like to be a wife. He was over there when I had my miscarriage and there were many times I resented him for all of that because I felt I was missing something from life.''

''But you said you always loved him,'' he argued.

''I did, but love isn't perfect,'' she replied honestly. ''Your father came home from the war a changed man and I had changed also. Thanks to the GI bill and both of us working, we were able to put him through law school, but it wasn't easy.''

''What if you could do it all over again? Would you?''

Abby sighed. She was afraid Matt would come up with that question. ''I might hope we would have more sense, but yes, I would do everything again, but that still doesn't excuse you! When Zach had those birds-and-bees talks with you he must have missed something,'' she grumbled under her breath.

Matt stared down at the floor, his hands clasped between his open legs. ''You don't want us to get married, do you? That's why you're being so negative.''

''If Beth wasn't pregnant I would definitely talk you two into waiting for a while, although with how stubborn you two are you'd probably just live together,'' Abby said candidly. ''But she is pregnant and you will not put off law school for another semester, because if you do, you'll never go. I will do what I can, but you will also have to do your share and get a part-time job to help out.''

''I had already planned on it.''

Abby sat there feeling the intense need to break down crying, but she knew this wasn't the time for it. ''Basically, that's all I have to say. You're an adult and all I've tried to do is be honest with you. I want you to be happy, Matt. Not a divorce statistic later on.''

''Just because Carolyn divorced Zach doesn't mean we'll end up that way. They weren't happy for a long time. I may have been a little kid back then, but I heard enough about the subject,'' Matt pointed out.

Abby nodded, remembering the stormy battles between the couple. "You probably should get to bed. It's been a rough day for all of us and it isn't going to get any easier."

"You're still going to help us with Zach?" he asked hopefully.

"I'll referee, that's all."

Matt stood and walked over, kissing her on the cheek. "I know I act like a bull at times, but I do love you, Mom," he said softly. "I know this hurt you, but we'll be fine, you'll see."

She managed a wobbly smile. "I sure hope so because there's been enough pain within these two families."

After he left she remained in the den. Hating the idea of being alone, she let Max out of his cage. Sensing she needed comfort, the large macaw walked across the couch and settled himself in her lap like a puppy and murmured to her while rubbing his beak across her chest.

"I'm sorry Max, but when I expected comfort I didn't know it would come from you," she laughed softly, hugging him.

"ARE YOU GOING TO STARE in the mirror all evening admiring yourself, or are you going to come out and greet your guests?" Estelle demanded, standing in the bathroom doorway.

"I'm looking for the new wrinkles and gray hairs all this has to have caused," Abby replied, applying a rose-colored lipstick and colorless gloss.

"Are you going to tell me the reason for this dinner or do I have to wait for the movie to come out?"

Abby picked up her cologne and sprayed it on her pulse points. "I have an idea you already know," she murmured. Estelle had given her a strange look after overhearing her invite Zach and Beth to dinner, and probably couldn't help noticing Matt's strange mood for the past few days.

The housekeeper sighed. "Then I was right. She's pregnant, isn't she? That's what they told you that night. Obviously Zach hasn't been told, which is why we're having this softening-up dinner, right?"

Abby nodded. "I thought a normal family-type dinner might help the situation."

"This isn't the right way to tell him, Abby," Estelle reproved.

She flushed. "Do you have a better way? It's not as if we're going to spring it on him during dessert. Beth is so upset at the idea of telling him, although I don't know why. He worries about her like any normal father, but he certainly isn't going to turn into a raving maniac. At least I hope not," she murmured to herself. "I just wonder if those kids know how much this will cost them?"

The older woman walked over and put her arms around Abby. She clutched her, feeling the need to cry as she had over the past few days. "An announcement like this should be a happy occasion," Abby whispered.

"It will be. Just keep a smile on your face and don't get in the middle of it. You've had your shock, now it's Zach's turn," she told her. "Now, dab your eyes carefully so your mascara won't run and get out there in the next two minutes. I'll serve him a stiff drink."

Abby smiled at Estelle. "I must have done something right to deserve someone as wonderful as you."

"Considering your lack of domestic skills, you were damn lucky," she grinned, walking out of the bedroom.

Zach knew something was up from the moment Abby had issued her dinner invitation. Part of him had hoped it would be only the two of them until she mentioned Beth's name, too. His suspicions grew when Estelle mixed him a drink guaranteed to melt the hair off his chest. "What's going on?" he asked Estelle when she told him Abby would be out in a minute.

"You're getting a free dinner, settle for that," she retorted. "I baked a ham with a pineapple glaze, new potatoes, applesauce, mixed vegetables, corn bread and I baked a lemon-meringue pie for dessert." She ticked off the evening's menu with pride.

"Now I know something's up."

"You're too suspicious, Zach," Samantha hugged him tightly. "But you're also a very nice man who's generous to a fault."

He sighed. "How much are you hitting me up for?"

She dropped a brochure into his lap. "Magazine subscriptions. No biggie, honest. I'd be happy if you would just choose one."

"And ecstatic if I choose more?" he teased.

"I wouldn't turn them down." She settled on his chair arm.

"Samantha, you promised not to ask Zach." Abby swept into the room with a broad smile on her face. She walked over to him and dropped a kiss on his lips. "You're allowed to ignore her."

Zach looked Abby over from head to foot, finding no fault with her soft lilac jumpsuit with a turquoise scarf wrapped around her slim waist. Her hair was pulled back with turquoise clips, and he noticed her makeup was a bit heavier than usual. He had a good idea she was up to something. "You look good enough to eat," he said lazily, keeping his eyes level with the slashed V-neckline. "Why don't we get rid of the kid and get down to business?"

"Kid?" Samantha shrieked, jumping up. "Zach, I'll be sixteen next year. In another month I'll be eligible for my learner's permit."

"God help us." He raised his glass.

She braced her hands on her hips as she leaned over him. "I'll have you know I'm taking Drivers' Training and doing very well at it."

"That's because you're not behind the wheel of a car." His eyes twinkled. "If your mother's smart she'll give you a Sherman tank for your birthday."

She glared at the man. "I'll be an excellent driver, you'll see."

"You better be one, because I hate to see how much my insurance rates are going to jump when I add you on," Abby spoke up, going over to the bar and fixing herself a mixed drink. "You may have to hit Zach up for a raise to help pay for the privilege of driving."

Zach raised an eyebrow at her choice. "If you're all out, I brought a bottle of wine with me."

She smiled but it didn't reach her eyes. "I thought I'd have something different. How has work been?"

"The same. You?"

"The same."

Zach opened his mouth to ask exactly what was going on, when Estelle appeared with the announcement that dinner was ready.

"I had the kids set the table," she explained Matt's and Beth's absence.

From the moment Zach sat down to the elaborate meal, he knew something was going on. Beth had been upset all week, Matt appeared more than a little uneasy every time Zach said something to him, and Abby was acting a bit too cheerful for his peace of mind. Samantha and Estelle were the only ones acting normally as far as he was concerned. He meant to find out what was going on soon.

"Estelle, you really outdid yourself this time," he complimented the housekeeper as he later helped himself to a second slice of ham and potatoes.

"I try." She smiled at him. "You just be sure to save some room for my pie."

"No problem there, although Beth will have to drive home because I doubt I'll be able to fit behind the steering wheel," he joked, noticing that although everyone laughed, it appeared just a bit forced on their part. He also noted Beth pushed her food around on her plate more than she ate.

After dinner Samantha was dispatched to help Estelle clean up while the others returned to the den for coffee and pie. Beth asked for a glass of water instead of the coffee. Abby exhaled a silent sigh of relief that she hadn't asked for milk, which would have been a giveaway.

"All right, I've been sated with good food." He shot Abby a wicked look that indicated he might have preferred being sated with something a bit more elemental. "What's the bad news?" He looked at the faces of the tautly smiling three.

"Oh, I wouldn't exactly call it bad news," Abby said airily, glancing toward her son. "Would you?"

Matt set his cup down very carefully on the coffee table in front of him and turned to face Zach. "Zach, Beth is pregnant and we'd like to get married within the month."

Abby closed her eyes. "Good, Matthew, be subtle about it," she murmured under her breath. "Ease your way into the subject."

Zach sat forward, breathing deeply in hopes of containing his fast-rising temper. Once he looked at Abby his anger dissipated and hurt feelings took over. "Obviously you've known about this." *And you couldn't give me any warning* was left unspoken.

"Yes." What else could she say? But her eyes told him how sorry she was for keeping quiet about it these past few days.

He nodded, understanding her mental apology, but the fact she hadn't warned him still hurt. "And this is the reason for the dinner."

"Yes."

"And you're obviously on their side," he commented, feeling his temper rise again.

"I'm merely present to make sure you don't kill anyone," Abby explained, recognizing the signs of his reddened face and darkened eyes. "And I think the only way this should be discussed is in a rational manner."

Zach jumped up. "Rational manner, my eye!" he shouted, his face purple with anger. "Your son got my baby pregnant and you want to discuss this in a rational manner?"

"Yes, I do." Her quiet voice was deadly. Abby leaped to her feet, striding over to him with murder in her eyes. "As I recall, *you* were the one to tell him all about sex. What exactly did you tell him back then? If anyone is to blame for this, it's you!"

"Me?" He thrust his face into hers. "I told him the basics, let him ask questions and I even discussed birth control, which he obviously didn't use. If anyone is to blame for this, it's him!"

"Beth was on the pill and it didn't work. Otherwise, Matt certainly would have used something because he's always been responsible."

"If he had been responsible he wouldn't have started something like this to begin with. As for the pill, everyone knows it isn't foolproof. You found that out when you discovered you were pregnant with Sam." His narrowed eyes echoed her own murderous thoughts.

Matt turned to Beth who sat curled up next to him crying quietly into a handkerchief he had handed her earlier. "Why do I feel as if this argument has gotten off track," he whispered.

"Because it has," she replied under her breath. "I don't know about you, but I don't want to be the one to break them up, either. They look as if they're going to start swinging at each other."

"I knew I shouldn't have had you talk to Matt about sex!" Abby blazed. "No matter how embarrassed he would have been with me explaining it, I'm sure I would have gotten the point across much better."

He took several deep breaths in vain hopes of calming himself, but he figured he deserved a display of temper considering the way his evening had been running so far. "This is not getting us anywhere."

"What is this?" Estelle entered the room and took in the battle scene in one calm gaze.

"You knew, didn't you?" Zach's arm swept the room's expanse. "You knew the reason for this dinner and what had happened thanks to *him*."

"Do you see me blaming Beth because she's pregnant?" Abby demanded.

"Oh wow, Beth is pregnant?"

The adults turned to the teenager standing nearby.

"Go to your room!" Abby shouted.

Samantha didn't look the least bit cowed. "I'd rather go over to Melanie's," she declared. "It'll be a lot safer over there."

"Samantha, not one word of this. Do you hear me?" Abby ordered.

"Mom, I'm not stupid. I won't say anything, but I sure hope the wedding will be soon, or everyone will figure it out anyway." She turned away.

Her entrance had been perfect for diffusing the tension crowding the room. Abby spun around in the direction of her chair. "This has to be discussed rationally," she spoke in an even tone, as if she hadn't lost her temper a few minutes ago. "One thing is certain, the wedding will have to be soon."

"They're too young to get married," Zach argued.

Abby smiled ruefully. "I'm afraid you're saying that to the wrong person. While I'm not pleased with this turn of events, either, I'm aware we have to make the best of the situation. I'm just glad this isn't viewed as a shotgun marriage. They're in love and I think with family support they'll do just fine." She privately hoped she sounded as convincing as she tried to look. She must have, since Zach listened to her words with a show of sincerity.

He turned away, his hands braced on his hips, his head tipped down studying the carpet as if he would find all the answers there. He swiveled his head, staring at his daughter. "My God, Beth, do you realize what you've done?" he asked in a quiet voice.

"Yes, I do." While her voice was low, it was also strong as she looked up at her father. "Matt and I love each other and we made a baby from that love. Is that so bad?"

Her statement left him speechless. He swung around to look at Abby, silently asking her for support.

She threw up her hands. "I've already had my say. This meeting is purely for your edification."

Zach studied Matt next. "I have a lot of reservations about this," he admitted. "Any father would. And I don't have too many warm feelings toward you right now. From the time Beth began dating, I started checking out the boys to make sure they wouldn't try anything with her. The only one I never worried about was you. It just goes to show how wrong a person can be."

Matt reddened under his regard but didn't pull away from Beth's side or release his hold on her hand. Together, the young couple presented a united front to their parents.

Zach shook his head. He raked his fingers through his hair feeling as frustrated as he looked. "I think we'll make an early night of it," he said finally. "Come on, Beth." Without a word or facial expression to indicate his feelings toward Abby, he walked out of the room.

Beth looked at Matt with soft eyes, then kissed him before she stood up. "I'll call you when I get home," she whispered, squeezing his hand before releasing it.

Abby looked down at Matt sitting on the couch. For a moment she was carried back to a boy who sat on that same couch looking forlorn because the first time he kissed a girl, she told him she would prefer to kiss a frog. "It's been a long time since then,'' she murmured, dropping down next to him.

"I don't think Zach gave us his blessing,'' he sighed.

"She's of age, don't worry about that. And I'll talk to him,'' she assured him. "Matt, I'm proud of you. You're taking on a big responsibility and you're showing some maturity. And I think you're not going to back down no matter how difficult it gets.'' She wrinkled her nose. "I just wish it hadn't happened this soon. The last thing I feel like right now is a prospective grandmother.'' She opened her arms and hugged him, now both of them laughing.

"I guess I now know what to get you for Christmas,'' Matt casually remarked.

"Dare I ask what?''

He appeared perfectly serious. "Easy. A nice maple rocking chair, a pretty wool shawl, maybe in a soft peach shade, that color looks good on you, and a lace cap to cover the gray.''

"Augh!'' She punched him in the arm. She suddenly sobered. She cupped his face between her hands. "Oh, Matt, I just hope we'll all be prepared for this.''

He smiled. "I guess we'll find out in about seven months, huh?''

Abby wrapped her arms around her. "Give me a break and let me feel like a mother for a little while longer before I have to settle for being the kindly gray-haired grandmother, okay?''

Chapter Twelve

The more Abby thought about Zach's reaction to the news and his cool silence toward her, she knew that he felt betrayed by her firsthand knowledge and the way the scene must have looked to him. As if the three were united against him. Taking the matter into her own hands she tracked him down at one of his salons.

"I hope you aren't springing any more surprises on me," he said coolly when she identified herself.

"I thought we could meet for lunch and discuss this." Abby was undaunted.

The pause from the other end seemed to go on forever. "All right. Tomorrow, one o'clock at Anthony's."

Abby mentally canceled her one o'clock appointment. "I'll see you there."

Without another word he hung up.

"That's Zach, polite to the end," she said wryly, barely hanging up the phone before it rang again. The way her day was going, she should have realized it was of her clients with a problem they felt only she could solve. Luckily, it was something she could easily handle.

ZACH ARRIVED at the restaurant early and decided to do his waiting in the bar. He knew he had handled Matt and Beth's announcement badly; an abnormally quiet Beth moping around the house for the past few days certainly told him that. He only wished he knew what to do to make it up to her. He was just finishing his Scotch and water when he watched Abby walking in.

"Hello, Zach." She greeted him with the kind of kiss she might give an old friend. "Drinking a little early in the day, aren't we?"

"If *we* wanted to drink early in the day *we* would have started at breakfast," he replied, getting up off his stool. "I made a reservation for one, so our table is probably ready."

It was, and the hostess led them through the crowded dining room. Both paused a few times to say hello to a business associate or friend as they worked their way across the room.

"Do you have a meeting with a client after this or did you just finish one?" Zach asked after the waitress had taken their drinks order.

She looked surprised by his question. "Actually, neither."

"Then I'm flattered you dressed up on my account."

Abby smiled wryly. "Actually, I did it for courage."

He nodded. "Abby, I have nothing against Matt, you know that, but we both know what can happen in young marriages, and I think there's even more pressure on a couple than there was in our day."

"That's true, but it still doesn't change the situation," she argued, pausing when the waitress set a glass of wine in front of her. She gave her order for fettucini, Zach asked for the veal Parmesan and they were left alone again. "They will certainly have more support than Jason and I did. After all, my parents weren't in favor of our marriage and his parents were divorced and just plain didn't care what we did."

He toyed with his Scotch. For a brief moment a look of pain crossed his features. "She had such plans. She wanted to become a physical therapist and especially work with children. She's talked of nothing else since she learned all about it after that time she broke her leg so badly, remember?''

Abby leaned across the table, speaking fiercely. "She still can, if she's willing to work for it. I got my degree, she can, too."

"You keep talking about support, how do you expect to do that?" he challenged. "With money? Time you don't have? What?"

"Matt and I have talked about the future," she replied softly. "Since his trust fund pays for his schooling, he'll be able to use earnings from a part-time job to pay for personal expenses. And Estelle, bless her, has suggested Matt and Beth take over the garage apartment and Estelle will move into Matt's room until he goes to law school."

Zach stared down at the snowy white tablecloth. "It seems Estelle's giving up a lot," he muttered. "It's not fair to her."

"That's what I said, but she feels that Beth should have someone nearby for the later months, not to mention they should be able to save some money by not paying rent."

He felt a little disgruntled that others were making decisions that he should have some say in.

"Zach, nothing definite has been decided yet." Abby read his thoughts. "We're just trying to come up with ways to make it easier on them."

He nodded. "I can understand that, but would it be possible for all four of us to get together and discuss this? Why don't you and Matt come over Friday night and we can hash some of this out?"

"I think that would be an excellent idea," she agreed immediately.

"I'm still not happy about this, Abby," he warned. "Young marriages don't work."

"Some do, as long as there's support and they love each other," she argued. "And they have that. All right, they jumped the gun a bit. Now there's a baby on the way, but

hey're handling the situation like responsible adults. I have
a lot of faith in them, Zach. I just wish you did, too.''

He sighed. "Abby, I do have faith. But I also know
what's ahead of them and so do you. Does Matt really have
it in him to manage a wife, new baby and school?"

She raised an arrogant eyebrow. "He's his father's son—
need I say more? Let's just wait until we all get together so
they can be in on this, all right? I just wanted to clear the air
between us. I don't want us to be at odds with each other,
Zach.'' She reached across the table and grasped his hand.

Zach turned his hand over so their palms touched, lacing
his fingers through hers. "Neither do I," he admitted. "I'm
probably acting like the overprotective father."

"It's more than allowed."

By the time their lunch was served, they felt more at ease
with each other.

"Beth has been dragging herself around the house as if
her days are numbered," Zach brought up. "I think she's
afraid I'll send her to some out-of-state clinic to have the
baby."

"Matt has taken up smoking."

Zach sighed. "One thing for sure. I hadn't expected to be
a grandfather so soon."

"You? Matt told me he was giving me a rocking chair and
shawl for Christmas."

Their eyes met and they both chuckled.

"It looks as if all of us will be making changes in our
lives," Zach commented. "What does Sam think about all
this?"

Abby grimaced. "She adores the idea of being an aunt
and has already offered to baby-sit. She also assured me not
to worry about her, because she doesn't plan to fall in love
until she's thirty so she can travel all over the world first."

Zach laughed. "That sounds like Sam all right. What did
you tell her?"

"To join the army and she can see the world at their ex pense instead of her own or mine."

Their shared laughter relaxed them more than anything else could. They were finally able to finish their meal and even enjoy a torte for dessert. When the waitress ap proached them with the check, Zach inclined his head to ward Abby.

"The lady is paying."

She wrinkled her nose. "Now I know why you picked such an expensive restaurant." She dug into her purse and withdrew her American Express card and handed it to the waitress. "I guess it's only fair since the bride's family pay for the wedding. All the groom's family has to do is be at the church on time."

Once the check was taken care of they walked slowly outside.

Zach stood on the curb, his hands jammed in his pockets while they waited for their cars to be brought around. "I'm glad you asked me to lunch," he said finally.

She tipped her head back in order to gaze up at him. "So am I."

Zach angled his head down and dropped the lightest of kisses on her mouth. "Let's get this straightened out fast so we can get back to ourselves," he murmured, glancing up when the parking valet brought his car.

Abby wasn't surprised she was always smiling when she was with Zach. He did that to her. "Just as soon as they're on their honeymoon," she promised, moving away when her own car was driven up. "We'll see you Friday evening."

"HE'S FORCING US to discuss this on his turf," Matt said darkly, walking up to the Randolph front door. "And I don't like it."

"As you intend to marry his daughter, he does have that right." Abby's tone was bland, although she silently won dered why she hadn't spanked her son more when he was ttle. "I suggest you don't walk in there with a chip on your houlder or this will be over before it's begun."

His shoulders slumped. "I just love Beth so much and he's miserable right now. I don't want her hurting any-nore."

"Neither do we." Abby used her forefinger to punch the oorbell. "Take a couple of deep breaths and just remem-er to use that common sense you were supposed to be lessed with."

Beth opened the door looking a bit pale, although the mile on her face was natural.

"Hi, honey." Abby greeted her with a kiss on the cheek nd put her arm around her shoulders. "Are you still hav-ng morning sickness?"

She nodded while taking hold of Matt's hand. "Except I lon't know why they call it that when I seem to have it any ime of the day."

Abby nodded. "I was the same way. I know how you feel bout the medication but you'll be much better off taking t. Where's your father?"

"In the den."

Abby slowly released Beth's shoulders, not wanting to pproach Zach looking as if the three of them were against im. She walked a bit slower entering the room a few steps ehind the young couple. Zach looked up from his position ehind the wet bar and smiled.

"Hello, Abby, Matt. Would either of you like something o drink?"

"A cola is fine with me," Matt replied, taking a seat in a earby chair with Beth perched on the arm after picking up glass filled with mineral water.

"Same here." Abby chose the couch.

Zach poured drinks and handed them out before seating imself next to Abby.

"I'm not going to beat around the bush," he said with-ut preamble. "I'm still leery about this marriage, and while

you kids aren't looking further than the next few weeks, I'm
looking quite a bit into the future. At first, I'm sure you'll
see marriage as a way to be together all the time and do what
you want. But then you're going to have a third person to
think about, and with that comes diaper changes, late-night
feedings, walking the floors all night because the baby has
the colic or is teething, not to mention an infant depends on
you for everything. It's a big—"

"And you don't think we can handle it," Matt interrupted.

Zach shrugged. "Only time will tell. But I don't want the
two of you to go into this without looking at both sides."

"You still don't want us to get married," Beth piped up,
angling her body so her shoulder touched Matt's.

Zach exhaled a deep breath. "No, I don't, but not for the
reasons you think. These next few years are important to
kids your age. Having the responsibility of raising a family
shouldn't happen to you so soon." He held up his hand anticipating Matt's argument. "Before you say anything, yes,
your mother did it and did an excellent job, even more so
after Jason died, but you and Beth are not them. And while
I may not approve, I won't stand in your way, or give you a
hard time."

"What is this right now?" Matt spoke up.

Zach's eyes narrowed. "The truth, and I suggest you
watch your attitude, Matt. You tend to get more than a little uptight when you're stressed. Attorneys live with stress
and you can't afford to let it overtake you."

Abby stared at her son, willing him to remain calm.

Matt took several deep breaths and nodded. "You're
right, I'm sorry. It's just that Beth has been upset over this
and I don't want her to cry anymore."

"If I've been upset it's because the two people I love
most, suddenly can't get along," Beth spoke up. "Daddy,
as much as you wish differently, I'm not your little girl anymore. Maybe I'm not the adult I should be but I'll learn, not

ecause I have to, but because it's time. So, please, no more
ighting. I want us all to be the way we were."

Abby turned to Zach silently saying *What do you say to
hat?*

Zach leaned forward bracing his forearms on his spread
nees, his clasped hands hanging between them. "Matt,
our trust fund should cover the cost of your schooling, am
right?"

Matt nodded. "And I intend to get a job. I figure I can cut
own on the number of classes I take. It may take me an
xtra year to finish but I'm not worried."

"Medical costs before and after birth? Setting up a
ousehold? While Estelle is wonderful to give up her apartment as long as Matt's going to school here, he'll soon have
o move away for law school and you kids will need an
partment, furniture. Not to mention I want to see Beth
inish school," Zach told them. "Of course, she might want
o wait until the baby begins school, and by that time Matt
hould be settled with a law firm and can easily pay for
3eth's education. Now, I have a suggestion. I am willing to
oan you kids enough money for medical expenses. And it
vill be a loan because there will be paperwork drawn up and
expect to be paid back once Matt has a position. The way
look at it, that will be one less thing for you to worry about
nd should give Matt the incentive to find a well-paying
ob."

"Oh, Daddy!" Beth cried, jumping up and running over
o him, hugging him tightly.

"It's a loan," he repeated.

Matt stood and walked over quite a bit slower. Standing
efore the older man he held out his hand. "I accept with
hanks," he said in a low voice. "My pride tells me I should
e able to do it on my own, but Mom keeps reminding me
'm supposed to have some common sense and I'm trying
ery hard to use it." He offered both parents a sheepish grin.

"I admit I've worried about making sure Beth has goo
medical care."

"One worry taken care of," Abby announced. "We ar
here to help you two but we won't do it all. Zach is right
marriage is a very serious business and requires a lot of worl
on your part."

"Abby and I could probably talk to you kids for the nex
six months about responsibility, but I think that time i
past," Zach said. "I guess if anything, we should talk abou
the upcoming wedding." He shot a wry glance in Abby'
direction.

Beth's face lit up. "I have so many ideas for colors an
flowers. I'll get them."

Abby smiled. "And now the fun begins."

Two hours later when it was time to leave, Abby and Zacl
walked out to the car first to allow the engaged couple a bi
of privacy.

"You in the mood for dinner out and a play tomorro
night?" he asked, standing next to the car while she leane
against the passenger door.

She shook her head, smiling regretfully. "Sam is going t
a dance tomorrow night. Perhaps you'd like to come ove
and give me tips on how to handle the idea of a daughte
dating."

"Sure, why not. I'll even come over early and check th
kid out if you'd like."

Her smile bewitched him. "Let's not scare him off to
quickly or Sam will never forgive us. Of course, you coul
just stand there and look fierce and he'd probably get th
idea. About six-thirty? Estelle is going to a pot-luck suppe
at her church, so we could send out for pizza."

"I'll bring it with me," he offered. He leaned over an
kissed her lightly on the lips before she got in. "I'd like t
kiss you a great deal more, but after the talk with the kids
don't think it would be a good idea."

"You're right, it wouldn't," she agreed. "Just remember, no anchovies on the pizza."

"It's Matt who likes the anchovies, I prefer mushrooms," he retorted.

"Okay, you two, break clean," Matt called out, laughter in his voice as he and Beth approached the car.

"See you tomorrow," Abby told Zach as she slipped inside the car.

In deference to Abby's ears, Matt kept the radio low as he drove.

"It's going to take time to bring Zach around, isn't it?" he said quietly.

"Yes, you'll have to prove yourself to him but I have faith in you." She smiled. "After all, you are my son."

"He'll see. I'll make Beth happy," he said with the confidence of youth. "Zach won't have anything to worry about."

Abby sighed. She could only hope so.

"DO I LOOK ALL RIGHT?" Samantha asked anxiously, swirling in front of her mother.

Abby swallowed the large lump residing in her throat. The soft pink gown was scoop necked with a ruffle around the neck and the calf-length hemline. Her medium-heeled shoes were dyed to match and her off-white stockings carried a faint design circling her slender ankle. She had loaned Samantha her pearl necklace and earrings and Zach had styled her hair earlier that day in a mass of upswept curls that managed to be sophisticated without making her look too old.

"I think you look beautiful," she whispered. "And I wish we could put this off for a few more years, say ten or twelve."

"Mom, I'm only going to a dance."

"Matt said that once," Abby mourned.

Samantha leaned toward the mirror applying a glos.
pink lip color. "Mom, when Kevin comes in, please don
ask him a lot of questions." She looked at her mother in th
mirror with an eloquent plea in her eyes.

"I think you'd better talk to Zach about that. He'll
here in about ten minutes."

Samantha groaned. "Oh, no! Mom, please call him ar
tell him to come later? He'll probably act like my father
embarrass me in some way in front of Kevin. I just know h
will. Look how he used to act with Beth. And he always sai
he'd be willing to do the same for me and I just know h
wasn't kidding," she wailed.

"I'll make sure he behaves," she assured her daughte
Abby stared at her, unable to equate this exquisite creatur
standing in front of her with the jeans-clad hoyden runnir
through the house every day. She felt as if her world wa
rapidly changing around her while she was standing still. Sh
straightened up when the doorbell rang. "That's probabl
Zach."

"I hope it's Kevin." Samantha stuffed necessary article
in a small purse.

Her wish wasn't fulfilled when Abby opened the door t
Zach carrying a large carton and a small bag.

"I stopped by the video store and picked up a couple c
tapes," he told her, stepping inside. "Where's the socia
ite?"

"Don't you dare say anything to Kevin, Zach," Samar
tha threatened, walking down the hallway.

He handed the pizza and tapes to Abby and walked ove
to Samantha, taking one hand and twirling her aroun
"You look beautiful, princess," he said in an awed voice
"This guy better appreciate what he's getting."

"Mom?" she pleaded.

"Zach, I want you swear you won't interrogate Kevin,"
Abby said, carrying the pizza into the kitchen and leavin
the tapes in the den.

"I can't even ask him if his intentions are honorable," he joked.

Samantha immediately feared the worst; especially when the doorbell rang. "Mom!"

"Behave, Zach," she ordered in a low voice, heading for the door before he could reach it. The young man standing on the porch was dressed in a dark suit, looking uncomfortable in the formal clothing and carrying a box with a corsage. "Hello, Kevin." Abby smiled at him stepping back to allow him to enter.

"Mrs. Townsend." He smiled as he walked inside, his steps faltering when he encountered the tall man standing near Samantha as if guarding her.

"I'm sure you remember Mr. Randolph," Abby spoke up, sending Zach a look that spoke volumes.

"Kevin." He nodded. "So the two of you are going to a dance?"

He swallowed. "Yes, sir."

"Who's driving?" He didn't wince when Samantha "accidentally" stepped on his foot.

"My father."

"What time will you bring her home?"

"Would you like me to put that on?" Abby cut in cheerfully, holding her hand out for the corsage.

He nodded, clearly intimidated by Zach's paternal demeanor.

Abby didn't allow Zach to say another word as she pinned Samantha's corsage on and hurriedly ushered them into the living room to take a few pictures. In record time she had them out the door and on their way after wishing them a good time. After she closed the door she leaned against it looking at Zach with exasperation.

"You just couldn't resist it, could you?" she scolded. "You had to go and act like the heavy. Sam will never forgive you for that."

"I wanted the punk to know if he tried to get out of hand there was a male figure to deal with him," he replied, unconcerned with her irritation at him.

Abby threw up her hands. "What do you think Matt is, chopped liver? Contrary to the battles he and Sam have on a regular basis, he is very protective of her. Besides, Kevin is a very sweet boy whose father is a neurosurgeon and his mother is a financial planner."

"He has a pierced ear." To Zach that said it all.

"But he wasn't wearing an earring tonight, and believe me, I would rather see my daughter go out with a boy with a pierced ear than one whose hair is shaved or streaked in twenty different colors."

Zach walked over to her, placing one hand on either side of her shoulders to prevent the idea of escape, although he doubted she would consider it. "What about you?" he asked silkily. "I don't have a pierced ear and my hair is only two colors although the gray is increasing every day."

"I definitely wouldn't allow my daughter to go out with you," Abby murmured, tipping her face. "You're more dangerous than a dozen Kevins."

"Then I guess I'll just have to concentrate on charming the mother, won't I?" His mouth brushed across hers several times before he deepened the kiss. His tongue traced the outline of her lips before forging its way inside. He moved closer until their bodies swayed against each other as he took his time nibbling on her lower lip. After tracing a path to her ear, he trailed kisses along the rim and fastened his teeth on the lobe, his tongue playing with the tiny gold earring.

Abby felt her so-called good sense leaving her as she returned his kiss with full-blown warmth. She wrapped her arms around his neck, leaning her body against his. She felt as if she could remain there for a long time, just allowing Zach to kiss her into oblivion unless she forced them back to the present.

"Pizza," she muttered.

"Hmm?" He was lost.

"Pizza. It's in the kitchen and I'm hungry."

Zach slowly returned to the present, tempted to tell her he was hungry, too, but not for pizza. "Right." He reluctantly released her and stepped back.

Abby took several deep breaths. "I was right, you are dangerous." She stepped around him and almost ran for the kitchen with him close on her heels.

"I'm surprised you felt confident enough to turn on the oven or is the fire department standing by, just in case?" He opened the refrigerator and withdrew a bottle of beer for himself and wine for Abby.

"Cute." She pulled the carton out of the oven and set it on the table before getting paper plates and napkins. "What tapes did you pick up?"

"I guess you would call it a variety."

Abby burst out laughing. "You have interesting choices there. At least you stayed out of the X-rated section."

He grimaced. "You've seen one, you've seen them all."

They carried the food into the den, setting the pizza carton on top of newspapers covering the coffee table. Zach inserted a tape in the VCR and settled back to watch the first movie.

"Pizza!" Max croaked at the top of his voice, wistfully watching Zach carry a slice to his mouth. The look on the macaw's face would have suggested he hadn't eaten in years.

"How does he do it?" he asked Abby. "I'm sitting here feeling guilty because I'm eating this and he isn't."

"He's got it down to a science." She carefully tore the crust away from her slice and fed it to the macaw. "No more begging, do you hear me?"

Max bobbed his red feathered head up and down then just as quickly shook it before gobbling down his treat and looking at her for more.

Zach sighed, "Here." He handed Max his crust. "Doesn't he ever eat real bird food?"

"Not if he can help it. Sam says the only reason she likes him is because he'll eat broccoli, which she's hated all her life." She looked pensive. "Oh, Zach, she isn't my little girl anymore. She just left on her first real date."

"She's still your baby. Wait until tomorrow when she's running around in clothes you wish she'd thrown in the trash and playing rock music so loud you're convinced you're going deaf," he soothed. "I felt the same way the first time Beth was all dressed up."

"The first time she was dressed formally was when she was six and a flower girl in Jay and Lisa's wedding," Abby reminded him. "That should have been plenty of warning of what would happen."

He smiled. "She did look cute, didn't she? She had on that lilac-sprigged dress, black patent Mary Janes and her hair done up in ringlets with lilac ribbons."

"That sounds more like a mother than a father," she quipped.

"Probably because I've been both for so long." He eyed her sitting comfortably with her back against the arm of the couch, her long jeans-clad legs crossed Indian style. Her dark gold oversized rag sweater hung loosely to her hips, but he still remembered how slender they felt under his wandering hands. And here Zach thought not too long ago he would never be interested physically in another woman. Where Abby was concerned, his hormones seemed to be working on overtime. "You realize we're going to be in-laws, don't you?"

"It's going to be a novel idea, but I think we can handle it." Abby finished her slice of pizza. "Of course, all of this would happen at the beginning of my busiest time of year. I'll have to work hard so I won't neglect the family."

"What about me?" he asked huskily. "Am I considered part of the family?"

She smiled, seeing his vulnerability in the question. "Yes, you are."

With that reply they settled back to watch the rest of the tape.

Chapter Thirteen

"How am I supposed to get married if I can't even find a dress in time?" Beth wailed, as she and Abby left a boutique. "We've been to five stores and I haven't seen anything I like yet."

"I guess you'll just have to wear something you already have in your closet." Abby thought very seriously of suggesting they sit down for a cold drink. When she had first been pregnant, she didn't have any energy at all while Beth seemed to have more than enough for ten people.

Beth stopped dead in her tracks and spun around to face Abby. "I can't do that!" Tears sprang from her eyes. "I have to find something special."

Abby sighed. Beth also had plenty of emotion. "Beth, I was just teasing. We'll find something, don't worry. Come on, let's stop for something to eat and drink and figure out where to try next." She practically dragged the young woman toward a nearby restaurant.

After they were seated and had ordered their lunch, Beth consulted the list she had drawn up that morning.

"I need shoes but I can't get those until I find a dress," she sighed, dropping the sheet of paper on the table. "So far, all I've found is a nightgown." She blushed a soft pink realizing she was not only talking to a woman who had been like a mother to her, but also her fiancé's mother.

"Trust me, he'll love it," Abby said dryly, thinking of the delicate lilac gown Beth had chosen that was more cob-webby lace than fabric. "Don't worry, Beth, we have two more shops to try here and it certainly isn't the only mall around. We'll find your dress today, I promise." *Or I'll die trying,* she silently vowed.

Beth smiled, reassured by Abby's matter-of-fact tone. "I really appreciate you coming with me at the last minute. I know the situation isn't what you wanted but I'm glad you're willing to help."

"So it's a few years earlier than we expected. Ever since I can remember you're who he's always wanted to be with," Abby replied. "Ever since he was a little boy Matt has al-ways known what he's wanted and gone after it with a sin-gle-minded purpose. He's wanted to become an attorney and wanted to marry you for a long time now. All I ask is that you help make sure his other dream comes true, too."

Beth's face lit up. "He'll be a wonderful lawyer, you'll see." Just as quickly her expression changed when a wait-ress passed by carrying two plates. "Just the smell of ba-con is enough to send me to the bathroom," she confided. "I finally gave in and started taking the nausea medication. I only wish I had done it sooner so I wouldn't have suffered so much!"

Abby smiled. "With me it was tea. Everyone told me to drink tea instead of coffee because it would be better for my stomach. Tea sent me reeling, coffee didn't."

"Did . . ." she paused, unsure whether to ask then forged ahead. "Did you have any strange cravings? The way they talk about in the movies and TV? You know the kind, pick-les and ice cream?"

She began laughing. "Did I? I had so many I drove Jason crazy. One day I might demand peanut butter on every-thing I ate, and the next day I would insist just looking at it made me sick. I once got Jason up in the middle of the night because I had to have chocolate-chip ice cream or die. He was the one who got sick when he watched me heap marsh-mallow creme, hot fudge and strawberry sauce all over it, but I ate every calorie-laden bite and enjoyed it." She settled back in the booth. "Beth, you are going to finish this semester, aren't you? There's no reason for you to throw it away when you've been doing so well."

"I want to finish it," she agreed. "In fact, I saw my counselor yesterday to rearrange my schedule a little. I have trouble making it to my early-morning classes so I switched over to the afternoon sessions."

"Did you call your mother about the wedding?" Abby knew she was bringing up a somewhat painful subject, but was aware it had to be done.

Beth shook her head. "Dad told me I should call her, but I don't see why. We all know she doesn't care about me. As it is, she only calls me at Christmas and I don't know why she bothers then."

"She's still your mother."

She looked bitter. "Is she? Then why were you the one to attend all the mother-daughter activities at Girl Scouts and at school? Who was the one to intervene with Dad the time I dated that guy he didn't like and we ran out of gas in Carlsbad? And that's only a small part of what you've done over the years. I never considered Carolyn my mother. You were the one there when I needed someone. Not her." The last two words were said in a whisper.

"Well, then I hope you can put up with me as your mother-in-law," she said finally, trying to inject a lightness into the somber conversation. "We're supposed to be regular dragons, you know."

"Maybe if you got together with my dad, you could mellow a bit," Beth teased then burst out laughing when Abby's face reddened. "I knew it, you have the hots for my dad!" she crowed.

She held up her hands. "Now wait a minute. I have never given anyone, most of all your father, the impression that I have the hots for him."

She didn't look convinced. "Give me a break, Abby. I've seen the way you two look at each other. Why don't you just give in?"

"Probably because I have other things on my mind such as helping you find a wedding dress and whatever else needs doing," she retorted, glancing up when the waitress set a Caesar salad in front of her. "Or when my feet give out, whichever comes first."

Luckily, Abby's energy level was restored after lunch and two hours later they found Beth's dress; a salmon-pink silk slip-style dress with a matching jacket. Beth decided to have flowers woven into her hair instead of wearing a hat or veil. She also bought several other outfits since her father had teasingly ordered her to purchase a trousseau.

"Buy plenty of underwear and bras," Abby advised. "For some reason that's usually the last item we purchase, although with the sexier styles out we are prone to indulge more often."

Beth looked down her slender build. "Think I'll get a bustline after this?"

"I did. Trouble is, it didn't stay," she chuckled. "Jason once kidded he was going to bronze my bras."

Beth giggled then sobered. "You miss him, don't you?"

"At times like this I do because he would have enjoyed seeing his son marrying his best friend's daughter," she admitted. "But there isn't the pain I felt in the beginning. Now I remember him in a different way. Now, no more talk about the past. We have a lot of plans for the future. And I'm hoping you'll indulge me by allowing me to buy the baby furniture. All you have to do is pick it out. I'll just write out the check."

"Abby, that's too much," she protested.

"No, it's not, because basically you two are going to be on your own without any in-law interference, so let me do this, okay?"

"Okay."

By the end of the day both of them were worn out from their shopping expedition.

"I just hope when Dad gets the bills he remembers he told me to go all out." Beth eyed the packages in the back seat when Abby parked the car in the Randolphs' driveway.

"Don't worry, I'll remind him." Abby got out of the car and pushed her seat forward to retrieve the bags from her side of the car.

"Good afternoon, Miss Howard," Beth called out to the older woman standing on the neighboring front porch. "How are you?"

"I would be fine if you and that boy wouldn't come home at all hours at the night," she said tartly. "The two of you would be better off married before something...unseemly happened."

"What a wonderful idea," Abby said cheerfully. "Isn't it convenient then that they're getting married in two weeks."

The silver-haired woman looked Beth over from head to toe. "I'll tell you that in nine months."

"For a spinster, she certainly has a dirty mind," Abby murmured as she waited for Beth to unlock the front door.

"Actually, I feel sorry for her," the young woman admitted. "The few friends she has are just as narrow-minded as she is. They were over one Sunday afternoon and two almost had heart attacks when Dad walked out front wearing his swim trunks. And it isn't as if he wears a European style." She grinned wickedly. "Now that would cause a few palpitations, wouldn't it?"

Abby pictured Zach in a sleek strip of cloth. "More than a few I'd expect. I'd even experience a few flutters if he strutted his stuff." She glanced down at her watch. "I better get going." She looked at Beth's pale features. "Why don't you rest a while and put your things away later?"

She nodded. "I am feeling tired." She hugged Abby tightly. "Thank you so much for your help." She considered her next words before speaking. "Abby, that night we told you about the baby, Matt didn't mean what he said. He wouldn't hurt you for anything."

She smiled. "Honey, I know that. It's just a shame he inherited my temperament instead of his father's, because we tend to fly off the handle at the same time. That wasn't the first time we've butted heads and it certainly won't be the last. But we've always survived our battles with a minimum of scarring. As to what he said, it was basically true and how can a person get angry at hearing the truth? I admit I had hoped you two could have waited, but I won't throw you to the wolves because you didn't. Now, you go and rest. Don't do anything more strenuous than writing out your guest list, all right?"

Beth laughed and hugged her. "Yes, Mother." She tried to present a demure picture but failed miserably.

"You're turning into a smart-mouthed kid like Matt," she grumbled, walking toward the front door. "I just hope my grandchild doesn't turn out like his or her father or we'll all be in trouble."

Abby nodded at Miss Howard on her way to her car and quickly left, looking forward to a hot soothing bath and a quiet evening at home.

"Did Beth get everything she needed?" Estelle asked when Abby walked in the back door.

She nodded. "Yes, thank God, and my aching body is testimony of what it took to find all of it. Would you believe she even wanted to browse through a maternity shop?" She poured herself a glass of iced tea and collapsed in a chair. "Do you know what I've realized lately. My son's sex life is more active than mine. That's really sad."

"You could easily remedy that," Estelle countered.

Abby eyed her above the rim of her glass. "Estelle, I'm surprised at you for condoning casual sex."

"Only with the right person. Besides, maybe the two of you will finally settle down and get together the way you should be."

"Maybe we will be able to do that," Abby murmured with a slight smile on her lips. She finished her tea and poured herself another glass. She stood up slowly. "But for now I'm taking a very long relaxing bath before dinner."

"You're not going out with Zach?"

"No. Besides, I wouldn't have the energy to do more than sit very quietly and very still on the couch."

Estelle said slyly, "A lot can happen on a couch."

"Yes, but I would rather suffer unrequited lust than get hurt when it was all over."

"You'll never know until you try."

Abby escaped Estelle's well-meaning advice. "No, thanks, I've had enough hurt in my life," she muttered, heading for her bathroom.

Two hours later, a hot bath and clean clothes revived Abby enough to eat dinner with Matt and Samantha. Matt informed her he was going over to Beth's for a few hours, and Samantha asked if she could go over to Melanie's for the evening.

"Whatever happened to spending an evening home with your dear old mother?" Abby demanded, feeling abandoned by her children's plans.

"That was when you wouldn't allow us to go at night," Matt told her. "Besides, Beth wants help with the guest list. We only have two weeks, you know."

"Yes, I know." And Abby knew she would be doing a great deal more work on the wedding than the mother of the groom normally did.

After Estelle retired to her own room, Abby settled down in the den with the stereo playing softly in the background and a book in her lap.

She looked up a few minutes later when the doorbell rang and put away her book with the feeling she wasn't going to be allowed to finish it that night. That feeling was confirmed when she found Zach standing on her front porch.

"Hi, I felt like a third party at home, and Matt mentioned Sam was out tonight so I thought I'd come over and keep you company." He held up a brown paper bag. "I even brought a bribe."

She looked suspicious. "What is it?"

"Let me in and I'll show you." He grinned, looking about as innocent as a devil. "You know the old saying, 'I'll show you mine if you show me yours'?" He moved forward until she was forced to step back and allow him to enter the house.

"You should be so lucky," she said tautly.

"I can always hope, can't I?" He was unperturbed as he walked through the house.

"What has happened to you?" Abby asked, following him into the kitchen. "You used to be so uncomplicated. And now..." she couldn't figure out exactly what he was, much less put it into words.

He set the bag down on the counter and pulled out the contents. "Maybe I'm finally waking up to the truth," he said quietly. "And you just happen to be the main part of the waking-up process."

Abby looked over his shoulder at his booty. "Oh my," she breathed. "You wonderful man. I'll probably regret it in the morning when I step on the scales, but I'm more than willing to suffer the consequences."

"Then maybe I should take it all home." He pretended to repack the bag. "I'd hate to be the reason for your downfall. I'd never be able to live with myself afterward."

"You try to walk out the door with all these goodies and you're a dead man." Abby picked up the jar of hot-fudge sauce, opened the lid and sniffed the rich aroma. "This is heaven."

Zach took the jar out of her hands and popped it in the microwave, setting the timer to heat the sauce. While it was warming he set Abby to getting out bowls, while he dug out silverware. Pretty soon French vanilla ice cream was covered with steaming hot fudge, whipped cream and nuts. By mutual consent they carried their bowls outside to the patio since the evening was a comfortable temperature.

"Pretty soon it will be too cold to do this," Abby commented, curling up on a chaise lounge with Zach seated near her legs. "And to think most men feel wine is what a woman wants when he comes calling." She closed her eyes in bliss as she savored the rich flavors exploding on her tongue. "This is sinful and I love it."

"Too bad it isn't cheaper than wine. I had no idea gourmet hot fudge sauce could be so expensive." Zach couldn't keep his eyes off Abby enjoying her rich treat.

"Maybe, but you don't get a hangover from eating hot-fudge sundaes."

"No, just a pretty sick stomach if you overdo it." He dug his spoon into the fudge-covered ice cream. "Thanks for taking Beth shopping today. She was pretty excited tonight showing me all her purchases. I know she's been a little nervous about the changes happening to her body, and I don't think she feels comfortable enough talking to her doctor or to me so I'm glad she could talk to you."

"Did she tell you that?" She was pleased by his praise.

He shook his head. "She just seemed a lot calmer tonight, so I assumed she'd talked to you."

"She had. I'm just glad I was able to help."

Zach set his bowl on the ground under the lounge chair so it wouldn't get in the way. "You know, they just might do all right," he remarked.

"Talk about a load of confidence," Abby said dryly.

"They do have one thing in their favor. They have parents who care."

"Zach, your parents were dead when you got married and Carolyn's were happy to get rid of her."

"And yours didn't speak to you for a long time after you married Jason."

She shrugged. "I was very young and even more foolish in the way I handled the situation with them. It took quite a few years to mend the fences and while they aren't as strong as they were in the beginning, there is a definite improvement. There are times when I wonder if I would do it again if I had the choice. Do you know it scares me that I have to even question myself. I should say yes without hesitation, but I can't. Maybe if we hadn't gotten married so young Jason would be alive today."

Zach grabbed hold of her shoulders and shook her hard. "Don't ever look at it that way. Jason's death was meant to happen then, whether you two married young or five or ten years later. The past is all over, Abby, and we're the future," he said fiercely. "You don't know this, but on your wedding day I wondered what would have happened if I had asked you out first."

She looked up with stunned surprise written on her face. "You did? I never knew."

He turned away, disgust with himself written all over his face. "You weren't meant to. It was the thoughts of a guy suffering from the typical bachelor-party hangover who saw a pretty girl and wished he had seen her first. It happens all the time, but I don't want to talk about that time. I'd prefer to concentrate on what's going on now. You promised to give us a chance and you're backing down. Let's get back to us, shall we?"

She could only look up at him. "All right," she whispered.

"I already feel as if we need another weekend away," Zach told her, nudging her over until he could stretch out on the lounge and pull her back against him.

"That was nice, wasn't it?" Abby mused, angling her head so she could rest it on his shoulder. "I felt as if we were in another world there."

He nuzzled her ear and gently blew in it. "We were."

Abby sighed. "But the real world always has to intrude. We never really did take time for ourselves, did we, Zach? Oh, we each had a few brief interludes in the past but nothing serious. Were we unconsciously running away from each other?"

He shrugged. "Perhaps. It's hard to say what we were trying to do. Still, in times of need we always knew who to turn to. Maybe we should have concentrated more on each other back then."

She looked up at the dark sky, feeling comfortable in Zach's embrace with his warmth seeming to surround her. "Did you ever think we would end up like this?" She could have sworn she felt his smile against her hair.

"No, but I'm not surprised. Kids don't have a monopoly on love, you know. We just haven't had the time to fully explore it yet," he murmured. "I do know I want you with me all the time. We share a rapport most couples can't even dream of, and I don't see anything wrong in our looking to a future together, do you?"

Abby smiled. "No, I don't see anything wrong in it at all."

Chapter Fourteen

"Are all wedding rehearsals that bad?" Matt asked, plopping on the couch and closing his eyes.

"Oh yes," Abby sighed in relief when she eased her shoes off and walked barefoot into the kitchen. She returned to the den with two glasses of wine, handing one glass to Matt. He accepted the glass, smiling his thanks. "They're supposed to be, so everyone will worry that something will go wrong during the ceremony, while actually everything turns out just fine.

"So my dear son, you are joining the ranks of matrimony tomorrow evening," she intoned. "Anything you care to ask your dear old mother before you take that giant step tomorrow?"

He chuckled. "I think most of the topics have already been pretty well covered. Right now I'm just trying to remain calm."

"The jitters are perfectly normal. I'm sure Beth is having a few of her own." Abby sipped her wine. "I know I did."

Matt rolled over onto his side, propping his head up with his hand, his other hand cradling the wineglass. "You know, Mom, you are something else. You could have called me all sorts of names and blamed Beth, but you didn't."

She smiled wryly. "You forget, I've been there. Besides, you were willing to stand by Beth, that's what really counted. These past few weeks have been hectic for all of us. You did more than your share and I love you for that.''

''I never realized how much work goes into planning a wedding. No wonder some couples are engaged for more than a year. It takes that long just to figure out a color scheme,'' he sighed, his face lightly lined with weariness. ''I'm surprised more just don't say the hell with it all and elope.''

''Reserving a chapel, ordering flowers and writing out invitations is hard work—thank goodness you two wanted a small ceremony.'' Abby groaned, remembering all the calls she had made to find a suitable reception room until Zach came through with a perfect one in a hotel. She smiled at her son. ''I want to thank you for tolerating your grandfather at the rehearsal. I know it wasn't easy.''

His face darkened. ''There was no reason for him to ask Beth if we were getting married because she was pregnant. He almost had her in tears.''

''That's just his way. I doubt he even realizes how rude he sounds. He was just as bad when your father and I got married.''

''Yeah, but Carolyn really took the cake,'' Matt grumbled. ''She's hardly even talked to Beth all these years, but tonight she acted like she was the all-time loving mother losing her treasured baby girl. Not to mention the way she crawled all over Zach.''

Abby remembered that part only too well and with a great deal of distaste. More than once during the evening she'd nurtured the idea of dumping champagne in the woman's lap. ''Yes, she did,'' she murmured, drinking more wine to ease the knots in her stomach. ''I had forgotten how beautiful she is.''

He laughed, but there was no humor in the sound. ''Beautiful? No, Mom, she's nothing more than a facade. You're the one who's beautiful, inside and out. When Dad died you took your degree and made it work for you in a way that allowed you to stay home with us when we needed you." He hesitated. "I know I never said it enough. I guess because the boy in me felt it wasn't macho, but I love you a lot, Mom. And not because you've been great about Beth's pregnancy and our wedding, but everything before that . . . and I haven't been exactly the best of sons."

"No, you have given me some rough moments," she whispered, vainly blinking back the tears. "Such as when you were positive you could ride down that hill on your bike and ended up with a broken collarbone. And then you had the nerve to tell me it was all the bike's fault. I wasn't sure whether to murder you or cry over your scrapes and bruises. Oh, Matt, we've been through a lot together. Your broken bones, Sam's broken bones . . ."

"Hi!"

They both looked over at the covered cage and burst out laughing.

"Max," Matt said dryly. "Remember the first time you dated after Dad's death, you swore you couldn't do it and I gave you what I thought was excellent advice."

"Ah, yes." Abby smiled, recalling a young Matt looking up at her with a most adult expression. "'Now, Mom, don't order any soup because you'll never forgive yourself if you spill any on you.' Very profound."

"And on my first date you told me to always open the door for the girl and to use my handkerchief when I sneeze."

She stared at her son. "There're so many things I want to tell you, but I wouldn't know where to begin, so I guess I'll just have to hope you can do well on your own."

He smiled. "I won't be on my own, Mom. I'll have Beth and if I need advice I've got you and Zach, so I'm not too worried."

He levered himself off the couch and walked over to Abby, dropping a kiss on her cheek. "I'm going to bed before I fall asleep right here or we get too maudlin. You better get to bed, too. Tomorrow's a big day."

She smiled up at him. "Yes, it is. I thought of an old saying tonight: 'A son is a son until he takes a wife, but a daughter is a daughter all her life.' I think I'll sit here for a little while and feel maudlin because I'm losing my only son."

"As Estelle is wonderful enough to give up the garage apartment for us until I start law school, I'd say you have nothing to worry about never seeing me again," he assured her. "Good night."

Abby poured herself another glass of wine and sat in her chair surrounded by the night's silence. She knew she was beginning to feel sorry for herself, and before she thought twice of what she was doing she grabbed the phone and punched out a number.

"Whoever this is, it better be good." Zach's irritated voice was husky with sleep.

She laughed softly. "How about I breathe heavy and pant into the phone? Will that cheer you up?"

He groaned. "Abby, do you know what time it is?"

She looked at the clock. "Just past two."

"Right. And I'm hoping to get some sleep so the bride's father won't have bags under his eyes tomorrow."

"You can sleep late to make up for it, Zach." Her voice was little more than a whisper. "Everything is changing around us and nothing will be the same again. The day we all went to the fair we talked how we wouldn't have the family get-togethers anymore and wondered what would happen when Matt left for law school next year. This isn't what we expected, is it?"

"No, it isn't, but I think it's because you and I know firsthand what starting out with a family is like."

"Yes, but you were older than Jason and I were."

"It didn't make me any more responsible, did it?"

"I don't know. Carolyn didn't seem to hold any bad feelings toward you during the rehearsal dinner." Abby knew she sounded childish but she was so tired, she was past caring how she sounded.

"Oh, so that's it." He settled himself more comfortably. "I'm even surprised she came, after the hassle she gave Beth over the phone when she called Carolyn to tell her about the wedding."

"If she acts like that during the wedding or reception, I'm going to pour champagne over her perfectly coiffed head," Abby said sweetly.

"Then perhaps I should keep a very close eye on you so you won't be tempted," Zach suggested.

A smile curved her lips at the idea of his staying close to her. "Are you sure you won't mind?"

"It will be my pleasure."

Abby could feel the weariness pour over her and knew if she didn't hang up soon she would fall asleep with the phone in her hand. "I should let you get back to sleep and get myself to bed," she said softly. "But I guess I wanted to hear your voice. I'm sorry I woke you. I'll see you tomorrow."

"Abby." The one word halted her hand. "I'm glad you called me."

"So am I. Good night."

When Abby went to sleep that night she fell asleep with a smile on her lips.

"MOM, ESTELLE SAID she has breakfast ready." Samantha knocked on her bedroom door. "She also said to hop to it because today's going to be real busy. And Zach called. He said to be at the salon around two so he can do our hair. We're to knock on the back door since he closed the salon today. Isn't this great?" Enthusiasm brightened her voice.

"Yeah, just wonderful," she muttered, crawling out of bed. It took her a few moments to find her robe; probably because it was hanging inside her closet instead of thrown across the bed as it usually was. Abby splashed cold water on her face and took the time to brush her hair before staggering out of her room.

"You've got circles under your eyes," Samantha told her.

"Thank you, my darling daughter, you have just made my whole day."

The girl followed her toward the kitchen. "One good thing about this wedding is that Max can't go."

"Oh, I don't know. All he'd need is a bow tie and he'd look quite dashing," Abby reflected.

"Mo-ther!" The pained expression on her face revealed that she thought her mother might be serious.

"It was a thought." Abby entered the kitchen.

"Here." Estelle handed her a large mug of coffee. "You look terrible. What time did you get to bed?"

"Around three." Abby glanced at the clock and moaned. "Seven o'clock? The ceremony isn't until six and you had the nerve to get me up now? I bet you're letting Matt sleep late."

Estelle shook his head. "He wandered out here an hour ago looking worse than you. I think the whole thing is getting to him. He's finally realized what happens today."

"Where is he?"

"Swimming laps." Estelle filled a plate with scrambled eggs and ham and set it in front of Abby before retrieving a basket of corn bread and a jar of honey butter. "I got fed up with him pacing the house so I ordered him outside to work off some of that energy. At the rate he's going, we might not see him until just before the ceremony. Now eat."

The last thing Abby wanted to do was eat. But with the way Estelle was looking at her, she knew she had no choice. After she finished, she carried her refilled coffee mug and another cup outside. She found Matt in the pool swimming laps as if he were working against a clock.

"Matt, you're going to end up growing gills by the end of the day," she called out. "Come on, I brought you some coffee."

He stilled, swimming over to the side and lifting himself out. Abby handed him a towel and picked up another one to dry off his back as he toweled his chest and hair dry.

"You were so calm last night I should have realized you'd fall apart this morning," she said conversationally. "Drink some coffee, it will calm your nerves."

He laughed, shaking his head at his mother's tone. "It used to be 'Drink some hot chocolate, Matt, you'll feel much better.' You always had your special cures, didn't you?"

"I try." Abby settled herself in a chair, adjusting the folds of her robe around her legs. "Did the swimming help?"

He shook his head as he picked up his mug and sipped the hot coffee. He took the chair next to her, stretching his legs out in front of him. "Unless you count that my arms and legs now feel like spaghetti. All of a sudden I woke up this morning and realized in twenty-four hours I'm going to be responsible for two more people."

She smiled. "Scary, huh?"

"Scary, yes!"

"I'm not worried. You've always had a good head on your shoulders." Her eyes lit up with a devilish gleam. "Besides, if you mess up, Zach will kill you."

Matt threw his head back laughing, looking more relaxed than he had a few minutes ago. "Yeah, he would, wouldn't he? Okay, Mom, your coffee and pep talk had the desired effect. Are you happy?"

She leaned over and kissed his cheek. "Of course I am. I can't have you getting cold feet, can I?"

"Why did we have to make it so late in the day?" he grumbled. "I can't imagine Beth is doing much better than I am. I called her before I came out here but Zach said it's bad luck to talk to her. I told him it was seeing her that was the bad luck, but he just laughed and hung up."

"Let him have this day with Beth," Abby advised, standing up. "It won't be the same for him, either. Don't spend too much time in the water. You don't want to tire yourself out, do you?'' She tweaked his ear.

EVEN THOUGH IT WAS her wedding day Beth insisted on fixing breakfast instead of Zach taking her out for brunch as he had wanted to do, and they ate on the patio by the pool. Their only concession for the special day was Zach fixing mimosas.

"I feel special. You're using the good stuff," Beth quipped, eyeing the champagne bottle's label. She forked another bite of her eggs Benedict. "I know you thought it would be nice to take me out to breakfast, but I didn't want to share this morning with anyone else. I wanted it to be just us."

He settled back in his chair watching her with a sharp eye. "You're not one bit nervous, are you?"

She shook her head. "No reason to be. I think deep down I've been waiting for this day for a long time. I know it happened sooner than all of us expected it to, but it's still what Matt and I want." She sipped her champagne-and-orange-juice mixture. "So, are we going to have the traditional father-daughter talk?"

"Not the way you're thinking." Zach pressed his fingertips together in the shape of a steeple. "You and Matt are getting married for two reasons—because you love each other and because there's a baby on the way. If it hadn't been for the latter you would have waited until Matt was out of school. At least, I hope you would have waited. Still, it's the love part that counts because that's what holds a marriage together. So, when the baby is crying its little lungs out and you've gone without sleep for so long you can't think straight and your household budget has gone up in flames, I want you to remember that love. Will you do that for your old man?"

"Among other things, yes," she murmured. "You've taught me a lot over the years, Daddy, and while Matt

sometimes flies off the handle, he has many of your quali-
ties. After all, he learned from you just as I did. Maybe
that's why I fell in love with him, because he reminded me
of you."

"I can only hope that turns out to be a positive factor,"
he said wryly, leaning back in his chair. "All I'm asking is
that you be happy and for you to know I'm always here for
you if you need me. And if he ever hurts you, I'll kill him."

"HE SHOULDN'T HAVE TO WORRY about doing anyone's hair
today," Abby protested, knocking on the salon's back door,
which opened immediately.

"It keeps me busy instead of pacing the floor," Zach told
her. "Hi, Sam, Estelle. Come on in."

"How's Beth doing?" Abby asked, walking inside.

"She's calm while I'm the one going crazy," he confided.

She grinned. "Is that why you turned on your answering
machine?"

He grimaced. "That and because Carolyn kept calling,
moaning she couldn't do anything with her hair and would
I please do something with it. That's pretty funny since she
used to hate what I do for a living and wouldn't let me touch
her hair."

Abby didn't think it was so funny. "Charge her double," she said tautly.

"I told her the only hair I was doing today was family and
as I didn't consider her family anymore she was out of luck.
I even gave her the name of another hairdresser. Sam, why
don't you put on a smock. I'll do you first."

"Hi," Beth greeted them with a broad smile.

Abby looked at her, recognizing that special glow only
brides have. "You look lovely," she told her.

Beth lightly touched the coil of hair on top of her head
with baby's breath threaded among the strands. "Thanks.

I told Dad I didn't want anything too elaborate and he came up with this.''

Abby sat with Beth and Carla while Zach worked on Samantha, then Estelle.

"What do you think?" Samantha sashayed around, her arms held out at the sides in a high-fashion model's pose.

Abby's eyes widened. Zach had pulled her hair back into an intricate braid with the end tucked up. While her hairstyle for the fall dance hadn't made her look sophisticated, this one easily added several years to her age.

"I can't take this," she moaned.

Samantha was too busy studying herself in one of the mirrors. "I look about three or four years older, don't I?" she asked to no one in particular.

"Don't worry," Beth assured her. "Tomorrow, she'll be back to her old self again."

"I only wish I could believe that," Abby said sadly, sorting through the collection of nail polish on a nearby table. She selected a color and carried it to the table next to Carla. Grabbing a bottle of nail polish remover she cleaned her nails and brushed on the new color that would coordinate with her dress.

"If you want to wait I'll do that for you," Carla offered.

"No, thanks, that's all right." Abby carefully painted the next nail. "Beth's the one who has to look extra special today."

Estelle was next with Zach brushing her hair up in a flattering style. Beth's makeup had been applied to add to her own inner glow, and she had left saying she'd see them later. Abby again marveled how calm the young woman appeared. Carla left soon after saying she'd see them at the reception.

"Next," Zach stood nearby, looking all too good in a pair of well-aged jeans and a delft-blue polo shirt. Abby followed him back to the shampoo sink where he tucked a towel around her collar.

"You're right about Beth, she's acting as if getting married is about as normal as doing the grocery shopping," she commented, stretching out on the reclining chair so he could wash her hair.

He adjusted the water temperature. "At least she's able to keep me from going too crazy." He squirted a dollop of shampoo in his hands and rubbed them together before tackling her hair.

"This is very nice of you to do our hair," she murmured.

Zach leaned down to whisper in her ear. "I only offered so I wouldn't sit around the house and go crazy. Being the father of the bride is a very unsettling occupation."

She couldn't help laughing. "Zach, you're incorrigible. You're handling all of this beautifully."

"That's what you think. To be honest, my knees haven't stopped knocking." He draped a towel around her wet hair. "Up we go. Do you have any image in mind for tonight?"

"Wash and wear because I'll probably cry my eyes out the minute the ceremony begins." She heard a little chuckle at her pronouncement. "Zach, I'm not kidding. Weddings always make me cry. I don't know why but I always seem to come unglued. Umm, that feels good." Her eyes closed as he used a wide-toothed comb to loosen the tangles in her hair.

In no time Zach had her hair combed back into an elegant French twist.

"If you say this makes me look older, I'll shoot you," Abby threatened, studying herself in the mirror.

"I wanted you to feel more like mother of the groom," he replied, standing back. "When you turn into a grandmother I'll add the more appropriate touches of gray. Perhaps I should say, extend those touches already there."

"Good thing you're out of reach or I'd sock you one for that crack." Abby stood up. She turned, caught in his green gaze. For long moments they stood there watching each other until Abby started to slowly move toward his arms.

"Mom, that looks really nice."

They both halted, wry smiles on their lips as they suddenly remembered they weren't alone.

Abby shrugged. "I guess that's our cue," she murmured. "And as your daughter and my son are getting married in about two hours we should probably be on our way to finish all those little things that suddenly crop up."

He sighed. "Unfortunately you're right."

Estelle appeared behind Samantha giving each of them an apologetic look as if she sensed they had wanted that extra moment of privacy. "Perhaps they aren't finished." She placed her hands on the girl's shoulders and spun her around guiding her toward the front of the shop.

Zach grimaced. "Unfortunately, I think we are. Come on, I'll walk you out to your car."

Once there, he slid into his Corvette and headed for home, anticipating a bit of relaxation before they left for the chapel. When he saw a sleek Jaguar parked in his driveway he could only curse under his breath and hurry into the house, expecting the worst. As he thought, his ex-wife sat on the living room couch looking as if she had never left while Beth stood a few feet away. He breathed a silent sigh of relief when he noticed his daughter's face showed no tension.

"Hello, Zach." Carolyn Randolph Sheraton treated him to a cool smile.

"Carolyn." He nodded his head, recalling how he once thought that icy beauty held an impassioned woman. It hadn't taken him long to discover differently. All he could thank her for is Beth. "What are you doing here?"

Delicately arched eyebrows lifted. "I came to see our daughter. After all, this is a special day for her."

"She wanted to see if I could be talked out of it," Beth spoke up, amusement lining her words. Considering her emotional state the past few weeks, Zach was proud of her composure.

"Honestly, Zach, didn't you ever talk to her about birth control and other ways of handling this kind of problem?" Carolyn drawled.

Beth turned on her. "Wait a minute, Dad has nothing to do with this. This baby has Matt and myself—that's more than enough. Now *Carolyn*—" she stressed the name letting the woman know she wasn't going to acknowledge her as a biological parent, "—when I needed a mother you weren't there. You walked out on Dad and me when I was a toddler because you didn't want to be tied down with a child and have a hairdresser-husband whom you were convinced wouldn't make it. Well, Dad did just fine without you. He took care of me when I was sick and he watched after me when I was well. He took me to school my first day and he did everything possible so I wouldn't miss having a mother. It wouldn't have mattered, because I couldn't miss what I hadn't had in the beginning anyway, could I?" She looked coolly at Carolyn who sat frozen. "Now, if you don't mind, I have a great deal to do before the ceremony."

Recognizing a dismissal when she heard one, Carolyn stood up with graceful economy. She turned to Zach. "You ruined that child," she said frostily. "I should have followed my first instincts and taken her with me."

"Save it, Carolyn. You had made it clear for a long time before you left you didn't want either one of us," Zach said bluntly.

Carolyn looked from one to the other. "I'll attend the ceremony and the reception because it's the thing to do."

"That's right, Carolyn, keep up the image," he said dryly.

Her eyes snapped with fire before the icy mask descended. She gathered up her purse and walked out of the house. Although the door closed quietly, she may as well have slammed it.

Father and daughter looked at each other.

"She didn't want to make amends," Beth explained.

"Just trouble. And I wasn't going to allow her to do that."
He smiled. "Now I do know my little girl has grown up."

ABBY DIDN'T KNOW how she survived the next two hours as she bathed and dressed and helped Samantha with her bridesmaid's gown of aqua chiffon. Abby stood back looking at her suddenly grown-up daughter with maternal pride mixed with dismay.

"Tomorrow we have braces put on your teeth," she decided.

"Mom, I had them taken off when I was thirteen," Samantha protested.

"I don't care. You're getting them again."

"I wish I had a cigarette." Matt raked his fingers through his hair, earning a reprimand from Abby as she carefully brushed it back into place. Dressed in a tuxedo he looked incredibly handsome to his mother's fond eyes.

"No, you don't. Just take several deep breaths and you'll be fine," she instructed, glancing at the clock. "I thought Kyle was coming here." She mentioned his friend who would act as Matt's best man.

He shook his head. "He's meeting us at the chapel." He grimaced. "I think I'm going to be sick."

"Take more deep breaths," Abby told him. "Look Matt, just say 'I will' when the time comes and everything will be fine. I hope," she muttered under her breath. "Come on, we better get going."

When they reached the chapel, Abby did a quick once-over to make sure the flowers were in their correct places even though she had done the same thing on her way home from Zach's salon when the florist had been there. She made her way to the rear of the chapel where Beth was ensconced in a small room with Zach, her maid of honor and two bridesmaids. Beth still looked as calm as she had earlier.

"You look lovely," Abby said softly, kissing her on the cheek.

She blushed. "Thanks." She looked up at her father. "I feel beautiful."

Abby blinked to keep the tears from falling. "Oh, I already feel the waterworks starting. I better get out of here before I succumb."

After that, time became nothing more than a haze to Abby from the moment she was escorted to her seat in the front pew until the time she watched Beth walk down the aisle on Zach's arm to be met by a broadly smiling Matt who obviously got over his jitters. Each word was spoken with love and no one present missed the deep commitment the young couple had for each other. Her tears still threatened to fall as she listened to the minister introduce the couple to the guests as man and wife.

Limousines carried the family to the hotel for the reception, and all the time Abby stood in the reception line she looked longingly at the waiters carrying glasses of champagne among the guests.

"This can't go on for much longer," she murmured to Zach. "Otherwise I'm going to shock everyone by taking off my shoes. They are killing me."

He glanced down at her jacket dress of soft peach and further down to the matching high heels. "Keep smiling. It won't be much longer. Besides, we still have dancing."

Abby smiled and shook the hand of a person whose name she missed. "I can't wait."

True to her silent vow Abby snagged a waiter for a glass of champagne and sipped her drink as she circulated among the guests.

"I have to admit you and Zach did an excellent job in handling this situation, Abigail." Leonard Hill, Abby's father, told her with an unsmiling face.

"They love each other and they're determined to finish school. I'm more than happy with that."

"I thought you would have made sure that kind of thing would have been nipped in the bud, considering your and

Zach's pasts. You, of all people, should know what can happen."

Abby looked around for a waiter carrying glasses of champagne, but found none. "Dad, you promised Matt you wouldn't say anything."

"I promised not to say anything to his girl, there was nothing about talking to you," he grumbled. "Still, she's a pretty enough thing and appears to have brains, so they might make a go of it. By the way, I wanted you to know that your mother and I are flying back to Phoenix late tonight."

Abby sighed. She should have known her parents wouldn't bother staying for any kind of extended visit. "I'm glad you could come." Her tone was ironic.

"Families have to stick together, no matter what." With that, he moved away.

"This is beautiful, Abby." Donna walked up and hugged her. "Can you believe those two? I know Beth was upset over his going away for law school so I can understand their getting married now, although I'm sure you weren't too happy about it happening so soon."

"All I care about is their happiness." Abby appropriated another glass of champagne.

Donna smiled. "I saw your father with his martyr's look. Don't worry about him. Buck up, kid. Everything is doing fine."

Abby remembered little as they all posed for the pictures, observed the cutting of the elaborately decorated cake and the dancing that began later in the evening.

"I must say you've done an excellent job in setting up this wedding, Abby." Carolyn Randolph, in a pale blue silk dress told her. "But my dear, it must have been a great deal of work for you. You should have called me and I would have lent you any assistance you required since I have so much more experience in planning formal gatherings. Although I do feel," she lowered her voice confidentially, "considering the circumstances, this is a bit overdone."

Abby looked at her with murder in her eyes. "Carolyn, if you do or say one thing to upset those kids I will personally escort you out of this room and it won't be done in a pretty way. Do we understand each other?"

Her ice-blue eyes narrowed. "You used to be a real sweet and naive kid, Abby. Obviously you matured in many ways over the years. I've heard you've been seeing Zach. Trust me, you wouldn't be happy with him. Some men just don't have it, and he never did."

Abby's smile showed just a hint of gleaming white teeth. "It usually takes the right woman."

Carolyn's facial muscles tightened until her face resembled a smooth mask. Without saying another word she moved away.

"Score one for me," Abby congratulated herself with a glass of champagne.

"What did you say to my ex-wife to turn her into the living mummy?" Zach's breath tickled her ear.

She twisted her head back and smiled up at him. "Let's just say she knows the battle lines are drawn and I'm not afraid to fire my weapons."

He picked up her hand and kissed the fingertips. "I'm not entirely sure what you mean, but I have an idea you fought for my honor and won the first round. I just hope you enjoy the prize."

"If you two can separate for a minute I'd like to dance with my mother." Matt stood in front of them, one hand holding onto Beth's, whose eyes glowed in happiness.

"Fair enough, since I'll have a chance to dance with my daughter." Zach smiled at Beth.

When Matt circled the dance floor with her, Abby looked up at him with pride shining in her eyes. "The first time we danced together you were five years old," she murmured, allowing the tears to roll down her cheeks. "And you wore a dark blue suit, complaining that your tie was choking you. But you looked so handsome and so grown-up.''

He chuckled. ''Aunt Lydia's wedding.''

Abby nodded. ''Your father and I had just finished dancing and you walked over to me with this very grown-up air and asked if I would dance with you. I cried then.''

''You cry at every wedding,'' he teased gently. ''And you told me even then I was a better dancer than Dad. Don't worry, this won't be our last dance. Wait until your grandchild gets married.''

Abby sniffed. ''Please, not now. I can't handle anymore.''

Matt hugged her. ''You're doing great, Mom.''

''As much as I would like to keep you with me as long as possible, perhaps it's time to change partners,'' she spoke softly around the lump in her throat as they approached the new bride and her father.

He kissed her. ''Mom, I never told you enough, but I love you.'' They danced near Beth and Zach and changed partners.

''This is the best reception I've ever been to,'' Abby told Zach.

He looked at her sharply. ''How much champagne have you had?''

She considered his question. ''Not enough.''

Zach softened, understanding her pain. He folded her closer to him. ''It won't help, you know.''

She managed a wobbly smile. ''I know.''

Abby had shored up her courage until she watched Matt approach Samantha and escort her onto the dance floor. As she watched her son and daughter waltz around the room she felt the tears stream down her face.

''Here.'' A handkerchief appeared in her line of vision. ''You're supposed to cry when Beth and Matt dance.''

"Yes, but those two have fought for so many years and look at them now." She dabbed her eyes, careful not to disturb her mascara too much. "Damn, I feel so maudlin."

Zach put his arm around her shoulders and hugged her close to him. "It's allowed. And as much as I hate to start the tear ducts flowing again, I think I'd better let you know they're going to be leaving in a few minutes." He had arranged a short honeymoon for them in New Orleans as part of his wedding gift.

"I think instead of rice I'll throw advice to Beth on how to handle his bad habits."

Zach kissed the tip of her nose. "Why don't you let her find out on her own. It will make it more fun that way."

"You can say that because you weren't the one to climb over the clothing littering his room and bed and find remnants of toothpaste on the bathroom counter. We won't discuss the aged food I used to find under his bed. He has never been the neatest person, and I happen to know Beth has her closet cataloged by color and items."

"They'll be the perfect balance then."

When the couple left the reception, Abby did allow her tears to fall as she hugged first Beth, then Matt.

"Zach, make sure she doesn't drink any more champagne, okay?" Matt asked his new father-in-law. "Mom gets pretty sad when she's sloshed."

"I'll keep an eye on her," he promised.

The two men looked at each other for several moments before moving together in a hug.

"I'll take good care of her," Matt murmured.

"I know you will," Zach replied under his breath. "I guess we're trading ladies."

Matt broke out into a broad grin. "Yeah, I think we are. I don't think you'll hear me complaining."

Abby stood back watching the others throw rice at the departing couple as their limousine sped away. She looked up at Zach.

"I'll be in for the gray treatment first thing Monday."

Chapter Fifteen

"Zach, I do not want to go to the zoo. I want to stay home and feel sorry for myself," Abby informed him on the phone. "My son was married yesterday. A mother is supposed to worry about things like that."

"Not if I have anything to say about it. I'll be by in half an hour. Be ready or so help me I'll dress you myself." With his threat hanging in the air, Zach hung up.

"The zoo," she grumbled, slamming the phone down. "That's what he thinks." But Abby still pulled herself together dressing in a pair of off-white cotton slacks and pale blue short-sleeved sweater. Aware how much walking would be involved through the large zoo she wore a pair of low-heeled shoes.

"I thought you were going to stay in your room today and feel sorry for yourself," Estelle commented when Abby walked into the kitchen.

"Zach won't let me." She glared at her housekeeper. "I would like to know how he knew what I was doing."

"Don't look at me. He just knows you too well, that's all."

Abby looked around. "Sam out?"

"She went over to that one girl's house. You know, the one who wears the glittery nail polish and wears eye shadow six inches thick."

Abby nodded. "Connie."

"That's the one. Her mother is driving them to one of the malls."

"That will keep her busy for the day," she said listlessly.

"Go back and put on some more blusher and lipstick," Estelle ordered. "You look like death warmed over."

Abby obeyed and by the time Zach arrived she felt a little bit more like herself.

"Is there any special reason why we're going to the zoo?" she asked, once settled in his car.

"We need the exercise," he said, backing down the driveway.

After parking, Zach led Abby to the ticket booth and entrance. "Which section first?" he asked, after practically dragging her through the turnstile.

"You're in charge, you choose." She waved a hand.

"Koalas." He turned right, pulling on her hand as they walked swiftly down the road toward the specially built enclosure for the enchanting and popular Australian marsupials. They stood inside a large gazebo that housed television monitors so they could observe the koalas inside the screen houses or they could lean on the railings and search the trees for the shy animals.

"They always look as if climbing the trees taxes their strength," Abby commented, after pointing out one gray furry beast with half-closed eyes as he munched on a eucalyptus leaf. "They look like something you would love to take home until you're reminded they have extremely sharp teeth and nails."

"You should talk. What do you think Max has?" he countered.

"Sharp nails when they haven't been clipped and an even sharper beak."

"That is something I'm very familiar with."

It was some time before they could tear themselves away. After that, Zach barely gave Abby a moment's rest. They spent time watching the ostriches and emus, laughing at the antics of the baboons and chimpanzees and admiring the majestic aura of the lowland gorillas.

"If you pull me up one more hill I will murder you," Abby threatened, as they trudged up a steep path.

"You didn't want me to sit around the house feeling depressed, did you?" Abby pulled on his arm to slow him down. "Ah-ha! You have that guilty look on your face."

Zach groaned. "I do not look guilty. All I did was save you from standing in the doorway of Matt's room, which always looks like a disaster zone, and mourn the loss of your baby boy when you should be glad to have gotten rid of him so easily."

She scrunched up her nose. "That is not a nice thing to say. Besides, my baby boy married your baby girl, remember?"

His teasing grin froze. "I know, and while I had hoped it would be a while, I'll accept it. At least they'll be living close to you."

Abby held up her hands. "Okay, no more talk about the kids or we'll be crying right here. After all, they're off enjoying their honeymoon."

"I just hope they'll see more than the hotel," he muttered.

She could feel the flush stealing up her throat to her face. "Let's go." Now she began pulling him down the path.

Zach dug in his heels forcing her to slow down. "How about the reptile house?"

Abby stared at him in disbelief. "You have got to be kidding."

He grinned. "Oh, that's right. You're not too fond of the little critters, are you?"

"Some of them aren't so little." She grabbed his hand. "Come on, we'll visit Max's relatives. I'll feel more at home there."

After leaving the cages housing the exotic birds, they saw a couple of the animal shows, wandered through the children's zoo and stopped in the gift shops on the way out, where Zach bought Abby a large koala.

"A memory of your day," he said, presenting her with the gray furry animal.

She buried her nose in the fur and looked at him over the top of the toy's head. "Thank you."

By the time they reached Zach's car, Abby had to admit she was pleasantly tired and the day did her more good than she would have realized. "You always know what's right for me," she commented.

"Just lucky guesses." He half turned in the seat. "I don't want the day to end, do you?"

Abby stared into his eyes and instinctively knew what he was trying to say. "No," she whispered, keeping her eyes on him. "No, I don't."

Without another word he put the car in gear and drove out of the parking lot. They remained silent during the drive to Zach's house. He left the car in the garage and they entered the house through the kitchen.

"Would you like some coffee or something else to drink?" Zach watched Abby walk across the den and look out the sliding glass door to the pool.

"Perhaps some iced tea," she replied softly.

She didn't turn around until he returned with two glasses, handing her one.

"I always liked this house," Abby still spoke in the soft tone. "Everything always looks so neat and in its place, whereas poor Estelle never has a chance of keeping things in order."

"But your house has a lot of love. That's more important."

Abby turned away long enough to set her glass down then took Zach's glass out of his hand and put it down. After that, she appeared unsure of what to do next.

She lifted her eyes, the smile on her lips tentative. "I'm sorry, Zach, I'm really not all that experienced in this," she murmured.

He smiled gently. "Neither am I. We're part of a generation that didn't take things lightly, Abby. Oh, I know I gave you a bad time about getting you into bed. Some of it teasing, the rest, well, I discovered my hormones hadn't been laid to rest after all."

He rested his hands on her shoulders, rubbing them over the softly rounded contours and slowly down her back, carefully bringing her closer to him until their chests barely touched. Abby sighed with contentment, laying her cheek against his shirtfront. She curled her arms around his waist, her fingertips splayed out over his back. When his motions turned from comforting to sensual she had no idea. All she knew was that one hand stroked close to the underside of her breast, and she wanted him to touch her and mutely showed him where. He pulled her shirt out of the waistband and moved his hand up her warm skin until he found the lacy edge of her bra.

"Does this have one of those complicated hooks that rivals a chastity belt?" he breathed against her lips.

"It once took me ten minutes to get out of this," she replied, running her tongue across his lower lip.

Zach groaned. "Then you won't miss it much if I rip it off you in a gesture of lust."

"Just kidding. If it was that bad I would have thrown it away a long time ago."

But he wasn't listening. He was too busy unbuttoning her shirt and pulling it off. He gazed at the pale blue lace confection that didn't cover as much as entice. He exhaled a shuddering breath.

"Wow. If I had any idea you wore lingerie like this, I would have tried undressing you a long time ago."

By now Abby felt more relaxed. Relaxed enough to take the initiative and pull Zach's shirt over his head and drop it to one side.

"I guess I've been a bit luckier," she murmured. "Because I've been able to admire this manly chest for many a year now."

His face split into a broad grin. "Really? You like my chest?" He shook his head. "I can't believe this, and here I was afraid you'd prefer someone more muscular."

"Honestly, Zach, when you start something you must finish it." She worked on his belt buckle and once it was unfastened, popped the button on his chinos, "Oops, sorry about that. I'll sew it on later," but when it came to lowering the zipper she lost her newfound courage. "I think the next move will have to be yours," she whispered.

"Why don't we give ourselves a bit more privacy?" he suggested, guiding her down the hallway to his bedroom. "Not to mention comfort."

Abby had never had a reason to see Zach's bedroom except the time he had been so sick with the flu four years ago. She didn't see any changes as he pulled back the burgundy and silver-gray bedspread. Zach straightened up, not missing the hesitation in her stance.

"If this isn't what you want, just say so," he said quietly. "I won't feel hurt—okay, I'll feel hurt, I may even kill myself, but I'll understand. All right, I might not understand, but I'll try. I just want you to know I have trouble with rejection, especially from you, but I'm an adult and I can take it." He looked for all the world like a hurt puppy.

A strangled laugh left her throat. "Perhaps not the most romantic thing to say to the woman you want to make love to, but it's the most honest. And I love you for it."

Zach could only stare at Abby standing in front of him in the tiny bra and even tinier matching bikini panties.

"I'm not as firm as I used to be and there's stretch marks. Having three children tends to do that and for all I know, since I'm afraid to look, I may have varicose veins," she spoke rapidly, afraid he didn't like what he was seeing.

"You are beautiful," he spoke in a hushed tone.

Abby had no idea when Zach had guided her toward the bed, but she did appreciate his slow and easy approach as if they had all the time in the world. He had figured out her bra's clasp and it soon lay on the carpet next to the bed— he had informed her that if he was only wearing his briefs, she should be dressed, or undressed, likewise.

"When you washed my hair that first time, I could feel tingles all the way down to my toes. I didn't want you to stop," Abby murmured, enjoying those same hands moving over her bare breasts and teasing her nipples.

"Funny, I felt my tingles somewhere else." His mouth now covered one dusky-rose nipple and pulled on it gently. Abby gasped with the sensation even as Zach encouraged her with throaty words. She ran her hands over his light brown nipples, delighted to watch them harden from her loving ministration and continued her exploration to see where else he was sensitive, enjoying learning about him intimately.

"This feels so right. I feel as if we've always done this," she said huskily. "I don't ever want to stop."

"Let's see how long we can keep this going then." He edged his fingers around the elastic edge of her panties and inside to find her warm and more than responsive to his touch. He kissed her deeply, his tongue thrusting between her parted lips where her tongue darted up to meet his and coiled around it.

Abby's arms clung to him as she felt him slide her panties down her legs and she released him only long enough to help him take off his briefs. When he again moved over her, she felt his slightly rough skin against her.

"I'd like to draw this out for hours but I'm afraid I'd die of a heart attack within the next thirty seconds." His heavy respiration rate was more than proof positive.

She smiled. "Now I can't allow that to happen, can I?" She reached down to guide him toward her as she lifted her hips.

Zach moved slowly, allowing her to adjust to him as he entered her as carefully as possible, aware she hadn't been with a man for a while. When he was fully embedded in her softness he paused, looking down at her face.

"You look so beautiful," he whispered in awe, brushing his lips across hers. "I only wish we hadn't waited this long."

"Then let's not wait any longer."

By then Zach knew he couldn't. As he became a part of her, he watched the play of emotions cross Abby's face and knew there was more happening here than two people making love. It was a new beginning for them; a beginning that would have a more-than-favorable middle and end. He had read in books about fireworks and lightning striking during love scenes and considered them nothing more than an author's idea of making something look even better. He was wrong, because he could swear he could even hear violins playing love songs and he wanted that to go on for a long time. But his body had other ideas. The last thing he remembered was seeing Abby's face glow with pure happiness as first she found that sensual nirvana and he soon learned what true lovemaking was all about.

"I feel..." Abby rolled over in bed, not caring if the covering sheet followed her. "I feel as if we just discovered something so wonderful I don't want to share it with anyone." She laughed with pure happiness.

Zach opened one eye and looked at her. "We did discover something wonderful and I don't intend to share you with anyone." He grabbed her head with his hands and pulled her back down for a lingering kiss. "As long as I make you happy, I'm happy," he murmured. "Fair enough? So how was I?"

Abby pondered. "On a rating of one to ten you were oh..." She shrieked when Zach's fingers hovered dangerously close to her bare sides. "All right, you were a five million!" she giggled.

He lay back looking incredibly smug. "That's better."

She inched her way across his body, the sheet following her. "There's something I want to confess to you. And you may think I was foolish back then, which I'm sure I was."

He smiled up at her. "You were never foolish."

She shook her head, her hair streaming down around both faces. "Oh, but I was. As to why I'm telling you this, I don't know. Maybe something about today brought back the memory." She continued staring into his eyes. "Remember when the four of us went to Lake Arrowhead? You and Carolyn had only been married about two months."

Zach nodded. "Sure I do. We borrowed a friend's cabin and it rained the first night we were there, and the roof leaked in both bedrooms. Who wouldn't remember sleeping in a wet bed?" he couldn't understand what she was getting at.

All of a sudden Abby wished she hadn't brought up the subject. She started to move away, but Zach held on to her forearms, refusing to allow her to escape.

"We went for a walk that second day." She refused to look at him now. "And you and Carolyn returned to the cabin to get everybody's sweatshirts, but you didn't come back for about an hour. And I remember Jason making some kind of joke about newlyweds. When you did come back Carolyn had this look, as if..." She paused. "And for a split second I felt jealous, because we all knew what had happened back at the cabin and I—" She curled her fingers. "I—"

Zach grasped her chin and raised her head so she had no choice but to face him. "Open your eyes," he ordered gently. "Abby, look at me."

"I was so damn jealous," she whispered, more to herself than to him. "Matt was going through the 'terrible twos' and he ran both Estelle and me ragged and I couldn't remember the last time I'd had a decent night's sleep or when Jason and I had the time to make love the way it should be done, and all I could do was look at the two of you and feel jealous."

Zach gathered Abby into his arms and held her tight. At first she tensed up, but soon the tension eased and she relaxed against him. He drew the covering sheet away and nestled her close to his side.

"I don't know much about it, but I'd say you were feeling the aftereffects of keeping track of an energetic toddler, a husband finishing up law school and wishing you could have some time for yourself. There's nothing wrong with that," he told her. "Besides, look what happened to Carolyn's and my marriage. Basing it on sex and my need to settle down didn't cut it. I saw what you and Jason had and I wanted the same thing. I should have realized that Carolyn wasn't you and saved us all a lot of heartbreak."

"Yes, but now I know what she had and threw away," she wailed against his neck. "She was a fool."

Zach turned over on his side so he could face her. "Are you going to throw me back?"

"No way."

This time when Zach made love to her he took his time, and before they climaxed Abby discovered lovemaking as she had never known it before. Nestled spoon fashion, they fell asleep in each others arms.

"THIS IS PURE DECADENCE, Zachary," Abby announced, watching him set a tray of snacks on the edge of the bed and proudly display a bottle of wine resting in an ice bucket.

"Sure it is. Are you complaining?"

She shook her head as she leaned forward filching a cheese-covered cracker. "Are you kidding? I feel too good." She yelped when a shirt covered her head.

"Put it on so you won't catch a cold," he advised, pulling on a clean pair of briefs before climbing on the bed. "Also so your naked body won't tempt me while we eat. It looks like I'm going to need all the strength I can get if we're going to make up for lost time."

Abby sat up cross-legged, dragging on the knit polo shirt. As she munched on another cheese-covered cracker, she asked reflectively, "Zach, you didn't do this because you knew I felt sad about Matt, did you?"

He scowled. "Give me credit, Abby. I'm not into that."

"Then why?"

"Because I felt the time was finally right and I was going to do my damnedest to make sure it didn't slip away from us," he said candidly. "And because we had admitted we loved each other and it was time for us to show that love in a physical sense. I wanted this day to be purely for us. I even called Estelle and told her not to expect you home until morning." He stared at her silently, daring her to protest his high-handedness.

A glimmer of a smile touched her lips. "What did she say to that?"

His smile echoed hers. "She laughed and said it was about time and she wouldn't worry if you didn't show up until dinnertime. I think we have her blessing." He leaned over to pour two glasses of wine and hand Abby one as she stuffed a cracker into his mouth.

"She would. She's always been on your side." Abby sipped the chilled wine with relish. "Don't you have more in that kitchen than cheese and crackers? I'm starving. After all, you didn't bother to feed me at the zoo."

"If you're that hungry, we're better off calling out for something." He snitched a cracker out of her hand. "What sounds good to you?"

"Chinese," she decided. "Zach?" He turned toward her. "Just in case you've forgotten, I love you, too."

"I haven't forgotten, but it's always nice to hear."

Zach disappeared for a few minutes and came back saying their order would be delivered in about fifteen minutes and he would have to wear a bit more in the way of clothing so he wouldn't shock the delivery person. After pulling on a pair of jeans he went into the living room.

Abby climbed out of bed and wandered into the bathroom to freshen up. She quickly brushed her hair and splashed her face with cool water and then stood back looking at herself in the full-length mirror covering a linen closet. Her cheeks were glowing, her eyes sparkled, and she knew she never looked better. For a long time she had denied her feelings for Zach as being love, but she knew that time was over. Now was the time to explore those feelings even further and enjoy them. After a quick gargle with mouthwash she walked down the hallway.

Before too long they were seated in the kitchen feasting on sweet-and-sour duck and ginger beef, along with varied dishes to tempt any palate. They laughed and talked as they never had before and fed each other with their chopsticks. After the cartons were emptied and thrown away, they returned to the bedroom by silent consent. Their day wasn't over and they were determined to enjoy it to its fullest.

Chapter Sixteen

"I don't feel cheerful and I don't feel Christmassy, unless you want to count that I happen to look like Santa Claus, and I don't want to deck any halls with boughs of holly," Beth complained. She shifted in the easy chair, trying to make a comfortable place for herself but unable to, while watching Abby sitting cross-legged on the carpet sorting through packages and colorful wrapping paper. Green ribbon hung around her neck like a narrow scarf. "I hate being pregnant."

"We all do at one point or another," Abby said absently, cutting paper to fit a long box holding a shirt for Matt. "I was convinced I'd never see my feet again."

Beth stared into her glass of mineral water, which she loudly announced to the world she hated. "I look like the Goodyear blimp."

Abby hid her smile. She didn't want to tell the young woman that just because she couldn't fit into her favorite skirt didn't mean she wouldn't be able to six months from now.

"Just be thankful you're not having twins. Then you'd be blooming like crazy," Abby said tactfully, carefully taping the edges of the paper before pulling the ribbon from around her neck.

Beth looked at her with a pout on her lips, not feeling too happy about anything at the moment. "You always love to wrap gifts, don't you?"

"Sure, it's fun to make bows from scratch and see if I can copy some of the fancy wrapping techniques they use in the stores." Abby looped ribbon around two fingers and looked around. "Where's the gold ribbon?"

"Pretty, Max," the macaw crooned, strutting around the room, strands of multicolored ribbons trailing behind him.

"Oh, Max." She looked at him with disgust. "Look at the mess you made."

Max lifted his head, looking as proud as any ribbon-covered macaw could look. "I'm pretty."

"You're a mess." She picked the ribbons off his head and from around his back and wings. "If you do this again you're going back in your cage. Understand?" Judging from his drooping head Abby knew he understood only too well.

"Do you and Matt want to stay for dinner?" Abby asked, attaching a name tag to the wrapped gift. "Estelle's fixing a pot roast, so there's plenty."

"We eat over here too much as it is," Beth protested.

"Matt's idea of cooking is opening a couple of cans, and you've been feeling pretty tired today. Besides, your father's coming."

Beth's face lit up. "Great! You spend a lot of time with Dad, don't you?"

Abby ignored the funny warm feeling in the pit of her stomach and the thought of Zach. "Always have."

"Yes, but now there are times when you go out and don't come home until the next day," she said slyly.

"That's what happens when your kids live with you," she mumbled, aware her face was beet red. "No privacy."

"There's nothing wrong with you and Dad having a sex life, as long as the two of you are careful," Beth teased.

"Believe me, at our age we're certainly careful," Abby retorted, happy to see Beth relaxing. "But I do suggest you watch what you say to your father. He's still having trouble adjusting to his little girl having a baby in a few months. If you start talking to him about his sex life, he'll definitely have a fit."

Abby had no trouble persuading Matt to stay for dinner where Estelle's pot roast was concerned and with Beth tiring easily. He already felt guilty enough that she'd had to drop her classes a few weeks before, although Abby and Estelle did their best to keep her cheerful and even suggested she maintain with her studies so it would be easier for her to catch up when she returned to school after the baby was born.

"Why don't you go to the movies with us?" Zach suggested over dinner. "We're going to see that new Mel Gibson film for Abby's sake."

"I'd never fit in a seat," Beth mourned.

"Sure you would. You've only put on a couple of pounds. Wait until you see yourself in a few months when you really start blossoming out. This is nothing," Zach said cheerfully.

Beth looked at him as if he had struck her. "Thanks, Dad. Thanks a lot." She rose from the table and ran from the room.

Matt looked around with a bewildered expression that equaled his father-in-law's. "What did I say wrong?" Zach said.

Abby sighed. "I suggest both of you begin walking on eggshells or there will be hell to pay. Matthew, go and persuade your wife that the best thing for her is to go to the movies with us. Go now."

Zach's idea seemed to be a good one until they ran into a couple of Beth's and Matt's friends at the theater. Abby noticed how Beth gazed with obvious envy at one girl dressed in tight jeans and a heavy pullover sweater, and how

Beth seemed to withdraw from the conversation as if she didn't feel she had anything in common with them anymore. After the foursome left the younger people, Abby took Beth to one side.

"I won't lie to you," she said softly. "There's going to be days when you'll be convinced you look like an elephant and you'll hate yourself and everyone else around you, but in the end you'll have a beautiful baby and this time will be forgotten. Hey, I'll even go to exercise class with you and you know how I hate to work out," she grinned.

Beth brightened up and hugged her mother-in-law. "Abby, I love you." Looking more like her old self, she returned to Matt and also hugged him. He looked over her head at Abby with a confused look on his face but she merely smiled. They all entered the theater in search of seats.

"If I get another broken seat, I'll never enter another movie theater," Zach whispered in Abby's ear.

"You say that every time we go."

"Don't worry about sitting with us," Matt told them with a broad grin. "I know how we old married folks can be a real drag on you youngsters."

"He stays home next time," Zach growled, pulling Abby to another row of seats and sitting down without letting go of her hand, which lay loosely in his lap.

"That was nice of you inviting them," she told him, angling her body against the arm rest. "Beth has been feeling a bit down lately and she needs to get out more."

"Actually my first idea wasn't us going to the movies, you know." He grinned wickedly. "But it wasn't difficult to tell Beth needed some cheering up. I just hope the movie does it."

"It will if dear sweet Mel bares his buns again." She raised her eyebrows. "That would cheer up anyone. Although," she leaned over to murmur in his ear, "your buns would certainly give him a run for his money."

He groaned. "Abby, please, not when I can't do anything about it."

"Don't worry, I'll behave," she promised.

Unfortunately for Zach, Abby did just that. He regretted their time apart and valued their time together, which wasn't as often as he'd like. Because of the upcoming holidays their work loads increased and they saw little of each other. For the first time, he wanted to be with a woman constantly and not just when it suited him. He tried to tell himself it was because their time together was so erratic, but he couldn't make himself believe that. It had a lot more to do with Abby. During the film, he contented himself with holding her hand and chuckling when she stole his popcorn or drank his cola and wished they were somewhere a great deal more private.

Abby's thoughts were following along similar lines. Zach had always been her friend and now he was her lover, sealing their bond even tighter. She just wished it could be more but felt a little too cautious in bringing it up.

"After we drop Matt and Beth off do you want to go back to my place?" he murmured, as the film rolled the ending credits.

She grimaced. "I don't know, Zach. If Sam's still up I don't have any kind of excuse."

"Abby, your daughter is almost sixteen and not naive. She knows what's going on and isn't the kind to think 'If it's all right for Mom, it's all right for me,'" he informed her. "We haven't had any time alone for two weeks. My God, you act as if I'm going to drag you off to my bed the minute we step inside the house."

She looked up under the cover of her lashes. "Aren't you?"

"No, I figured we could just talk."

"Pity. I wore my sexy underwear for nothing."

Zach considered her words. "That blue teddy that was nothing but lace and you?"

Abby looked smug at attracting his attention. "No, this one matches my skin tone."

He groaned. "We're still going to talk."

"Then I'll drive over to your house a little bit later on."

He argued to no avail. Abby was still determined to check on her daughter before leaving for Zach's house. Deep in her mind she knew Sam was well aware what was going on but she still wanted to do it her way, if only for her own sake.

After bidding Matt and Beth good-night, Zach bid Abby a sardonic good-night and drove off. Abby walked into the den to find Samantha watching television.

"I thought you'd be going over to Zach's," she remarked, keeping her eyes glued to the television screen.

"Why?"

"Because you usually do."

Abby sighed, thinking, so much for keeping up appearances.

A WELCOMING LIGHT was burning over the front door as Abby left her car and headed toward it. The door opened before she got there.

"It sure took you long enough," Zach groused, pulling her inside.

"Zach!" she exclaimed, snatching a look over her shoulder and noticing the ever-present lace curtain twitching at the front window next door. "You're giving yourself a bad name!"

"I'm a crusty, or is it lusty, old bachelor living alone." He enfolded her in his arms for a long hug. "It's allowed."

"Zach, you're incorrigible." Abby laughed when he released her and guided her into the den.

After watching her settle herself on the couch, he poured her a glass of wine and sat down beside her.

"Now this is the way for us to spend the evening," Zach told her, looking a bit too smug.

Abby slipped off her shoes and curled her legs under her. "Tell me how your work is going."

He sighed, resting his head back. "Busy. I hired two new cutters for the third salon. Oh, Darcy is pregnant." He mentioned the name of the receptionist for the third salon catering to the younger set.

"Is she?" she chuckled, recalling the young woman whose multicolored hair was a source of amazement to everyone since they never knew what color would next strike her mood. "It will be interesting to see what color hair she goes with."

Zach grimaced. "Half is pink and half is blue. She claims she doesn't want to look as if she favors one sex over the other."

Abby shook her head in amazement. "What scares me is that I can see the logic in that."

Zach leaned over curling a lock of hair around his fingertips. "Of course, if you ever try that I'll turn you into a bleached blonde," he said mildly.

"Good thing pink has never been my color." She winked. "Besides, I think that would be more in Beth's line, not mine."

He stared down at his hands. "Did you ever think about having more children?"

Abby looked startled by his question. "To be honest, I never thought about it one way or another. Besides, even though other women may be having babies at my age, I don't know if it's something I would want to do. I think I have more than enough on my hands at this time."

Zach nodded, not giving away his thoughts on the subject. "Then how would you feel about spending a couple hours of frenzied coupling in my bed?"

"Frenzied coupling?" she repeated. "Zach, you have to quit reading the tabloids scattered around your shop. They're giving you sordid ideas. You're just lucky I like the one you brought up."

It didn't take Zach long to change Abby's mind. He lay among the tumbled bed covers watching her brush her hair.

"What would you think about us getting married?" he asked casually.

Her hand stopped in mid-motion. "Is this a trick question?" she asked quietly, putting the brush down before she dropped it.

He shook his head. "I'm damn serious. We've got a lot going for us, Abby. I know you love me as much as I love you, and we share a lot of the same interests. We're the perfect couple!"

Abby plucked at the frilled neckline of her camisole. She wasn't sure why his proposal bothered her unless it was because he told her they were a perfect couple and shared the same interests. Couldn't he talk about love more? she asked herself. Add some hearts and flowers to his words? Would that be too much to ask? She knew she was probably overreacting about this, but she was unable to stop herself. "Is this because of Beth and Matt getting married or because you love me so madly you can't stand being away from me for more than five minutes? What, no quick answer? Thank you for your romantic proposal, but no thanks." She jerked on her loden-green cords with a savage motion and pulled the matching striped sweater over her head. "Damn you!" Abby blazed, suddenly turning and throwing the brush at him. Only his quick reflexes kept him from getting hit. She stormed out of the room, grabbed her purse from the couch and headed for the front door.

"What did I say that was so wrong?" Zach demanded, hopping from one foot to another as he tried to pull on his jeans without falling on his face.

She didn't slow down as she grabbed the doorknob. "Think about it." She slammed to door behind her.

Zach ran outside after her, hissing at the cold air attacking his bare chest.

"I propose to you and I get this?" he shouted, watching her unlock her car door and slide inside. "What did you think was going to happen to us? We'd just have a hot-and-heavy affair and say so long when the time came? I don't know about you, but I'm tired of all that. I want more than you just coming over here a few nights a week to hop into my bed for some lovemaking, then your leaving so Samantha doesn't realize you have a sex life. Although I bet she knows exactly what we've been doing. We're not getting any younger you know. How many proposals do you expect to get in the near future? I read somewhere that a forty-year-old woman can expect to get killed by a terrorist before she'll get a marriage proposal."

"Then I'll take the terrorist!" Abby jammed the key in the ignition and turned it with a savage twist. When nothing happened, she tried to turn the key back but it refused to budge. As she realized what she had done, she swore long and eloquently. She knew Zach stood nearby crossing his arms in front of his chest in order to keep warm, and she hated herself for having to get out of the car in order to use his phone, but she knew she had no choice. Taking a deep breath, she left the car and walked up the driveway.

"I can't believe you'd change your mind that easily."

"I just need to use your phone," she said coolly, sweeping past him into the house. Abby found the yellow pages and soon dialed a number. In a concise tone she explained her problem and asked how soon someone could come out. When she hung up, she stared long and hard at Zach's impassive features. "Don't say one word."

"I wouldn't dream of it. How long before the locksmith arrives?"

"Twenty minutes. I'll wait outside."

"Not in that cold you won't." Zach disappeared down the hall long enough to retrieve a sweatshirt from his bedroom and pull it over his head. "I thought you were going to buy a colored top for your key so you could tell it apart from Matt's car key.''

"I never got around to it." She now looked more angr at herself than at him.

"Abby." Zach's quiet voice compelled her to turn to fac him. "I wasn't trying to be funny or even sensible when asked you to marry me. You've always been very importan to me. I consider you a friend and now you're my lover. I it so terrible that I want you as my wife?''

She could feel tears starting and hated herself for that too, since she rarely cried.

"No, but would it have hurt to phrase it just a bit mor romantically than going on about how well we go to gether," she muttered, picking up her purse. "The lock smith should be here pretty soon. I'll wait outside."

"Romantically?" He looked at her, feeling more bewil dered by the minute. "What did you expect? Me to get dowr on one knee?''

Abby merely gave him a telling look before she walked away.

Zach didn't follow her but he kept watch by the fron window, seeing a man in a truck pull up behind Abby Within moments her key was extracted and she had paid the man. During that time she didn't look up once at the shad owy figure standing at the window.

"I DIDN'T REALIZE you did Pac Man's taxes." Donna stoo behind Abby who sat in front of her computer, using the joy stick to play her favorite computer game. Other game disk lay scattered across her work area.

"I didn't want to be disturbed," she grumbled.

"Estelle told me you've said a lot of things over the pas few days. And as you've ignored my calls, I decided to driv over and see what was going on. Since you started datin Zach I hardly see you anymore," her friend told her.

Abby sighed. It was clear Donna wasn't going to leave until she found out what was bothering her. So far she had been able to evade Estelle's questions and hadn't been above using Samantha and anyone else as a buffer, but now that Donna was here she knew she didn't have a chance because once her friend got her teeth into a problem she didn't let go.

Of course, she also had to contend with the silence on Zach's end. He hadn't called since she left that night, although she hadn't expected him to. But then, she hadn't expected to receive a dozen red roses every day, either, and they arrived like clockwork. There was no card but she hadn't needed one to know who sent them. Was he not contacting her directly because he decided she would have to come to him? Considering her mood lately, it would be a cold day in hell before she would make the first move even if she wanted to admit she just might have overreacted. Her emotions had been on a seesaw the past week, which hadn't improved her mood one bit.

"Estelle said you've been in a foul mood since you returned from Zach's almost a week ago," Donna commented, perching herself on a corner of Abby's desk. "Which leaves us with two conjectures. Either the two of you had a fight to end all fights, or you decided to take the initiative and proposed to him and he turned you down. And I can't see Zach turning you down."

Abby blinked rapidly to keep back her tears. "Who says he wouldn't be the one to propose." She hated the choking sound in her voice. Come to think of it, she hated a lot of things lately, including herself.

Donna leaned forward. "I see. He proposed and you were stupid enough to turn him down and now you hate yourself."

Abby jumped up and paced the length of the office, waving her arms around. "Me, stupid? He was the one who spouted off how we were so good together and since we were a suitable pair we may as well get married. The way he

sounded you'd think we were merging two businesses!"
Deep down she knew she had left out a few facts but she was
past caring.

"Something tells me there's a great deal more to it than
that," Donna said gently. "Zach's not the kind to propose
without love being involved, and you can't tell me that the
two of you don't love each other."

"Love doesn't make everything perfect." Abby kept
wiping her eyes with the back of her hand but the tears kept
falling. "Damn," she sniffed. "I never cry. Lately, I've felt
as if I've turned into Niagara Falls."

Donna chuckled. "And you thought there wasn't enough
love between you two," she chided. "You certainly never
cried over the others. Call him. Make things right between
you."

On this point she was determined to be stubborn. "Since
he hasn't called, he must not be as interested as he claimed
he was, so why should I be the one to give in first?"

Donna glanced at the vase of roses sitting behind Abby's
desk and remembered seeing another vase on the table in the
entryway. "Where did the roses come from?" She smiled at
Abby's flushed face. "I see. Those roses say a lot."

"There was no card."

"There didn't have to be, did there? Look, why don't you
shut down that computer and go out to lunch with me?" she
suggested. "And afterward we'll go on a shopping spree."

"You're right, I'm not doing anything useful here," Abby
said with a sigh. "Except let's forget lunch and just head for
the stores."

As they walked through one department store Abby
couldn't help noticing a frenzied mother trying to deal with
her reluctant toddler.

"Zach asked me if I had wanted more children," she said
softly. "There was a time I wouldn't have minded one or
two more, even with all the work involved. When you're
bone tired from the middle-of-the-night feedings and stay-

ıg up because of colic or teething, you tell yourself you'd
ever go through it again. But when the time comes, you
orget all about that and just look forward to the joy of
vatching a new person evolve."

"You really love him, don't you?" Donna asked softly.

She saw no reason to evade the issue. "Yes."

"And he loves you."

"Yes."

Donna nodded as she dragged a confused Abby out of the
tore. "Then that's all that matters. Although if I were you,
would get this settled as quickly as possible. Otherwise
ıere won't be any roses left in the state!"

She laughed, feeling freer than she had in several days.
"You're right. I've been an absolute fool for no reason at
ll. In fact, I'll make sure you get the first wedding invita-
on."

"I should hope so!"

"YOU HAVE GOT to be kidding!"

"I'm sorry, Abby, but no matter how much it shocks you,
. does happen to women your age. Biology doesn't look at
omeone's birth certificate," the gray-haired doctor in-
ormed the stunned woman seated across from him. "Why
ot relax and go with the flow? Give it some time and you'll
oon be feeling your old self. I should have the results of
our tests within a few days and we'll go from there. All
ight?"

She uttered a hollow laugh. "Oh, sure, that's easy for you
› say. Why is it that men think all of this is a snap for us
vomen? I think the fair thing to do is let the male sex go
hrough this and see how you like it!"

The older man chuckled. "I do believe I've heard this
rom my wife a few times."

"Why don't I find that comforting?"

Chapter Seventeen

"Zach, you have to talk to Mom," Matt insisted, following his father-in-law around the busy salon.

"If she wants to talk to me, she knows where I am."

He exhaled a deep breath, frustrated with both stubborn parents. "You know how she is. She's convinced she's right and you feel you're right—what the hell are the rest of us supposed to do while you two battle this out in your separate courts?"

"Nothing. This is strictly between your mother and me." Zach rummaged through the bottles of hair color until he found the one he wanted. He stood at the sink consulting an index card for the formula needed.

Matt turned away, raking his fingers through his hair, then spun back to Zach. "Okay, look, I didn't want to tell you this but I think you should know because Mom is so bullheaded she would try to make up some ridiculous story."

He looked up. "What should I know?"

"That Mom's pregnant."

Zach wasn't aware of the bowl falling into the sink, the dark brown contents splattering the white enamel.

"Are you sure?" His tone was hushed as if he couldn't believe what he was hearing.

Matt nodded. "She went to see Dr. Milford, her GYN a few days ago and he called yesterday about some test re

lts. Beth happened to be over there and answered the
one. When she tried to talk to Mom about it, she refused
say anything and just wandered through the house all day.
nd she's been acting funny lately, not at all like herself.
hat else can it be? No woman goes to her gynecologist for
cold.''

Zach shook his head, unable to take in everything.

"Zach?" Susan called out. "Your customer is wonder-
g what's going on."

"I'll be right out," he replied, then looked at the mess in
e sink and swore softly. "This is going to require some
avy thinking, Matt, but don't worry. I wasn't going to al-
w your mother to slip through my fingers no matter what
e thought."

Satisfied he had done his best, Matt slipped out the back
ay, leaving a very confused Zach behind.

"I'm too old for this," he sighed, picking up the color
ottles. He would worry about the mess later.

ACH DID THINK long and hard about what Matt told him
he paced the length of the living room long into the night.
he more he thought about it, the angrier he got that Abby
dn't felt she could come to him. And the angrier he got,
e more he wanted to march over to her house and de-
and the truth. In the end he could only come up with one
lution. Uncaring it was past midnight, he drove over to
bby's house and pounded on her front door. He was going
get this settled whether she liked it or not. He stood at the
ont door and punched the doorbell allowing it to ring
ntinually.

"Who is it?" Abby's grumble sounded through the door.

"Abby, let me in."

"No."

His eyes narrowed. "Abby, you let me in or I'll break this
oor down!"

"Try it."

Taking a deep breath, Zach stepped back a few paces an ran toward the door. His shoulder met a great deal of resi tance and his howl of pain could be heard throughout t neighborhood. Abby flung open the door watching him wit a mixture of concern and amusement on her face as he swo with great fluency.

"Just because I said to try it, didn't mean you had to, she observed.

"Why didn't you remind me that door is solid?" groaned, rubbing what he was convinced was a broke shoulder.

"Since you hung it, I assumed you'd remember."

Zach brushed past her. "You're a hard-hearted woma Abigail Townsend. You also look like hell. What have yo been doing with yourself? You've lost weight you can't a ford to lose and your skin tone is pasty. If you weren't t mother of my child and my prospective wife, I would prob ably think about murdering you for not taking proper car of yourself."

She stared at him wondering if he had lost his sense "What?"

"You heard me." He put his face to hers, nose to nos "I'm sick and tired of all your crazy reasons why w shouldn't get married. We love each other, we certainl know each other's good and bad habits and there shouldn be any surprises, unless you want to count your most re cent one. Just because you happen to be pregnant ha nothing to do with this. I love you, damn it! Doesn't tha count for anything?" He waved his arms around for em phasis.

"Of course it does, but if that's part of the reason you'r marrying me you're off the hook," she shouted back. "Be cause I don't know where you got the idea I'm pregnant, bu I'm not!"

"No excuses...." he halted. "You're not pregnant?"

She shook her head, standing in front of him with her arms crossed in front of her. "No, I'm not and I'd like to know who who told you this fairy tale?"

"Matt. He said you saw your GYN and there was something about tests." Zach felt the steam leaving his temper. "And what the hell do you mean by fairy tale?" He suddenly thought the worst. "Is it something else, Abby? Are you ill?"

Abby chuckled, seeing the humor in the situation. "No, I'm not ill and, yes, I saw the doctor. I admit the idea of my being pregnant had entered my mind at the time because my system wasn't as regular as it usually was. What it turned out to be is early menopause, so you're off the hook. That's right, the parts that make me a woman are beginning to fall apart. Another sign I'm not getting any younger, as you so politely pointed out one time." She looked disgruntled at the idea.

Zach burst out laughing and hugged her tightly. "You thought you were pregnant and saw your life going crazy all over again. I thought you were pregnant and saw it as a chance to talk you into marrying me. Matt and Beth thought you were pregnant and wanted me to make an honest woman of you. I don't want to be off the hook, Abby. I want us to get married as soon as possible because we should be together and I want to do it up right. Sound good to you?"

Her face lit up. "Yes."

He grabbed hold of her shoulders. "Just like that? No arguments?"

"No arguments. I was a fool who wasn't listening to her heart. My emotions were going through a strange time. The doctor said it had to do with hormones and it was expected. All I knew was that I hated myself for saying and doing things that made no sense. Including turning down your proposal because I chose to read it the wrong way," she admitted. "If I had used my common sense I wouldn't have put us through all this misery." She linked her arms around his neck. "I'm sorry I did, but I'll more than make up for it." She bumped her hips against his.

"I don't think you'll get any grumbling from me," Zach murmured, lowering his head for a much-needed kiss. He had been too long without her touch.

"Do you guys mind?" An aggrieved Samantha intervened. They turned to find her standing nearby. "Some of us have to get some sleep so we can go to school and do well in our history test so our mother won't yell at us for flunking. So can you keep it down?"

"You going to mind if I marry your mother?" Zach asked her.

Samantha was too sleepy to get excited. "Right now I don't care what you guys do as long as you let me get some sleep." With that she turned on her heel and returned to her room. "Although I wouldn't turn down an increase in my allowance. Or a cat large enough to intimidate Max. Or a car on my sixteenth birthday." Her voice drifted back toward them.

Abby looked up at Zach. "We just received Sam's blessing," she murmured.

He looked as if he had another idea up his sleeve. "Would you consider sealing the deal another way?"

A smile curved her lips. "Why not? I'm sure Estelle won't mind setting another place at breakfast. In fact, knowing her, she probably knew it would work out like this. She was probably the one to talk Matt into seeing you."

MATT PACED BACK AND FORTH, his eyes never leaving the bank of elevators. Every time a door opened he scanned the interior only to meet the eyes of a nurse or orderly exiting the car. Few visitors were allowed in the hospital at four in the morning. He checked his watch again when he heard a faint metallic ping and the doors slid open and two people stepped out.

"Mom? Zach?" His voice held disbelief as he gazed at the two people who could have stepped out of a James Dean movie.

Abby's hair was pulled up in a ponytail with the ends of a turquoise scarf dangling against her nape. Her off-white jewel-neck sweater and turquoise circular poodle skirt along with bobby socks and saddle shoes were pure nostalgia. Zach's flattop haircut, jeans and black leather jacket complemented Abby's outfit perfectly.

"Matt!" Abby squealed, hugging her son tightly. "How is she doing? What are you doing out here? You should be with Beth," she scolded. "My poor baby. We got here as soon as we could."

"It happened a lot faster than either of us expected. Even the doctor was surprised by the easy delivery. She had a girl an hour ago," he stumbled over the words. "What is this?" He stared at their clothing wondering if he wasn't dreaming.

Zach's grin broadened. "A girl! What's her name?"

"Jennifer." He still looked bewildered. "Why are you two dressed like that?"

His mother and father-in-law looked at him quizzically then down at themselves.

"Oh, we were attending a fund-raiser. They decided to put on a sock hop and we were to dress accordingly," Abby explained.

"How is Beth doing?" Zach asked.

"Fine." Matt was still finding it difficult to realize the two standing in front of him were his mother and father-in-law. "Come on, I'll show her to you." He offered a weak smile to one of the nurses standing nearby. "Our parents," he explained.

Within minutes the proud grandmother was holding a tiny pink-blanketed bundle while the new grandfather and parents looked on.

"I still can't believe I'm a grandmother," Abby told Zach as they admired the red-faced squirming baby, unaware two nurses stood in the room's doorway watching them. "Isn't she beautiful?"

"If it will make you feel more like the part, I'll buy you a rocking chair. Except right now you look far from the picture of a grandmother." He smiled into her eyes, reading the love shining in the teal depths. He leaned down whispering something into Abby's ear and from the way she laughed throatily and blushed, it had to be highly provocative.

"You two never stop, do you?" Beth's amused voice could be heard teasing them.

"They sure don't look like any grandparents I know," one nurse said to the other, watching Abby hand the baby back to Beth and then sit next to the bed talking animatedly while Zach stood behind her, one hand on her shoulder.

"Maybe not, but they sure seem to know how to love," the other one sighed.

"Don't you mean know how to live?" she corrected.

"No, I mean love."

Harlequin American Romance

COMING NEXT MONTH

#285 HOME IS THE SAILOR by Kathryn Blair

Sarah Mitchell was a strong believer in the power of love to heal. It was behind her every move at Puppy Power. Her dogs had brought a lot of happiness into people's lives, but they were not enough to fill the emptiness of her own—until she placed a puppy with her new neighbor, and the elderly woman's merchant marine officer son came into her life to challenge her convictions and her heart.

#286 TIES THAT BIND by Marisa Carroll

When Kevin Sauder came to Lisa Emery's quiet world on the wooded shores of a Michigan lake, he was looking for a sanctuary. But the young conservation officer and her little family, consisting of a teenage brother and sister, opened their lives to him—and Lisa opened her heart. And soon Kevin realized he may have found more than the courage to face life—he may have found love.

#287 FEATHERS IN THE WIND by Pamela Browning

Her face had been her fortune, but Caro Nicholson couldn't rely on her beauty anymore. She wanted to run, to forget what had happened. Mike Herrick was a man determined to make her feel alive again . . . alive in ways she thought long buried. But was he a man willing to wait for the woman he loved?

#288 PASSAGES OF GOLD by Ginger Chambers

Linda Conway knew there was only one way to save her family legacy . . . and Amador Springs, California, held the key. Gold, shiny and yellow, was there, and Linda had the fever. She would be strong and unafraid. That is, until Tate Winslow entered her heart and made her reveal her deepest fears. . . .

CHRISTMAS IS FOR KIDS

AMERICAN ROMANCE PHOTO CONTEST

At Harlequin American Romance® we believe Christmas is for kids—a special time, a magical time. And we've put together a unique project to celebrate the American Child. Our annual holiday romances will feature children—just like yours—who have their Christmas wishes come true.

A reddish, golden-haired boy. Or a curious, ponytailed girl with glasses. A kid sister. A dark, shy, small boy. A mischievous, freckle-nosed lad. A girl with ash blond braided hair. Or a bright-eyed little girl always head of the class.

Send us a color photo of your child, along with a paragraph describing his or her excitement and anticipation of Christmas morning. If your entry wins, your child will appear on one of the covers of our December 1989 CHRISTMAS IS FOR KIDS special series. Read the Official Rules carefully before you enter.

─── OFFICIAL RULES ───

1. Eligibility: Male and female children ages 4 through 12 who are residents of the U.S.A., or Canada, except children of employees of Harlequin Enterprises Ltd., its affiliates, retailers, distributors, agencies, professional photographers and Smiley Promotion, Inc.

2. How to enter: Mail a color slide or photo, not larger than 8½ × 11″, taken no longer than six months ago along with proof of purchase from facing page to:

> American Romance Photo Contest
> Harlequin Books
> 300 East 42nd Street
> 6th Floor
> New York, NY
> 10017.

Professional photographs are not eligible. Only one entry per child allowed. All photos remain the sole property of Harlequin Enterprises Ltd. and will not be returned. A paragraph of not more than 50 words must accompany the photo expressing your child's joy and anticipation of Christmas morning. All entries must be received by March 31, 1989.

3. Judging: Photos will be judged equally on the child's expression, pose, neatness and photo clarity. The written paragraph will be judged on sincerity and relationship to the subject. Judging will be completed within 45 days of contest closing date and winners will be notified in writing and must return an Affidavit of Eligibility and Release within 21 days or an alternate winner will be selected.

4. Prizes: Nine Prizes will be awarded, with each winner's likeness appearing on a cover of our December 1989 CHRISTMAS IS FOR KIDS special series. Winners will also receive an artists signed print of the cover. There is no cash substitution for prizes. Harlequin Enterprises Ltd. reserves the right to use the winner's name and likeness for promotional purposes without any compensation. Any Canadian resident winner or their parent or guardian must correctly answer an arithmetical skill-testing question within a specified time.

5. When submitting an entry, entrants must agree to these rules and the decisions of the judges, under the supervision of Smiley Promotion, Inc., an independent judging organization whose decisions are final. Sponsor reserves the right to substitute prizes of like substance. Contest is subject to all federal, provincial, state and local laws. Void where prohibited, restricted or taxed. For a winner's list, send a stamped self-addressed envelope to American Romance Photo Contest Winners, P.O. Box 554, Bowling Green Station, New York, N.Y. 10274 for receipt by March 31, 1989.

Photo-2

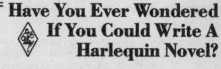

Have You Ever Wondered If You Could Write A Harlequin Novel?

Here's great news—Harlequin is offering a series of cassette tapes to help you do just that. Written by Harlequin editors, these tapes give practical advice on how to make your characters—and your story— come alive. There's a tape for each contemporary romance series Harlequin publishes.

Mail order only

All sales final
